D0005433

THE STORM

THE STORM

Margriet de Moor

TRANSLATED BY

Carol Brown Janeway

ALFRED A. KNOPF NEW YORK 2010

THIS IS A BORZOI BOOK
PUBLISHED BY ALFRED A. KNOPF

Translation copyright © 2010 by Carol Brown Janeway

Knopf, Borzoi Books, and the colophon are registered trademarks of
Random House, Inc.

Originally published in the Netherlands as *De Verdronkene* by
Uitgeverij Contact, a division of Boekenwereld, Amsterdam, in 2005.
Copyright © 2005 by Margriet de Moor.

Library of Congress Cataloging-in-Publication Data
Moor, Margriet de.
[Verdronkene. English]
The storm / by Margriet de Moor ; translated [from the Dutch] by
Carol Brown Janeway. — 1st American ed.
p. cm.
Originally published in the Netherlands as De Verdronkene in 2005.
ISBN 978-0-307-26494-7
1. Storm surges—Netherlands—Fiction.   2. Sisters—Netherlands—
Fiction.   3. Disaster victims—Netherlands—Fiction.
4. Psychological fiction.   I. Janeway, Carol Brown.   II. Title.
PT5881.23.O578V4713 2010
839.3'1364—dc22   2009037578

Manufactured in the United States of America

First American Edition

*For my sisters, Bernardien, Maria,
Fridoline, Simone, Josefien, and Leida*

It's as if time no longer recedes ahead of us,
but runs between us on parallel tracks.

—William Faulkner, *As I Lay Dying*

The dogs, they bark, the chains they clink
The people asleep in bed don't blink.

—Wilhelm Müller/Franz Schubert, *Winterreise*

I

Weekend Excursion

II

This Is What They Call Sleep

III

There's Always Weather

IV

Family Novel

V

Responsorium

I

Weekend Excursion

I

On a Raw Morning They Said Good-bye

One of them, Lidy, stood at the window and looked out. It was one of those midwinter mornings when it's just getting light and last night's storm no longer makes you feel cozy indoors, it's like a whine that gets on your nerves. She held her little daughter in her arms and her coat was already buttoned. In the process of leaving she hesitated for this one moment like someone who's glad to be on her way, if that's what comes next, but would be just as glad to stay home. That the whole plan wasn't hers to begin with, but Armanda's, was irrelevant. At this moment, all she was thinking was: I really want to drive a car again. Today and tomorrow, Armanda, you can take care of my daughter, and go with my husband to the party being given by your friend, who also happens to be his half sister. Tomorrow afternoon at the latest, I'll be back.

The living room occupied the second and third floors of one of the imposing houses fronting a little park in a less imposing neighborhood. Lost in thought, she looked out over the treetops, bare and black against the rectangle of house façades. She didn't see that diagonally opposite, the figure of a man was groping along a roof gutter until suddenly a flag flapped loose from his hands and immediately stood stiff and shivering in the northwest wind. It was the last day of January. If anyone had said to her that with Nadja held tight and safe in her arms she should take a good look all around because her farewell was a final one, she would have known deep in her heart that this was possible at any moment in life, but she wouldn't have believed it. After all, she was only twenty-three.

So without turning around, she asked casually, "Do you think it's going to snow?"

And Armanda, as she stood up from the table with a mug of coffee in her hand, answered, "Of course not, the wind's too strong," without the least pang of conscience in her voice. She began to pace up and down, slurping her coffee the way she always did. Not least because she'd taken off her shoes and was wearing a skirt and a knitted cardigan. She was the one who seemed at home here in the high space with the plaster rosette on the ceiling, not Lidy. There was hardly any light. In the back room the furniture was almost in darkness. The only things illuminated by a green standard lamp were a table pushed against the wall—on it a few objects, a teapot, a telephone, a briefcase with a protective band of tape around it—and the door to the hall and the stairs. The house had seen better days, like most of its big neighbors around the park, and the beautiful hardwood doors had been burnt for firewood during the war. But mostly in the rooms up on the third floor that smelled of beds and clothes and soap and cosmetics, it was still possible to recognize the original details of the house's fin-de-siècle style. In the bedrooms, leaded panes of glass in the upper half of the windows filtered the light.

A squall of rain exploded against the panes and streamed downward. Lidy peered out through the drops. Okay, she decided, I'll take the coast road. Once I'm past Rotterdam I won't go over the Moer dike, I'll head for Maassluis and take the ferry across the Nieuwe Waterweg. She still hadn't really thought about the whole route, but she knew there were maps in the car. I'll figure it out. Between another two squalls it was so silent for a moment that she heard the floorboards creak under Armanda's feet, and as that sound also ceased, she knew that Armanda too was peering out at the foul weather.

"It's funny really that I don't know these people at all," she said.

"It won't matter to them," said Armanda, now standing at the window by her side. "They haven't seen me for a year either." She sniggered. "Perfectly possible that when you go into the hotel, you know, the Hotel Kirke in the Verre Nieuwstraat, they'll all make the same mistake and won't realize right away that you're not me, but, um, actually you."

The same little irritated grin on both their faces.

They looked alike. Everyone thought so. They were tall girls with narrow, strong shoulders, always a little bent, which gave them a worried appearance that was quite misleading. And if they had turned round at that moment the double portrait would really have been striking: dark hair, almost chestnut-black, falling smoothly down their backs, exposing delicate little ears, and cut in a straight fringe that concealed the forehead completely. Nobody would ever see their foreheads. But everything could be read in the two pairs of eyes: merriment, sadness, mockery, indifference, passion, and also the speed of their shifting moods, yet what conveyed itself most clearly was that the two sisters appeared to see the world in exactly the same way, and to judge it.

Lidy set Nadja down on the floor and gave her a hug. Never mind the deceptive similarities, she was the mother here. "Mind she doesn't catch cold," she murmured, as she squatted down and pressed her nose against the child's neck with a certain feeling of self-confidence born of the countless times she had brought the little girl into bed with her from baby days onward, while whispering to her husband to slide over a bit and maybe snore a little less loudly.

She stood up again. "Did you give me the car keys or not?" As she groped in her coat pocket, she looked around.

Both began to go through the room. They hunted all over the furniture till Armanda realized she'd left the key at home.

"Then I'll get going," said Lidy. "I'll pick it up there."

In the hall Armanda said, "Don't forget their present," and handed Lidy the package. They gave each other a fleeting kiss. As Armanda said, "Give them my best," they both laughed.

Lidy clutched the umbrella to her chest, lifted the hem of her coat in one hand, and went down the stairs with her luggage. As she opened the front door, she wore a somewhat solemn expression and her forehead creased. As if she knew that she had to be serious about their exchange of roles, even if it was only for a day.

At the corner, by the street with the little shops and cafés that led to the market, she saw people with their shopping bags walking through the slanting sheets of rain: everyday lives, banal perhaps, but weighed down with work, she could identify with that, most of life got taken up with trivialities. So today she took an adventurous detour. She crossed the street. On the long side of the park, in front of number 77, her father's car was parked in its usual place.

"Anyone home?"

She had used her key. Now she was crossing the marble-tiled hall to the stairs, where she trod carefully to muffle her footsteps, the way one does unconsciously in a house whose occupants seem to have left. Down below, the door to the waiting room stood open, and her father's consulting room, as always, was closed. So where were they all? She supposed her father must be doing his rounds of the beds in the Binnengasthuis right now. And her mother must be shopping for food in town. As if she had all the time in the world, she went through the rooms on the first and second floors. In Armanda's room, the one with the balcony that had once been hers, she wanted to take a customary quick look in the mirror, but the wall next to the window was suddenly empty, and refused to allow her any reflection of her face. After that for some reason she couldn't resist a quick trip up to the attic. All dark, and what a hellish noise the wind was making against the roof. And of course there on his mattress under the low eaves she found her brother sleeping the way thirteen-year-olds can sleep, as if he were going to keep it up for all eternity. The little skylight was misted over. Daylight fell on the pillow. She looked at the pleading expression on the boy's face and thought: Why wait any longer?

Eventually she found the car keys on the desk in the consulting room.

A few minutes later Lidy, in a black Citroën, left the district where she had been born and raised and drove down the Ceintuurbaan toward the Amstel. At first, unfamiliar with the car, she had to grope for the gearbox. She practiced giving it gas a few times, used the engine to brake, gave it gas again. There was the crossroads, with the dilapidated church on the corner, then turn right. This was all part of a concatenation of different circumstances that had been set in motion the previous Monday, the 26th, when Armanda, in the grip of one of her spontaneous whims, had called Lidy to make her a proposal.

At first Lidy had hesitated. Staring at her fingernails, she had said, "Well, I don't really know . . ." to which Armanda pointed out that such an unexpected and comical excursion could really be fun. At that point there was silence for a moment as both of them recognized that the answer, given their relationship, was going to be yes. The younger could talk the elder so convincingly into something that what began as a tiny glimmer soon became an idea and the idea in turn became a wonderful idea.

"You can have Father's car, I've already wangled it for you," Armanda coaxed Lidy, who was always ready to be persuaded, and already seeing in her mind's eye a map of the western Netherlands stretching to the great arms of the sea.

It had happened late at night. Lidy had gone to bed, but stayed awake until she heard her husband come home. He had undressed in the bedroom without turning on the light and immediately tucked himself in close beside her as he always did. Peace reigned all around them. There were no noises of traffic out on the street, and the trees in the park at the front of the house stood there as if they had never strained in a north or southwest wind. Nevertheless, at this very moment, thousands of miles away, a depression had been set in motion, a tiny area of low pressure. Forming above the Labrador Sea, it had moved quite rapidly in an easterly direction, picking up one or two other depressions as it advanced.

When Lidy took the highway toward The Hague, she was able to turn off the windshield wipers after fifteen minutes; it was dry. Nevertheless she felt herself being buffeted insanely. The wind, which during the night had torn across Scotland with hurricane force, uprooting entire forests, and cleared the east coast of England at around dawn, was for her no more than a constant pressure that forced her to keep steering against it slightly, to the right. It was something you got used to after five minutes and then didn't think about again.

Shortly before she reached Maasshuis she stopped for gas. A young man in blue overalls filled her tank and washed her windows. Lidy followed him into the little office, which smelled of coffee and cigarettes. The news had just started on the radio.

"How do I get to the ferry?" she asked as the young man was closing the drawer of the cash register.

He indicated with his head for her to follow him and stood in the doorway to point the way. While Lidy nodded and took in the road that ran straight as a die until it finally curved slightly as it met a crossroads, the news announcer in the background began to read an announcement from the Flood Warning Service in a voice that projected no greater or lesser urgency than usual.

". . . Very high water levels in the area of Rotterdam, Williamstad, Bergen op Zoom, and Gorinchem . . ."

Lidy thanked the man and stepped back out into the wind.

"You can't miss it!" the gas station guy called after her.

And indeed she found her way quite easily. In no time at all she was at the harbor. She shielded her eyes with one hand. The water was very narrow. Nonetheless the far bank really was another bank, a gray line that seemed closer to being rubbed out than to holding firm. Her scarf tied round her head, she went to the pier, where there was a board with the ferry schedule on it. She read that the ferry coming from the other side wouldn't dock for another half hour. There was a little hut, up a couple of steps, where she ordered coffee. Dim light, the radio again, she let herself slide into the general mood of passive waiting. Just sitting there, nothing more. Dozily she put a cigarette between her lips.

What am I doing here, for heaven's sake? Who or what brought me here?

The Sisters

A quarter of an hour after she'd seen her sister alive for the last time, Armanda was walking across the market. She was pushing a stroller with a clear hood, and under the hood was Nadja. Because she was going to a party this evening, Armanda wanted to find a comb to wear in her hair. Because it was so windy and indeed the wind was picking up, many of the market people were packing up their goods and rolling up the awnings of their stalls. The pieces of cloth flapping around the poles contrasted with the anxious faces of the customers still peering inward in their winter coats gave Armanda the impression of a wild contagious abandon. She bought a comb and then added a couple of elastic hairbands decorated with tiny pearls. She pushed back the hood of the stroller and while the Syrian stallholder squatted down and held a mirror in front of the child, Armanda made two little ponytails on top of Nadja's head and wound the hairbands around them so that they stood straight up; Nadja now looked like a little marmoset.

"Look how pretty you are. . . ."

She loved the child. Nadja was something miraculous, the impudent trick Lidy had stunned her by pulling roughly two and a half years ago. Naked, in the room with the balcony, Lidy had poked herself gently in the belly with her forefinger. Armanda could still call up this image whenever she chose: tall, white Lidy, meeting her eyes in the mirror as she recounted how she'd been to the family doctor that afternoon, where she'd had to spread her knees embarrassingly wide over a pair of wretchedly hard stirrups.

"Oh, but . . ." Armanda had stammered after a pause. And then, "Didn't you take precautions?"

Overcome by a strange, dejected feeling that she'd lost something forever, she had looked at Lidy in the mirror, as Lidy turned toward her with a motion that for Armanda was synonymous with hips, shoulders, soft upper arms, breasts: a woman far gone in a love affair. It had been the beginning of summer, the middle of May, and just as Armanda was working out that it must have happened at the beginning of March, the phone rang. She ran out into the hall. After the spacious brightness of the room, it was suddenly dark, like a tunnel. Suddenly uncertain, she stopped, facing the wall with the ringing telephone, then reached for the receiver and heard the voice of someone she knew well and consequently could immediately see right there in front of her but now suddenly as if for the first time: long-limbed, good-looking, blond, a strong face with a fascinatingly intelligent nose. I always liked to talk politics, money, and English literature with him, I always liked it when he kissed me in that seductive, dangerous way you see in French films, God, it was fine with me back then: he kissed my throat, made a funny snorting noise as he pounced on the nape of my neck, he breathed into my ears, and after he'd done all that, he looked into my face, and I saw that his eyes were terribly serious. Good. But when nothing happened in the days that followed, no letter, no phone call, nothing . . . why didn't I wonder about it for a single moment?

It was Sjoerd Blaauw, a friend of hers who was now going out with Lidy. Still completely shaken, she greeted him with the first words that came into her head: "Sjoerd, while I've got you on the line, maybe you can tell me . . ."

Before she was able to ask whether the new Buñuel movie had opened at the Rialto, Lidy, in an unbuttoned checked dress, had snatched the receiver from her hands. There was a lot of breathless whispering, but Armanda was already out on the balcony, looking at the rear of the house on the Govert Flinkstraat, and it was dawning, dawning on her, as dawn it must, that she was already nineteen. A part of life she'd now missed out on, she thought. A shame, but don't keep looking at it, that part has turned elsewhere.

Below her in the gardens and inner courtyards the afternoon sun shone on sandboxes, sheds, dogs, bicycles. And in the foreground, in the decking of the balcony, were Lidy's freshly whitened tennis shoes, set out neatly to dry, and looking not white but orange in the reflection of the sun's rays. The two of them wanted to fall in love, okay, they've gone and done it and not by half measures either. I'm not pretending to myself: I'm really truly shocked! She had fiddled with her skirt, stared up into the air, and followed an imaginary bird with an old-spinsterish look in her eyes. Meanwhile her very simple thought was: I still have my life ahead of me, while she felt an unease that declared in essence, okay, maybe there are still terrific things in my future, but indications are that I lack the talent to experience them, or even recognize them when they're right in front of me.

Armanda went on studying English at university. Lidy broke off her degree in French language and literature to marry her hands-on lover, who already had a job with good prospects at Bank Mees & Hope. In the months that followed, there were no more comments about how much the two girls looked alike, because Lidy's belly was starting to swell. And not just the belly: her arms and legs also transformed themselves into soft, rounded masses of flesh. Her face, in which her eyelids drooped mysteriously, took on a look of plump melancholy. For the first time they looked totally unalike.

Once they had a conversation about this.

"What does it actually mean," said Lidy as she poured herself a glass of lemonade after taking a quick look at Armanda's still-half-full glass of port, "what does it actually mean to look alike? That we have the same color eyes?"

"I think so."

They took a short look at each other, as Lidy, in a way Armanda felt was significant, remarked, "Eme-rald-green."

It was the end of an afternoon in November. From the living room on the street side of the park, where Lidy now lived with her husband, it was almost possible to see the house where she and her sister had grown up.

Armanda drained her glass. She said, "Everyone loves the idea of brotherhood and sisterhood. God, it's lovely and all that but . . . I mean, why is it so lovely?"

"What do I know? Nesting instinct, some kind of memory of cuddling and being cuddled, and so on, being wise to all someone else's tricks, even the most innocent ones, you know . . ."

"And maybe that we're all going to die someday?"

"Oh God! Who knows—yes, that must be part of it too."

Armanda glanced down at the old Persian carpet from home, with the blue birds and the garlands, which oddly enough seemed much more familiar to her here, and also much more beautiful. As she stared at the blue birds, she said to herself: Once upon a time there were two girls, who wore the same clothes when they were children, who went to the same school when they turned six, and to the same high school when they were twelve. She looked up and continued out loud. "The Vossius Academy. Because both of them were good at languages, they decided to make this their specialty, and the older sister's textbooks could be passed straight on to the younger one two years later."

Lidy stared at her for a moment, nonplussed. "Hah, bound together by fate," she said, and poured Armanda's glass so full that she had to stick her head forward quickly and lap a couple of mouthfuls.

"Damn." Armanda had sat down again, her hands flat on the table on either side of her glass. "Your underlinings were still in them," she said. "Words of wisdom in Goethe, revenge and curses in Shakespeare, everything so frightfully beautiful and true. So my eyes would keep wandering to the same things you'd seen a couple of years before, the very same lofty, grandiose things."

She felt the alcohol going to her head.

A little hoarsely she went on: "Don't think I read all those beautiful things the same way you did."

The two of them were silent for a while. But the two of them had known each other so long that their observations and retorts continued unspoken.

With fat Lidy facing her like an idol, Armanda said rather sadly, "You can never feel what someone else feels." And as Lidy only nodded absentmindedly, she went on in the same tone, "The movements that little monster makes in your stomach, do you feel them the same way you feel your tongue moving in your mouth, only bigger?"

"What nonsense!" Lidy shot to her feet so uncontrollably that she had to hold tight to the edge of the table.

"Careful!" said Armanda affectionately but without moving an inch.

Lidy trudged awkwardly out of the room.

When she came back a few minutes later, Armanda's mood had changed. Taken aback, even deeply moved, she looked at Lidy's body as she spread her legs and laid her hands on her belly to sit down again beside her.

She leaned forward. Quietly and emphatically, like someone who has known something for a long time but only just found the way to put it into words, she said, "You know, quite objectively, I really can't stand myself."

"What?"

"True. If I had the choice, I'd prefer not to have that much to do with myself."

"Well, that's your bad luck."

"Don't laugh, it's true, even when I was a child I hadn't the faintest sympathy for myself, not the faintest."

Since she was a little drunk, she had trouble getting the words out, but her gesticulating hand spoke volumes.

"Those dresses with the smocking on the bodice never looked good on me."

"Oh, stop it."

"Forehead was too high for a child."

"True. Mine was too."

"Didn't suit me."

"Nonsense." Lidy contradicted her without paying much attention, but Armanda kept going, that most people felt really tender toward themselves. Not her. Which was why it really wasn't so bad, not bad at all, to have an older sister who was sitting here right now, right here opposite her with a body so much more voluminous than her own and so pleased with herself that it was totally infectious.

A sudden surge of love went through her that curiously she experienced first and foremost as love for herself.

"Not bad at all," she repeated warmly, looking up at her sister, unembarrassed, with tears in her eyes.

Lidy turned her head to one side.

"Be quiet."

Armanda also pricked up her ears. Downstairs the front door had opened and shut with a bang. She jumped to her feet. "Is it that late already?"

The staircase in this kind of house was narrow. If you hit the light switch with the automatic timer downstairs and started up, you could bet that the light would go out by the time you reached the half-landing. In the pitch darkness Armanda, still buttoning her coat, met Lidy's husband on his way upstairs with a rustling newspaper. Both of them had to laugh. Armanda felt his breath on her face.

After she'd done her shopping, Armanda took Nadja in the stroller back to Lidy and Sjoerd's house on the short side of the park. While she climbed the stairs one by one, holding the child by the hand, she was thinking about the evening to come, and the party, murmuring: After nine. He's not allowed to pick me up before nine. This time she really wanted to arrive a little late. Betsy often gave parties in her loft on the Nieuwezijds Voorburgwal. At first Armanda had been unable to believe that Sjoerd was the brother of this friend, who was quite a bit older than she was, and whom she admired for her narrow, intelligent face and curly black hair. Then she discovered that they were stepbrother and -sister, with the same father but different mothers.

She reached the top panting, having carried the child up the second flight of stairs. Why, the question suddenly struck her as she took out the little decorative comb in the living room and looked at it again, why had she set her heart on going to this party? Although she had already committed herself to a visit to Zierikzee (her annual pilgrimage of love, which until now had always been such a joy and which meant she really couldn't go to the party) on Monday evening she had gone out into the hall. Some decisions just make themselves. A firm plan—she wanted to wear the blue dress with the tight skirt—drew her to the phone and secured her sister on the other end of the line.

"Mrs. Blaauw."

Very funny even now. She cleared her throat sarcastically.

"Hello, it's me."

Lidy hadn't been able to get it at first and found it all a little strange: Armanda's goddaughter was turning seven and was determined that her aunt and beloved godmother, who came to visit once a year, must make the long trip to the little provincial town, bringing ballet shoes as a birthday present. And now Armanda was asking her to go in her place? Oh. But why?

"All right, okay, I guess it sounds like a nice idea," Lidy finally said after five minutes of to-and-fro.

It had been a sudden stirring, a blind impulse that had come to her the previous Monday from out of the blue, and which, just like that, she had allowed to take hold.

When Sjoerd came home shortly after midday, the table was covered with papers, and Armanda was hunched over her diploma thesis. She put down her pen and greeted him with a smile signifying that she and Nadja, who was at the head of the table with two fingers in her mouth, drawing a bear, had spent a wonderful morning together. She quickly poured him a cup of coffee; a plate of rolls sat on a dictionary between them. The mood was companionable as Sjoerd tried good-naturedly to report on the urgent meeting he'd had to have in the office this Saturday morning with a client involving a mortgage loan of many hundreds of thousands of guilders that would have to be converted in a flash on Monday into a 6 percent bond, but the thing didn't interest her, and conversation soon moved on to Betsy's party.

"Fine by me." He stared at her for a moment, and then said with the same indifference, "I'll pick you up at nine fifteen."

The rain had stopped, but the wind was still raging.

"Seems to be getting worse," he said, without turning to look at the window.

"Yes?"

Armanda observed his face, which was almost being erased by the background behind it: rattling panes of glass in the west-facing window, and behind them treetops swaying wildly in a chaos of branches. She was suddenly overcome by the feeling that everything was happening in almost farcical parallel with the story that had been occupying her for half the morning in her work, for the part she'd been working on involved a play in which a storm, conjured up by human powers, broke out and tore across an island. So—and why should that be impossible? By human powers? Out of revenge, out of holy outrage or some such? Now, as she thought back over it again, it didn't strike her as *not* at all unthinkable. In earlier times—and we can be sure that the human race was no dumber back then than it is now, maybe it was even a little more intelligent—people believed absolutely it was possible, highly possible, that mental energy, the mad heart of pure invention, could trick an event into becoming real. God, in short, and why not? Who says that everything that is fated to happen must first be properly thought out? Thought out and, maybe, written down in the most convincing way possible? She closed her books. While she was thinking that an event, if it announces itself, discovers that a place has already been made for it and hence connects so familiarly with the imagination that those it touches, i.e., us, respond accordingly, she gathered up her sheets of paper. Dialogues, gestures, scenes, everything already predigested by a literary memory.

She made an unconscious movement. Her pen rolled onto the floor. He bent down faster than she did.

"Thank you."

She saw something in his eyes as they flashed at her. What kind of marriage did the two of them have? she wondered, and at that moment something so wicked tightened around her heart that she didn't even try consciously to understand it. She stood up and started pushing her things into her bag.

"Okay," said Sjoerd, also getting to his feet.

Armanda bent down to fish her shoes out from under the table. She heard the house creak under the force of a squall. My God, she thought, with the detachment of the incurably candid, what a terrific, homely sound! Just think, the weather is going to get so much worse in the night that some of the ferry services will certainly get interrupted, and the captains can thumb their noses at the idea of working tomorrow, maybe even the day after tomorrow, maybe even till hell freezes over. Just think!

Looking distracted, she said good-bye.

As she and Sjoerd got out of the taxi that evening on Nieuwezijds Voorburgwal, Betsy's front door was standing open. Sjoerd took the four narrow, almost vertical flights of stairs so fast that they had to pant at each other speechlessly for a moment when they reached the apartment door at the top. He took the coat from her shoulders. There was already a mountain of wet clothes hanging over the banisters. Betsy discovered them, called out a welcome, and led them into the attic room that once upon a time had served as a secret church; it had very high ceilings and was already filled with the din of voices. Armanda was in seventh heaven. It felt so good to walk in with a carefree Sjoerd in his old tweed jacket. And naturally there were any number of more casual acquaintances who did a double take when they first saw her.

"Armanda," she had to say more than once. "I'm Armanda."

3

Landscape?

For the first time today she was crossing water. The Nieuwe Water-weg is a deep but fairly narrow channel—the ferry only needs ten minutes to get from one side to the other—but the fare between the two landing stages is still a quarter guilder. Lidy saw a shockingly old peasant's face loom up by her left-hand window. She understood, wound it down, and put the demanded coin in the ferryman's paw. As all the windows in the car promptly steamed up, she got out and was startled by the wind, which seemed to her to be extremely strong out here on the water.

She looked around, and was amused to see a broad-shouldered man in a captain's uniform up on the bridge, standing at the wheel and looking serious. I really am on a ship. Little waves all around, at an angle ahead of them an oceangoing steamer making course for the open sea, and over to the left the freighter RO8, headed toward the harbor in Rotterdam. Leaning against the car, she was standing in the blurry light of an imminent rain shower. Under the roof of the gangway, people with bicycles and people on foot. Her eye fell on a chest standing next to the railing, with *Life Vests* painted on it in white letters, as if to make absolutely clear to her once more that she really had left dry land. A few minutes later and the ship was already swinging round and coming to a stop. The loading ramp landed on the quay with a loud crash. And yet: as Lidy drove onto the island of Rozenburg, the crossing, regardless of how short it had been, had succeeded in placing a greater distance between her and home than she had expected or intended. This little outing was supposed to be only a fantasy, wasn't it, a little exercise in tyranny on the part of her sister, Armanda, one that she herself had almost no part in?

Right, but in the hours that followed there was no pretense of a proper road to follow. A labyrinth of little side roads, locks, and bridges demanded her total attention. Impossible to think anything else in life more important, even for a moment, than the route, which seemed to have a will of its own and cared very little about the map spread out on the passenger seat. Near Nieuw-Beijerland she had to take another ferry, and a quarter of an hour later she reached the sea dike with a narrow asphalt road along the top. She stopped and ran in the wind to a faded street sign on which, luckily, she was able to decipher the name Numansdorp. That was where the harbor must be, at the Hollands Diep, which was the departure point for several ferries that made the crossing of the long arm of the sea.

The sea itself was not to be seen. But she had its unmistakable smell in her nose as she hit the gas again and put her face up close to the windshield, peering out at the landscape with the first stirrings of alarm. Landscape? In contrast to the huge arch of space above, the ground was almost erased. The solid rain cover had been shredded by the wind. Clouds with glistening edges were being pushed in front and behind one another like flats of scenery across the panorama on the other side of the windshield. To what extent were there any inhabitants in this panorama? She overtook only two disheveled cyclists with the wind at their backs, and once a farmer waiting on a side road with horse and cart waved when she honked at him. Tops of steeples, farmsteads, windmills with flying sails, a horse behind a fence—everything buried by the sky all the way to the dike, which wasn't that high but still drew your eyes away from the sea. Ghostly, she thought. The harbor took forever to come into view. She wished she could see both land and sea at the same time. This was still the province of South Holland, a sort of betwixt-and-between area with bare black polders that was, however, familiar to her. Her plan was to get to the harbor in Numansdorp and take the ferry across to Zeeland, a province she had never set foot in, but whose shadow she had already been sensing all morning, because it was the goal of her journey. That her compass needle was pointing her toward a group of completely unknown people, a family in a little rural town that didn't interest her, had never interested her, and doubtless never would, was something that she was gradually coming in the course of these few hours to find completely normal.

And when were they actually expecting this godmother?

It was now two o'clock. On the coast, the wind was strengthening to thirty knots, which corresponds to a full 7 on the Beaufort wind force scale, and from now on, was going to increase at the rate of another Beaufort number every hour. Lidy reached the port and drove into the town square. To her delight, she saw that she could continue her journey exactly as she had planned it that morning. Next to a couple of rocking freighters, the ferry, *Den Bommel*, was waiting at the quayside, and there was space to load her car. That part of the jetty was completely submerged didn't strike her as being in any way out of the ordinary.

Nor indeed was it. Twice a month on average the water in the Hollands Diep rose to the level known as the boundary-depth gauge, and even regularly topped it. That brought with it the regular local flooding without anyone making a fuss about it. She got out. The way to the booth where the ferry tickets were sold was blocked by an uprooted tree. She clambered over it and made sure she worked her way into the lee of the wind by the harbor office. As she joined the queue, her face was as flushed as the faces of the other passengers for the Numansdorp-Zijpe ferry, all of them talking cheerily, even with relish, about the weather. We know what storms are. When it blows, it blows, it's pretty strong today but we've seen worse!

Ten minutes later she reversed down a pretty steep ramp and over the metal plates in the hold, and got out of the car. An iron interior stairway led her up into the passenger lounge, which had a billiards table and a bar. The ferries were stable old tubs. *Den Bommel* registered 10,000 tons and had a 400-horsepower diesel engine that could power the ship at ten knots all the way to Schouwen-Duiveland in two hours. Bad weather, i.e., a storm out of the west or the northwest above gale force 9 in this treacherous area, demanded great skill from the pilot. Wind speeds of forty to sixty knots could transform the waters of Haringvliet, Volkerak, and Grevelingen into seas of steep, relentlessly oncoming waves. No boat should if at all possible present itself to them broadside.

Find a fixed point and keep looking at it. The feeling is worse than being drunk. Sitting at a table with a fried egg sandwich and a hot chocolate in front of her, it didn't take her long to realize she'd be better off in the open air. The tilting floor and the heaving of the world outside the windows bore no relation to what she was perceiving with her eyes or any other of her senses. Deathly white, she hurried to the middle deck, where more passengers were standing in the shelter provided by the engine room and staring fixedly at the massive volumes of oncoming water.

Her sick feeling vanished in an instant. Then she became aware that she was being observed from the side. A passenger standing next to her was just opening his mouth to say something to her, but she pointedly kept her eyes fixed in the distance. Reading the map in her mind's eye, she knew that what she was crossing right now was the junction of Haringvliet and Hollands Diep en route to the smaller arm of the Volkerak, but the tide was on the rise, and it was clear that the North Sea was now the master here. Genuinely beautiful. The surface of the water was coming at her in wave after wave of blue light, overlaid with such white streaks of foam that it was impossible to understand where the reflection was coming from.

Why can't I see any shoreline, why aren't there any steeples or roofs? Surely there's land all round me?

"Just look at that!" a voice said next to her.

It was her fellow traveler. A bear of a man with a red face was pointing something out to her with an outstretched arm and a serious expression. She looked at where he was pointing and nodded thoughtfully as she was told that there was usually excellent rabbit hunting on the foreshore of the dike, but the whole thing was now underwater. Then, as if in answer to a question, the man told her his occupation. "Chief engineer with the Royal Hydraulic Engineering Authorities."

What? Ah. Disinclined to diminish the spectacle of the sea with idle conversation, she nonetheless replied, "So that means this magnificent view is—your field of work?"

"Yes, exactly."

The chief engineer bent closer to her. She got a strong whiff of alcohol. "What you're looking at, miss, is a tide that will rise way above the depth gauges at a whole number of monitoring stations, I can tell you from experience."

She said nothing and frowned.

Her companion was now looking at her intently. "What you're seeing here," he said slowly, emphatically, "is the rising sea level, nothing special in and of itself, since it occurs with every tide. Obviously you're familiar with this. An affair of the sun and the moon, which exert a pull on the water." He balled both hands and lifted them to demonstrate. "But sometimes, umm, the tide speaks the language of the wind, not of astronomy."

"Excuse me?"

"Yes. Sometimes it's the storm that gives the water here along the coast an additional brute of a shove and lifts it higher."

She wasn't looking away anymore. She turned halfway toward her interlocutor, which didn't mean that the expanse of water that the ship had now left behind was ceasing to have an effect on her—on the contrary, she reached for her lingering sense of direction and transformed it into a kind of anesthetic, through which the voice of the chief engineer echoed with all the logic of a dream. . . .

"My God," she said.

"I take it that you're ready for me to give you a few facts and figures. Or . . . ?"

She nodded.

"Well . . ." The chief engineer glanced upward for a moment to focus his concentration. "This century has already seen quite a number of storm tides, and most of them were minor; we get a minor storm tide here almost every year, and things are underwater all over the place, you know. Medium storm tides, which is what we call them at the Hydraulic Authorities, pack a bigger wallop, they occur, let's say, between once a decade and once every hundred years. Remember the winter of 1906, when a hurricane drove the North Sea near Vlissingen up almost fourteen feet above the Normal Amsterdam Water Level, causing enormous damage. I'm sorry? No, nobody drowned. Or maybe just one or two."

The chief engineer massaged his hands. She saw that his face was changing, saw that minor and moderate storm floods were visibly giving way to something more drastic, and here it came: "The third category that we distinguish is the high storm flood. A frequent phenomenon? No. Occurs merely once every hundred to a thousand years. Good, I see you're nodding. The Hydraulic Authorities have never actually measured one as such, let alone broken it down into accurate statistics."

He paused for a moment. Then, with a kind of enthusiasm that mystified her, he explained that science did recognize a supreme category of storm tide, a four-star ranking, signifying a catastrophe that, however unlikely, could not be written off as impossible just because it might occur in this part of the world every ten thousand years.

He leaned forward with his head and mouthed something, but she didn't understand.

"Sorry?" she asked, and the answer came in a roar.

"The extreme storm flood! Oh! Can you just imagine it? Have you never heard anything about the hellish catastrophes in the old days? The Saint Elisabeth's flood in the fifteenth century, that swallowed up our entire province of South Holland? A century later: Saint Felix, even worse, a storm that felt called upon to restore all the mussels and crabs to the twenty villages around Reimerswaal in perpetuity. And then, darn it, forty years later, in the blink of an eye, statistically speaking, enter the All Saints Flood, and people are thinking all over again that it's the end of the world!"

The chief engineer laughed for a moment. Then: "Nature's fits of rage, every one of them responsible for enormous numbers of deaths!" Did she also grasp that this entire spectacle often ran its course with such extreme results not merely by force of nature but because of the shiftless maintenance of the dikes? Only a mountain contained its own mass unaided. Please would she believe him if he assured her—it was clear that he wanted to utter some unvarnished truth, the kind that makes your ears prick up—assured her as an insider, that the crests of the dikes even today failed to meet the norm?

He was looking at her with the peremptoriness of a man who knows the figures pretty damn well.

"Umm . . . you're a nice young lady. Am I alarming you?"

Not at all, though now her eyes were fixed on something else. A little ship, tiny in fact. It was about sixty yards away, chugging along in the opposite direction. She squeezed her eyes shut. Sometimes it disappeared up to the wheelhouse in the waves, and then she would be able to see the black tarpaulin and read the name, *Compassion*, before it plunged back into the depths. Rays of light piercing down through the cloud formations gave the scene a theatrical air.

"I . . . think it's really beautiful."

"Indeed, it's impressive," the chief engineer admitted. Then, after a pause: "Cosmic and earthly powers from unimaginably distant regions are converging right in front of us."

She gave a searching look into his slightly bloodshot eyes. He wasn't grinning.

"Lofty words."

"Am I boring you?"

"Absolutely not. Actually, this is my first time here." And like someone who in a chance moment recognizes that the heavens are the eternal, everlasting, primeval landscape of our minds, she said, "Yes, we say it's beautiful, but just think of everything that lies behind it all, you know?"

"True, true."

Unanimity. Which the chief engineer took advantage of to turn the conversation to the jet stream, the great band of wind racing through the topmost layer of the troposphere. Six to eight miles up it sweeps across continents and is capable of compressing the atmosphere into a single area of unbroken low pressure, or pumping it into an area of high pressure, just like a balloon.

"Picture it like a gigantic bicycle pump."

She did, but meanwhile kept peering at the horizon: for some time now they had been sailing parallel to dikes on which occasionally a little building was to be seen, and even a church steeple poking up here and there. On one of these she spotted a wildly fluttering flag. That's already the second or third today, she thought, until it dawned on her that it was Princess Beatrix's birthday. How old was she? Fourteen? Fifteen?

"And finally we get to the weather," said the chief engineer. "Rain, wind, yeah. Weather is never-ending, isn't it? Strictly speaking, weather and wind are the backdrop to our entire lives."

"Odd thought."

"Air, that does nothing but stream from an area of high pressure into an area of low pressure."

She smiled at him over her shoulder almost companionably, but he curbed this immediately. In a tone that was suddenly almost authoritarian he said, "Umm, as you will feel, the force of the wind is picking up by the minute!"

Meantime the ship had clearly changed course, and was beginning to pitch and toss. She noticed that the shorelines in either direction were farther away again and that they were sailing straight into the wind. The voice of the chief engineer, almost impossible to understand now, was still delivering his fantastical nature lecture at her. When she didn't react, he tapped her on the arm.

"And do you want to know about this racket? Believe me, if the monstrous eye of this storm is gathering itself over the North Sea and sucking everything up with all its force—do you get it?—that's what it'll take—that's when we can look forward to a really major show."

This seemed to end the conversation. Seemed to, for Lidy, who was actually thinking, God, fine, now how can I just get rid of this man, stood for several seconds staring back at him.

"Yes?" asked the chief engineer.

She shook her head and looked away.

As far as the eye could see, the oncoming flood tide. Both of them looked at it, until the chief engineer turned to her again. Emphatically, as if imparting a conclusion, he said, "Vlissingen. Hook of Holland."

Yes?

Could she imagine that after a weekend like this he was going to be really dying to know what the monitoring stations over there were going to produce as today's measurements?

Feeble laugh. Her back half turned to him, she didn't say anything in reply. The chief engineer moved so that he was in front of her again. She clasped her hands, rubbed them, and blew on them. Now what?

"I think I'm going to lie down."

If that was okay with her. He said he was going to stretch out on one of the benches in the passenger area, the wedding he was coming from in Hoeksche Waard had gone on till dawn. There was nothing he liked better, he explained, than to sleep in storms and bad weather. So he was going to give himself a little foretaste of tonight. Hadn't she had enough of the cold and the wind? Okay, he shook her hand and then in the same gesture threw his arm wide.

"Over there is England, that way at an angle is France, up there are the West Frisian Islands, and we're in the middle. Imagine a sculpture made of water, an ocean mountain range, relatively low at the outlying foothills but rising to a monumental height in the middle, and then draw a vertical line from there to here!"

The chief engineer laughed as he headed for the stairs. His voice and the wind had been piercing in her ears.

Dusk. An afternoon in January. Lidy, on a ferry on the Krammer, knew roughly where she was. The Krammer is the southeastern part of the Grevelingen, and the Grevelingen is the arm of the North Sea that divides South Holland and Zeeland.

Known facts that could put up no fight whatever against what was playing out before her eyes, and not only before her eyes. Underneath her, in the depths, and behind her something was also in motion that could not be marked on a map or a chart. It did not even reveal itself to the eye. Huge and deafening, it seemed to survey its own surroundings, with intentions that no human being could put into words, for the simple reason that no human being had even the smallest role to play in what was going on. You could at best try to transcribe it as: a cold wind is blowing in off the sea—and leave it at that.

Birds were still flying. She watched the gray-black specks sail out from under the layer of clouds. They must have convincing reasons to fly even short distances in this witches' cauldron. As she looked from the birds to the waves, which were piling yards high and yet somehow remained beneath her feet, she made the discovery that "under" and "over" no longer existed. And because it was getting darker by the minute, she was soon unable to make out any wider space anymore, nor any expanse of water, only streaks of foam. Whitish, azure green. Into which the ferry plunged in the circuslike glare of its floodlights, disappearing into them, then surging up again as it continued a journey that had lost all relation to time. All it had now was circumstances.

She gave a start and quickly began to think of home, for suddenly she had seen herself, bundled in her winter coat, on the middle deck. A strange, thoughtless young woman. Everything vital to her overtaken by the spectacle surrounding her. In such a place the thing to do is to blindfold oneself and think of home. Think where the chairs and tables are.

Which ones? She noticed that she was totally muddling up the furniture in number 77 and number 36. These carpets went here, the others went there, mustn't mix them up. She began pro forma to picture Sjoerd's bachelor apartment on Korsjespoortsteeg, where she had followed him one winter afternoon. Back then, after the first time they'd made love, she had lain in bed watching the curtains in front of the sliding windows wave softly to and fro in the draft, but now this was a soulless memory. Love had come quickly. She had met him only the week before at one of the tennis courts in the Apollo Hall, just reopened for the first time since the war. Beginning of February? In January there had been freezing weather seven days in a row, yet suddenly the very idea of going skating seemed over. She had sat with a little group on a sort of terrace at the side, watching a mixed-doubles match. Armanda and Sjoerd, Betsy's half brother, against Betsy and some partner or other. When the game was over, Sjoerd had looked at the chair next to her, as if he'd known the whole time, and indeed kept an eye out, that it was free. And after that, the date. And Sjoerd, after a short stroll in the exceptionally mild winter weather that was supposed to last for weeks now according to the weather forecast, took her to his intimate little pad on the fourth floor and didn't waste any time in making clear what he wanted. She had been ready for the taking, she still remembered, and she also knew that she always would be: the frankness of male sexuality. Horniness, flattery, and getting-to-know-you-better all in one. His hands had found their way under her skirt in the nicest way.

She held on tight. The ship suddenly tilted twenty degrees to port, if not more. An enormous sea towered up off the starboard bow and rolled without breaking in a dark green mass over the ship, which began to spew water like crazy from all the scuppers.

A cold wind is blowing in off the sea. . . .

Of course it spoke to her. Thrillingly inhospitable world, thrillingly bad weather! What could be more irresistible? Particularly when it was a question of mother-love. Can one ever look in to check on one's sleeping child more adoringly than when the wind is howling and the shutters are banging? Determined to counter the present uproar with something of her own, she thought: Nadja. She also thought: Since you arrived, everything has been more complete. But what she saw as she was thinking was that this was a photo, an unsuccessful snapshot, in which she is standing with the child against her neck, looking into the lens and staring back at herself with empty, blanked-out eyes.

Leave it alone. This air and this arm of the sea contain no trace of you. The young woman—you—who left home this morning must get hold of herself for a moment and take a long look at her own happiness. Her hands and face were stiff with cold. Then—the ship had swung around and, propelled by a squall, flew right toward the Zijpe dock on Schouwen-Duiveland—she was shocked out of her thoughts. Den Bommel had crashed against the fenders with a sound like an exploding mine.

No other ferry captain in the coming days would attempt to make the crossing.

4

So *You* Go

They left around 1 a.m. Although the party was nowhere near winding down, Armanda had said, "Shall we go?" to Sjoerd as she laid her fingers on the lapels of his jacket.

"Good idea," he said in a way that suggested that he had just had the same idea himself, and the fact that as he said this he took hold of her for a moment, simply grabbed her by the hips, was nothing surprising, because they had got on incredibly well all evening to the point where they were feeling basically intimate.

Parties: parties underline life's festiveness, as Armanda had felt from the very first minute this evening. The attic room was heated by a cylindrical oil stove with a pipe that ran clear through the entire space, and this alone—the contrast between the glowing warmth and the filthy weather outside—had immediately put her in the mood, relaxed, free from . . . what, she didn't know. When their hostess came over after about twenty minutes to ask her and Sjoerd, "Hey, where's Lidy?" Armanda had already greeted a lot of people and smiled and finished her first glass of wine.

"Lidy?" she repeated.

Through the voices and the soft jazz playing, Betsy asked again, "Why didn't Lidy come with you?"

They were standing in a circle, Betsy, Sjoerd, two or three other guests, and her. Oddly, just as she was about to answer, she was distracted by the red velvet band that Betsy was wearing around her neck, and indeed by Betsy altogether. Her friend, ten years older, was extraordinarily pretty, she was struck by this all over again, a grown-up kind of pretty, and her dress with its tight bodice, fashionably up-to-the-minute, looked fantastic on her. Luckily she didn't look too bad herself, for a moment she saw herself standing in the front of the mirror at home a few hours ago and then as she was here, now, in the candlelit attic room in her little cocktail dress, skirt three-quarters of an inch below the knee, rounded neckline, from a pattern she'd found in *Marion*. Sometimes people said she looked like Vivien Leigh, and this evening she thought there was maybe something to it. The faintest hint of the characteristics of someone else to enhance what one was already . . . a little bewitched by her own image of herself, she stretched out her hand toward Betsy and touched the red velvet band.

"Lovely!"

The little group was standing next to the sideboard, where every imaginable kind of food was already set out. Armanda leaned to the side, took a little toast square with smoked salmon on it, the sort of thing that you can pop into your mouth whole in a perfectly genteel way, and noticed, as she was chewing it, that the others were still looking at her expectantly. She swallowed hastily.

"Lidy's in Zeeland," she said, out of breath.

"Why on earth?" asked Betsy.

"Oh . . . I think she wanted to get into the car and just go. Yes, she wanted to be behind the wheel again. You lose the knack so quickly, don't you?"

She saw someone in the group nod.

"Actually I had something to do with it," she went on. "I have a goddaughter out there, you didn't know that, did you? A little treasure, today's her seventh birthday, she set her heart on getting a pair of ballet shoes from her godmother."

Betsy smiled as she eyed her, but she also raised an eyebrow. Meanwhile someone had turned up the volume on the music, a slow clarinet solo. Armanda raised her voice accordingly, but also because this time she'd be able to give the right answer to the question.

"But when we were talking on the phone, Lidy and I, at the beginning of the week and the subject of this little trip to Zeeland came up, she was immediately all fired up about it. Wouldn't you really rather go to Betsy's party, my beloved sister asked all casually, but I know her. First I just let her ask about how far it was, and the state of the roads, and the possibility of doing most of this magical journey on a boat, and then finally I gave way. Okay, fine, I said, then why don't you go in my place."

This was what Armanda said, and then looked past the others into the room in a slightly confused way, watching a few of the guests already slow-dancing a barely recognizable fox-trot to the lone clarinet; when she brought her gaze back to the group around her, she realized Sjoerd was watching her closely, with a rather ambiguous look. She looked right back at him, and immediately caught herself remembering the one time he had kissed her on the mouth, in black and white, a movie still. She quickly registered that his expression was softening.

I'm a little dizzy, she said to herself, but it feels good. Everything around me looks a bit blurred, it must be the cigarette smoke, all those blue rings and snaky white garlands going up to the ceiling in the heat of the candle flames. Besides which I feel hot. Is this life?

She had openly given him a very loving look.

The slow fox-trot was suddenly broken off with a scratching noise—someone had decided it was too early to set that mood—not to sound out again, even more mistily, until hours later, when everyone, as if at the wave of a wand, was ready to listen as the clarinet wove its tale of desire, consent, and the tenuous boundary that divides them. Armanda and Sjoerd sought each other out without hesitation and pressed themselves together. After spending the entire evening in such close proximity, it felt right to them, and everyone else, to dance cheek to cheek. Outside all was stormy night, and neither of them cared what anyone might think who saw that here, under the wood-beamed ceiling, a man was cradling the sister of his wife in his arms, his mouth pressed to her ear. The mood that held them both captive was unmistakable.

She descended the stairs behind him. He had called for a taxi, and as the stand was close by, they were already on their way downstairs.

The front door was stuck. He reached past her in the hall and used force. Rain immediately stung her face. The taxi didn't come. She kept taking quick peeks out from behind the half-closed door at the dark street and at a gaggle of dripping cyclists leaning against a lamppost. Apart from that, absolutely nothing was going on.

Ten minutes later, as they were running down the little side street, she was still holding his hand and they both laughed at the whole show. At the dam there wasn't a taxi to be seen. They crossed the road fast and stood in the doorway of a clothing store, though it faced north and provided little protection. She was absolutely freezing, shivered as she raised her collar, but held herself a little apart from Sjoerd. As she peered across the square, she could barely recall the happy atmosphere at the party, full of promises of the sort that don't necessarily raise expectations that they're going to become reality.

"Here comes one," she called, and ran with her shawl over her soaking wet hair, hanging down in rats' tails.

The taxi driver, like all taxi drivers in this city, was a talker. Huddled close together again in the soft backseat of the car, Armanda and Sjoerd had to put up with being told that the situation of the traffic this evening was extremely precarious. At the Keizersgracht an uprooted tree had blocked the road from Raadhuisstraat all the way to Berenstraat; in Bos en Lommer the balcony of one of the apartment houses still under construction had been ripped off and came crashing down on the streetcar rails; and in the square in front of the main train station, the taxi driver said, keeping up a steady speed automatically, he had had to swerve to avoid a 200-foot crane that was swaying toward the water at the edge of the open harbor while firemen raced to and fro.

"Dangerous weather," said the taxi driver expectantly, turning round to them for a long moment. As he kept them under observation in the rearview mirror, he told them all about a deadly accident on the Kattenburg earlier in the evening and was about to report on a traffic jam on the Wallen when he hit the brakes and went into a skid. The engine died, the driver snarled a curse, restarted it at once, and drove, craning his neck in curiosity, slowly past a crumpled motorbike with a sidecar lying in the middle of the pitch-dark Vijzelstraat.

"A Zündapp," he said. "Beautiful machine." And, as he shifted back into top gear, he went straight into his report about the state of traffic on the Wal, where the usual mob of drunks was letting vehicles pull up right in front of the doors of the bars, because they didn't want to take a single step outdoors with all the roof tiles flying around loose in the narrow streets.

"Typical drunk's thinking," said the taxi driver. "They totter smack into a canal without their brains sending out the slightest warning, but they have a real respect for roof tiles."

Chunks of wood, shards of glass, bits of bicycles, branches, newspapers, umbrellas, cardboard boxes, everything lying in the rain, which had meantime slackened to a gentle patter. Armanda and Sjoerd, stunned, looked out over the front seat at the city, glistening in the headlights. The well-known bridges. A little circuitous path along the river. And there was De Pijp with its precise grid of streets. As they got out at the corner of the park, Armanda felt the street plan of her home city coil around her, life-threateningly, darkly, wetly, capturing numbers 77 and 36 in its grasp, the one on the long side of the park, the other on the short.

They were standing facing each other. Armanda yawned. Through a crack in the clouds, a ray of light from the hidden full moon fell onto her storm-ravaged face.

"I'm tired."

"So go to sleep."

Sjoerd, his arm round her shoulder, accompanied her to number 77, where the outside light was burning. She asked if he'd like to come to breakfast tomorrow. A nod, yes, maybe, but she shouldn't count on him. Speaking of which, what time should he pick Nadja up? She groped in her coat pocket for the key. Oh, whenever it suited him.

He waited till she was inside and had closed the front door behind her.

How good it felt on a stormy night to slip into your bed in flannel pajamas! It didn't take Armanda five minutes to get ready and then go into the next room to check on Nadja, who was sleeping stretched out like a kitten; now she was closing her eyes. First she cast her mind back for a moment to the party, conversations, images, then for the umpteenth time began to ask herself if her life wasn't fundamentally colorless and bland, a pale reflection of something that certainly existed in her heart but clearly had no parallel in reality. What do I want my life to be?

Twenty-one already, she thought sleepily, but still no experience of life, and still a virgin, dammit, and I know a whole bunch of my fellow students who are no longer obliged to say the same. Then, as if riffling through a photo album, she saw the faces of friends and acquaintances merge, simply become details that gradually combined themselves into *one* anonymous face that she gazed at provocatively, brimming over with the sheer excitement of her own vital energy. You think I'm a fool, she thought in her dreams, just as she sometimes thought when she was wide awake. *What*, is that what it's about? Are those the adventures that hide behind your secretive faces, that I've been avoiding for reasons I don't understand myself? Doesn't compare very well with the things that are going to happen and that I don't actually know yet from direct experience but still I know are possible. She turned on her side. With a sleeper's acumen she picked one face out of the array of those staring at her.

Lidy Blaauw-Brouwer. Who had given birth in the early onset of winter in 1950–51 to a little daughter, Nadine ("We're going to call her Nadja"), thereby also giving herself an enchanting task that would last her the rest of her life.

She was now deeply asleep. As one ear continued to register the satisfying sounds of the storm, her brain was still lingering a little on Lidy, who had walked around her living room one winter evening with a nursing infant on her arm as if nothing, absolutely nothing in the world, could come close to equaling this experience. In the same room with her were two admirers: her husband and her younger sister, who had just realized that if things had gone a little, just a very little differently, this man could as easily have been loved by her, immoderately.

The sleeping girl lingered over this truth, which frightened her not at all; on the contrary, it left her in a state of private yearning as the hours slipped by unmarked. Toward dawn, she was rewarded with an erotic dream. She was startled awake, in a state of euphoria, only to plunge back into the dream's continuation. It was dark, and Sjoerd was seizing her shoulders to turn her around. It wasn't an embrace.

Rather he was pushing her away from him by the shoulders, but this was made difficult for him because she refused to take a step back. This image was followed by a series of uninhibited details that jolted her mind as she woke up again, roused this time by a child's solid little knee planted in her stomach. It was morning, and Nadja had climbed into bed with her aunt. Armanda pushed back the bedclothes and let the child snuggle up against her.

When she appeared for breakfast at around 10:30, everything still seemed perfectly normal, cozy, small-format. It was Sunday, and at home people listened to the national news on radio only on weekdays at 8 a.m. She said good morning to her mother, kissed her father, and laughed at Nadja, who was using both hands to push a rusk sprinkled with a crumbled lump of aniseed sugar up to her mouth. She sat down next to her father at the side of the table in the bay window on the second floor, which allowed a view of most of the street.

"Yes," she said in reply to a remark of her father's about the storm. "Just awful." She followed his eyes to the broken branches on the cobblestones as she stretched out an arm to take the cup of tea her mother had poured for her.

It was a peaceful moment, despite the stormy weather. Armanda was wearing a blue bathrobe; her parents, smelling of shaving soap and eau de cologne, were already fully dressed. Jan Brouwer and Nadine Langjouw: people with fixed habits and habitual sunny dispositions, made even sunnier this morning by the presence of the little girl. Armanda couldn't remember ever having heard her parents raise their voices to each other.

Shortly after eleven, they saw Sjoerd marching toward them through the swirling debris on the street, coattails flapping.

"In Zandvoort the sea's lapping up over the boulevard," he reported as he came in. Coffee was ready on the table. He sat down with them, saying that a friend had called to say why don't we go and take a look at IJmuiden, the water's lifted some of the ships right up onto the quay.

Armanda was wandering around restlessly, pouring coffee, sitting down again, running her fingers over the embroidery on the tablecloth, and when she looked up, she met the eyes of her mother, who asked, "So when's Lidy getting back?" as if she was supposed to know.

"We didn't settle on a specific time," Sjoerd answered for her. And then, after stubbing out his cigarette and beginning to get to his feet: "Should I give her a call, maybe?"

Upon which the rest of a day began, which would fix itself permanently in Armanda's mind as a series of household tasks whose simple familiarity concealed something utterly sinister.

Sjoerd came back into the living room from the hall. He hadn't been able to get through to Schouwen-Duiveland.

"The line to the island is stone dead."

At almost the same moment Armanda saw her father bent over in the corner, turning the knobs on the radio. The dial glowed green. She heard the voice of the announcer, heard him say that Army Central Command had ordered all military personnel on weekend leave to return to barracks at the same time as she waved hello to her brother, Jacob, who had finally slept himself out and was now in search of breakfast, still looking a little pale but already sufficiently awake to pay attention to the news.

"Oh, it's war." He took a roll.

Sjoerd left the house. Armanda went to get dressed and to tidy her room, in order to have something to do. While her hands were busy with the bed, the washbasin, and the wall cupboard, the radio was still on in the living room. The male voice calmly reported collapsed dikes, floods in the cities of Dordrecht and Willemstad, even danger to human life. At six o'clock, she and her mother began to make dinner. Darkness came early today. A Beechcraft from the military airfield at Gilze-Rijen had done a reconnaissance flight during the afternoon over West Brabant, Zeeuws-Vlaanderen, Walcheren, and Goeree. Everything was underwater.

As for Schouwen-Duiveland: no word.

She lay awake in the night; she was sick of the storm, which was still raging. Lidy hadn't phoned once during the whole day. It would be good, she thought rather crossly, if you checked in tomorrow, Sister, surely you must realize we're worried to death about you!

Near morning the newspaper thumped through the letterbox. She heard it and went downstairs. Switching on the lamp in the hall, she stared at the huge headline: ZEELAND WIPED OFF THE MAP, and then read a report that struck her as being no report but a complete fantasy.

"The Dakota flew low over the boiling waters of the Krammer in the direction of Schouwen-Duiveland. The island, battered and then overwhelmed, has ceased to exist. Entire villages lay strewn like driftwood along the broken dikes. Zierikzee was crying its death song. The spring tide has destroyed the harbor, and the North Sea has poured in from behind to attack the surrounding polders in a surprise rearguard pincer movement that has annihilated them."

Shivering, she went up the stairs, had a brief thought of How was I to know . . . and then blocked it out. She crawled back into her warm bed, but stayed sitting upright. Her mind in a daze, suddenly aware of this one tiny point in time against the background of the endless roll call of place-names, she looked at the alarm clock on the night table beside her. Half past six. Eyes open and then squeezed tight shut, Armanda for the first time saw her sister as she would appear to her, pitilessly from now on. Tragic, even heroic, in front of a landscape reduced to a wasteland.

5

This Was Once a Town

As Lidy reached Schouwen-Duiveland in late afternoon, not tired at all, indeed wide awake, the flood tide had already passed the high-water mark, and the Flood Warning Service had immediately decided to put out one of their rare radio alerts. It spoke—in anticipation of the night to come—of a "dangerous high tide."

She had taken the last ferry of the day to risk the crossing from Numansdorp to Zijpe. The entry into the harbor was so rough that it triggered a short-lived outbreak of screaming and running around on the decks. Nevertheless it wasn't ten minutes before she was raising a hand in greeting to the boy who had lowered the ramp, and she drove unhesitatingly onto the island of her destiny.

The heavy cloud cover was breaking here and there. By the light of the hidden moon, she followed a little road that offered no resistance to the storm. During the war, the island had been flooded by the Germans, killing both trees and hedges. The drainage ditches to left and right were full to the brim. Wherever she looked, cold, wet, dark land stretched away in all directions, but this didn't depress her. After all these hours, she accepted the howling wind, the cold, and the wet as part and parcel of her little odyssey. Even when she had to swerve as she rounded a bend to avoid at least ten hares racing along the road in the same direction as the car, she didn't take this as a sign.

"Hares!" she said, nonplussed as she switched back into her lane, for she had taken the animals for huge cats at first glance.

To her right were streetcar rails. A distant bell made her aware that a streetcar was coming up behind her, then for a few minutes it was moving alongside. If she looked to the side she could see travelers buttoned up in their coats in the well-lit interior, playing cards and eating sandwiches. Then the streetcar overtook her, and shortly thereafter forced her to a halt when it stopped to let off a few passengers, who then crossed the road.

View of a village. A streetcar stop, a brand-new streetlamp, a row of low houses closed tight, and a bicycle against a wooden fence; a day later all this would be gone, vanished forever, but for now it was still a perfectly normal Saturday evening in winter, the nicest night of the week. Another twenty-four hours and the first house walls would be collapsing outward, the storm would continue unabated, snow would be falling, all this was inevitable. What was also inevitable was that Lidy accelerated again, passed the back of an instant coffee factory, left the built-up area behind her, and three miles farther on could see the little provincial town with its oversize late-Gothic church tower spread out in front of her.

She drove in through the Noordhaven Gate.

A sparsely lit backdrop. An inner harbor with quays, lined with splendid ancient houses, each with a flight of steps leading to the front door protected by a balustrade. Houseboats in the water. Here and there were pedestrians to be seen striding along purposefully in the wind or slowing down, if they were in a group, to have a discussion about something that involved lots of gesticulation. She drove slowly past the grand houses, some of which had subsided, their windows pitch-black, and turned at the end of the harbor into the first street she found. She knew she was supposed to be here in this town, no longer remembered quite why, and so followed her impulse to take a little tour first.

How narrow and dark it all is; she forced her eyes wide open. The town, like any town first seen by night, surprised her with its unfathomably mysterious outlines. Streets and alleys crisscrossed one another in a tight pattern of straight lines, but every time she thought, Now I'm stuck, now I really can't see a thing anymore, the street plan made room for her and conjured up a magnificent church or a fish market or presented her with a sixteenth-century town hall.

She had had enough of driving. And she was hungry. As she was deciding to ask someone the way—there were enough people on the street—she saw a woman stop with her back to the houses, as if she knew she was needed.

"The Verre Nieuwstraat?"

The woman screamed the question back at her, to show that she had understood in spite of the wind.

The two of them looked at each other through the open window of the car. Lidy saw a round face not six inches from her own, wearing extravagant makeup; somehow it seemed to fit right in with the storm. She wasn't at all surprised by the green eyelids and the tragic scarlet mouth, but was given an explanation nonetheless.

"We had dress rehearsal this afternoon. I'm the duke's daughter!"

The woman advised her that the best way to go was along the new harbor.

That way lay danger, impossible not to see it. Lidy was offered a lively, almost entertaining view of this when she had to wait for a moment at the Hoofdpoortstraat before being able to make the turn onto the quay. Men were busy lifting the planks of a sort of wooden fence out of some concrete footings that had been positioned against the house walls on both sides of the street. One of them was nice enough to explain to the unknown girl who had climbed out of the car in the howling wind, clutching her hair with both hands, that the high tide would start retreating at any moment, should have done so already, actually, so they were taking down the fencing until the next high tide, later tonight. Give it a minute and she could be on her way again!

Distracted, her mind a muddle, Lidy stared into the man's enthusiastic face, which seemed to be captured on film against a background of hell and damnation. Ink-black sky, a row of fragile little houses, and high above the quay a whole fleet of heaving ships.

"Wow," she said to herself quietly a moment later, "people in this town keep working really late."

She drove slowly behind an old Vauxhall along the quay, which was underwater, just like the one in Numansdorp. The whole atmosphere was like an autumn fair, she thought, the same sense of people caught up in every sort of activity in a cold, wet twilight.

Indeed, a lot was going on here on the south side of town, where the tidal basin with its moorings for regular ships, cutters, and the direct daily service to Rotterdam had access to the Oosterschelde by way of a canal. At this hour on a Saturday the pubs were full of customers. Excited by the storm, many of them were raising their glasses toward the windows, outside which things were raging most impressively in the dark sky. In front of the houses a little farther down, figures were to be seen kneeling and crouching. Inhabitants of the wharves, who had erected the wooden flood barriers in front of their doorsteps a few hours before, inspected them again, smeared them with handfuls of clay, and then straightened up again, to have conversations with one another about whether the windows, which the Flood of 1906 had almost reached, might not be able to use a board or two this evening as well. Diagonally opposite, under the lamp with its yellow light, which looked lost against the huge soaring bulk of the corn mill with its fixed sails behind it and to one side, stood a little group of fishermen watching the boats. They were worried, understandably, but not excessively so, since the wind, thank God, was pushing the boats away from the quay. And now the harbormaster appeared, downstage right. He was holding his hands in front of his mouth like a megaphone. Although everyone already knew this, nobody took it amiss that they were getting another official announcement that according to the depth gauge, the water this evening was going to remain high, instead of turning into an ebb tide.

Bizarre, but it was common knowledge that according to fishermen's physics it was true more often than not that when there is no ebb tide, no high tide will follow, either. So who could have guessed that at two thirty in the morning the newly reinserted boards along the Hoofdpoortstraat and the other side streets leading off from the quay would burst open like folding doors, that a wall of black water crested with ash-gray foam would come crashing down and sweep away the modest houses, and that fifteen inhabitants, sound asleep in their beds on the first floor, would be drowned, to their great surprise? Still, the Royal Hydraulic Engineering Authorities had already calculated that if there were a confluence of all possible negative factors—spring tide, wind direction, wind force, duration of wind force, and water levels in the major rivers—the sea would not be held back by a single one of the dikes in this region, and certainly not by some puny board fence. . . . They could all have figured it out. But this was the place where they had not only been born but had lived their lives untroubled until today.

She had reached the end of the quay. There was only one way to go now, left into a street that sloped away steeply. Making her way down from the level of the dike to the level of the polder, she drove into the town again and at six fifteen finally found her way to the Verre Nieuwstraat. Like all the other streets, it was not completely empty of people, but it was still very dark. As she drove carefully behind a couple of pedestrians, she found a building halfway along the closed fronts of the houses that had three rows of brightly lit windows, one above the other. A sign hanging outside said Hotel Kirke.

As Lidy went into the hotel that was the agreed venue for the party on Saturday the thirty-first of January, 1953, she had the feeling that although her journey had merely taken a day, she had been on the road for weeks. She entered through a revolving door and went past the empty reception desk with her purse and a little suitcase. The hotel had a large, warm lobby, and it was bustling. The wooden ceiling bounced back both the light of an old matte copper chandelier and sounds of laughter and conversation. The warmth, the voices, and the smells of food all suddenly triggered a yearning in her for a few words of personal greeting, which she had certainly earned after such an epic journey. She peeked from the reception area into the jammed and noisy rooms that all opened off the lobby, then, as she heard someone call the familiar name "Armanda!," she turned around, relieved.

"Yes!"

She quickly set down her suitcase.

6

The Godmother

If being happy means being in the right place, surrounded by people you want to belong with, then this evening she was happy.

The table was in the Winter Garden and had been set with a blue cloth, a flowered dinner service, and old, slightly battered family silver. The company around it numbered twelve, all of them in the best of spirits: this was a celebration. And in their midst: her. "Shall I refill your glass, Lidy?" said the sixty- or sixty-five-year-old man with the gray cap and the gray eyes, whom she'd come to sit beside. She immediately nodded, full of sympathy as she looked at her table companion's emaciated face. Everyone had accustomed themselves by now to the fact that her name was Lidy. She'd explained things right after her arrival and admitted who she was, whereupon each of them had repeated the name most warmly and then passed it on. A young man jokingly identified her as a secret agent.

Candle flames flickered restlessly. She looked over into the dining room. People were all shouting at the same time, salvos of laughter erupted, there was singing. This was the island's evening off. "I feel like a million dollars," she said to Jacomina Hocke, the godchild's mother, who was sitting one chair down. The woman, freckled, round-faced, and curly-haired, promptly leaned over toward her and told her, smiling, to look where she was looking. Between them, at the right-hand corner of the table, two armchairs had been pushed together and a thin child in a stiff little white skirt was lying on them, asleep, with ballet shoes on her feet. Despite the lack of incisors, the open mouth suggested the little muzzle of a cat. At such a moment, a nice guest smiles along with the mother. Lidy, so preoccupied by the details of her adventure that she had blocked out all other memories of her previous life, felt dizzy for a moment. As she yawned, the other woman stretched out her arm and took hold of her wrist.

"Soon! It'll soon be time for you to go upstairs and have a good sleep, but not yet!"

And in fact she herself was conscious that she had to shake off her sleepiness. She perked up and looked around the table: relatives and husbands and wives of relatives of the sleeping girl, friends, two younger brothers, who had crawled under the table. A godmother is also definitely a member of the family. At the head of the table, side by side, sat the maternal grandparents. They were the owners of this little hotel, whose main source of income was the parties given here, rather than the occasional commercial traveler or civil servant passing through for one night. It was a tradition that anytime a grandchild had a birthday, the whole family ate in the hotel and spent the night.

If someone beside you is inspecting your face, you can feel it.

"Yes?" she said, turning back to Jacomina Hocke.

"Oh, I know it all so well," the latter said.

Taken together, the words and the look, focused on the child again, made it clear that since she was here as a representative and lacked the relevant shared past, she must listen as all the missing details were told to her. So, please, Lidy, here's a memory for you, in three parts. To bind you for this evening to an earlier time that doesn't actually belong to you. A summer holiday camp shortly after the war. And she, Jacomina, had been one of the leaders, despite the fact that she was pregnant. A little helper from Amsterdam, about fourteen years old, had followed her around for four weeks like a page.

Oh, of course, she thought.

"A sweet, shy child. Doctor's daughter."

After a few minutes she had almost ceased to listen. The meal was very heavy. When she looked up from her plate to see what was going on around her, she felt the way she often did when she was in company: lethargic, shortsighted, although her eyes were fine. The Winter Garden creaked and groaned in the squalls, and each time one hit, the gently swaying hanging lamps dimmed, then flamed up again with a larger, brighter light. The people at the table were changing places more often, and there was also a lot of coming and going between the Winter Garden and the dining room. The news bulletins that reached them now and again from the town fit the party mood, for such an atmosphere has a natural affinity for the wilder dramas of real life. A chimney had come down in the Meelstraat; the water in the Old Harbor was already washing across the bluestone pavings; a fire had broken out in the Hage dairy; the streetcars were no longer running. However, she did also notice here and there in the dining room that people had risen to their feet, and hadn't come back.

And the chair next to her at some point was no longer occupied. A tiny isolated space in the midst of the racket both indoors and out. At the other end of the table she saw Izak Hocke adjusting the lens of a camera. She hadn't talked much with him, but had already talked about him. So she knew that he had a farm about eight miles from here. This was a man who hadn't wanted to get married until he found a woman he could be sure would not concern herself either with the land or the business: both were the province of his mother, who lived with him. Jacomina had been a teacher until she married. He was ardent, jealous, and prudish, she'd told Lidy woman to woman. If he wanted to have sex during the day, first he checked the hall, then locked the bedroom door, and hung his shirt over the knob to cover the keyhole!

She saw him stand up. Chairs were pushed aside, the sleeping child was wakened, but before she and her two brothers were taken up to bed, a few more photos were in order.

Excellent. "And now one with you, Lidy . . ."

She laid her napkin on the table, went to the two armchairs in the Winter Garden that had been set out for the purpose, and sat down willingly, her hands in her lap. The godchild, beside her, was busy spreading her fingers and licking them. Then came the moment, and she smiled, taking care not to look directly into the lens but a few inches above it. She saw Hocke, the shutter cable in hand, staring from the viewfinder of the Ikoflex to her and the child from a distance of about ten feet. He knit his eyebrows: black, bushy, overshadowing the roundest, heavy-lidded eyes, which gave the face a melancholy, introverted look.

He looked down into the camera again and then squeezed the cable.

Suddenly someone came up to him. She saw a man in a jacket, soaked to the skin and giving off the stench of mud, who seized the chair that Izak was offering him with a gesture, and yanked it out from the table. His back half turned to her, they began a conversation that she could overhear in part, though she was still posed for the photograph. The man was talking about a sluice in some inner dike, and the words he was using—"rust," "garbage," "criminal negligence"—couldn't fail to have their effect.

Hocke nodded. He groped in his jacket pocket and handed the man his car keys.

"Okay, if you think it's necessary."

The other man promised to bring the car back within the hour.

She went back to her place at the table. Someone new was now sitting beside her, a tall young man with intelligent eyes fringed by pale lashes, who opened the conversation by saying, "Nothing special!" She looked at him cheerfully and laughed, as a way of easing the conversation about the sea and how it was skipping the ebb tide this evening for a change.

"Excuse me," she said after a while and leaned toward her new table companion to ask where his predecessor had gone. She was very sleepy again and had already wondered a couple of times when she could politely head for the room where she had changed from her traveling clothes into a dress hours before and laid out her pajamas ready on the bed.

"Where is he?"

"Simon Cau?"

"Yes."

The young man looked around. Simon Cau, he said, was the dike sheriff or superintendent of one of the large polders here, and had certainly made a quick trip to the harbor to check the water. The six o'clock news on the radio had spoken of "dangerous high tides" and that almost never happened. Dike superintendent, the highest authority on the dike, a noble office, some people took it seriously, others not at all.

"Yes," he went on, "what kind of a person is each of us inside . . . hmm . . . you, me, all of us? Does any of us have a choice? But sometimes someone manages to be that person he wants to be deep in his heart."

Lidy learned that Simon Cau was the last of three brothers, tenant farmers who had put their lifelong efforts into acquiring the beautiful eighteenth-century Gabriëllina Farm. Finally he had succeeded, and nobody even today had been able to work out how he had assembled the money. By saving, borrowing money, and loaning it out again, sharpening one knife against the other? Afterward he had succeeded in making it into one of the best-run businesses in the area, everything done in the most up-to-date way imaginable, except for the one instance in which he refused to go along with the times: he wouldn't allow any tractor on the farm. He was doing mixed farming, and everything, even the binding of the corn, was done using horses. For Cau, as the young man explained, loved horses, horses were his god, and it didn't matter what the neighbors thought, the new landowner, who had started out as a farm laborer, built a second stable right up against the house. And with a batch of old clinker he paved the area all the way from the barn doors to the road. And last: two new pedigreed mares who were given such a thick layer of straw in their stalls that after the day's work they couldn't resist the temptation to stretch out like dogs and lie on their sides to sleep. Even though they were heavy Belgian shire horses.

Lidy, who was listening with only half an ear, swallowed a yawn.

"Heavy horses," she murmured, her eyes damp. "Belgian shire horses."

And then, as if her words had conjured him back to the party, in the mirror next to the stairs that led to the upper floor, she suddenly saw Simon Cau cutting his way through the dining room. The light in the background made his figure stand out clearly: small and gray, hurrying, in an anthracite-colored coat with a cap on his head that people of his type usually take off only to hold in front of their faces while praying. Someone seized him by the arm in order to ask him something. Cau stopped, listened restlessly like a man interrupted, and shook his head several times.

Lidy, who had been feeling for some time that she was no longer awake but dreaming, got to her feet. The godchild and her brothers had already disappeared from the stage. She excused herself charmingly from Jacomina and Izak Hocke, shook hands in thanks with the grandparents and an arbitrary assortment of people, and in less than fifteen minutes was lying flat in bed under the noise of a creaking ceiling.

Deep in her sleep, despite the roar of the hurricane or perhaps because of it, as the noise had been an integral part of events, she continued the party in the hotel Winter Garden in her dreams. But when she was jerked awake by a hammering at her door, she thought she was back at home. She groped three times but couldn't find the light switch. She recognized the voice behind the door only when she opened it—"Ah, Jacomina"—and her eyes were immediately drawn to the two men standing behind her. Everything changed in that moment, and the day, decked out with the most alarming details, forced its way back into her memory.

She waited.

7

You're Not Her

It was a few days later. Armanda put on her coat in the hall of her parents' house, then her hood, fished in the basket that stood on the table under the mirror for a pair of mittens, and for a moment, out of habit, took a hard look at herself. A minute later the front door banged shut behind her. She crossed the street to the opposite sidewalk, which ran along the side of the park. Someone had told her that the newsreel in the cinema on the Ceintuurbaan was showing the most recent updates about the floods, and she wanted to see them.

Late afternoon. Dusk was falling, making the city look dirty, as cities so easily do in winter. But the broken branches and broken roof tiles had already been cleared away.

Vaguely disturbed, she walked past a bakery, a cobbler's workshop, and a bridal outfitter. Her unease was connected to the fact that everything seemed to be so normal again that it made one begin to wonder if the whole tumult had been necessary. It was still blowing, but not exceptionally hard, and the wet snow had stopped falling today. But the sky was as dark as it had been the previous month, too dark for the time of year. Frequently it had been misty for days at a time. The weather bureau in De Bilt had registered only twenty-five hours of sunshine for the whole of January, a record low, for which one would have had to go back all the way to the records of 1902. In addition, it had been cold. The mercury, a perpetual four degrees below normal, had signaled a winter freeze of a kind that people had forgotten in recent years.

She pushed open the door to the movie house and felt welcomed for a moment by the lights, the plush carpet, and the sense of hallucination. At the counter she asked if the show had already begun and held out a few quarter guilders. The cashier glanced sideways for a second, murmured, "In a moment," and gave her a ticket for the parterre. An usherette led her into the darkness with a little cone of light. Just in time. The *World News* headline anthem sounded . . . and there it was, a single expanse of water, filling the screen. Unbuttoning her coat, she sank into a seat.

A drowned village, a section of broken dike, against a sound track of howling wind Armanda saw a handful of soldiers in long coats, with berets pulled down over their ears, shoveling sand into sacks. She looked at the water lapping at their boots in little waves, completely disconnected from the whistling wind in the film, and at the surface of the water with the roofs of the village poking up out of it, looking oddly calm; water that looked like a normal sea, except that one simply didn't understand how it had got there. Soon the familiar newsreel announcer's voice came out of the music accompanying the storm to tell her more authoritatively than any messenger in a play what she was seeing and what she was to make of it.

"Something that is more tragically familiar to our country than any other in the world."

The picture showed groups of refugees being loaded onto buses, a herd of cows stampeding full tilt through a shopping street that had turned into a river, a cart pulled by a mournful-looking horse on which some women were sitting; the camera zoomed in so close that only one remained visible, filling the screen as she looked directly at Armanda out of another world, infinitely removed in space and time. The deaths didn't number in the dozens, the newsreel voice continued; alas, the previous figures had to be revised, the tally was in the hundreds. This is Oude-Tonge and Overflakkee—a dirty gray picture appeared—where three hundred people lost their lives in the floods. This is 's-Gravendeel in the Hoeksche Waard, where fifty-five people drowned. To the accompaniment of urgent music, a whole series of disaster zones now appeared, as abstract to Armanda as the names of places in ancient stories where mythical events had unfolded. Dordrecht, Willemstad, West Brabant, the Hollands Diep, they carried a message that was far beyond her grasp as they collected around a white space in her heart: she and Lidy, and their roles in a drama that had taken on a life of its own.

Drops of sweat formed on her forehead and cheeks. It was very warm in the movie theater and both the music and the announcer's voice kept getting louder. All around her she could sense the other moviegoers, packed tight, staring at the screen, which made no mention of Schouwen-Duiveland, not even once. So she slowly began to believe that Lidy had gone someplace that had absolutely nothing to do with these images shot through with flashes and wavy lines but was simply wandering around somewhere on solid ground with grass coming up between the paving stones, where people lived normally in houses, cows stood in the cowshed, and horses trotted around in green meadows.

"Helicopters with English, Belgian, and Dutch pilots buzzed around like huge wasps. . . ." She stood up.

As she left the cinema, the wind from the movie was still howling in her ears, but when she got out onto the street, she realized that a song was going around and around in her head. It was a mournful, incomprehensible song, and the words "The winds they whirl, the winds they whirl all around the boatman's girl . . ." came in a tragic voice that was Lidy's voice. Lidy, who was the musical daughter in the family, who practiced on the grand piano with full pedal, but in certain moods let herself go in such pure schmaltz, singing along at the top of her voice, that the family couldn't listen to her with straight faces.

She crossed the Ceintuurbaan with Lidy's voice still in her head, singing the song that had always succeeded years ago in inducing a feeling of inexplicable sorrow in her younger sister. It was about a girl child, one who was "only" a boatman's girl, and the song broadened and deepened the pathos of this with a melody that commanded Armanda's most painful awareness. Even the first words naturally struck a nerve; "the winds they whirl, the winds they whirl," sung in a hasty rhythm, put the child, who was only the boatman's girl, in a fearsome storm. Wind and more wind, gust after gust. Then the song continued with an appeal to which no one in the world is immune:

"Come here . . . ," the last word sung emphatically by Lidy at her little sister, who was already melting away, and then followed by something that never failed to pierce her to the core. Her name. "Come
here, Manja," sang Lidy, substituting Armanda's baby name for that
of the girl in the song, so that she could end the line of the verse, now
richer and more personal, with "you're my sister, you're my sister,"
and then, with even greater emphasis than on the line about the wind,
sing it all over again.

As Armanda entered the park, she stepped aside to avoid a wild-
looking man who was coming toward her with his peddler's tray of
socks and eyeglass cases, but she felt as softhearted as a little lamb.
For the first time in days, she saw her sister in an old familiar sce-
nario, namely with brass polish in one hand and a yellow cloth in the
other. As she polishes the faucet in the hall—very nice of her, there
are bound to be visitors tonight—her voice rings out in the second
verse of the boatman's daughter song, which begins "O Hell's spawn,
O Hell's spawn, my sister is gone," then commands again, "Come
here, Manja," before turning suddenly in a way that still gives
Armanda goose bumps, as it did then: "You're not *her*, you're not
her," sung to the same despairing waltz that had swirled around
"you're my sister," but now with these words, seems to reveal its
deepest intentions.

Lidy. When she was around twelve. Busy in the doctor's house,
polishing the brass faucet. As Armanda goes past her on her way
upstairs, Lidy wails out the song all the way to the end at the top of
her lungs, and casts a mock-despairing, cryptic glance at her that
appears to signify that everything is going to end badly. As Armanda
closes the door to the room with the balcony behind her, the final
words of the song, "Yes, yes!" like an exclamation, echo in her ears,
and her eyes fill with tears.

She put the front-door key into the lock. In the hall she cocked her
ear for a few moments. At first she thought there was no sign of life in
the house, then she heard her mother upstairs, talking to someone.

Nadine Brouwer-Langjouw and Betsy Blaauw were sitting in the
back room at a low table along the side wall, lit by a shaded lamp in

the corner. In front of them tea was laid out. Cigarette smoke hung in the air. As Armanda appeared in the doorway, she saw them both look up without reacting, which is to say that Betsy, who was talking, continued rather formally, as if she were forcing herself not to leave anything out.

Armanda heard: "He told me that they sailed the boat around in the night and you just couldn't imagine that the area had ever been inhabited. He saw the corpses of every kind of animal floating about, and tables and chairs and bales of straw, and most of all he saw the ship's navigation lights shining on waves with big white crests that came rolling in between the remains of the farmhouses as if they belonged there."

Armanda had come into the room, pulled up a chair, and now asked her mother firmly, by way of interrupting the conversation, "Is there any left?"

In the silence that followed, Nadine lifted the lid of the teapot, made an anxious face, and glanced up to see her daughter's pleading look. Sjoerd, she explained, had called Betsy today to tell her he'd managed to get on board a lighter in Zierikzee with the help of a couple of students from Utrecht. Armanda nodded—she understood—but was shocked for the umpteenth time this week by the dreadful alienation in her mother's eyes, a look that was quite foreign to her, and chilling, and the blue vein that was pulsing visibly in her temple.

Betsy, her face closed, waited for their conversation to end. Now she drew a deep breath. As she resumed her report on the report, slowly but without a single pause, Armanda felt it was as fantastical as the movie images she had just seen.

"They used the ship's horn. They surveyed all the attic floors and rooftops so that they could steer for them if there were any signs of life. He said they took a total of eight people on board in the course of the night, which was hellishly hard to do, given all the floating debris crashing against the hull, and the current, but they were all completely apathetic and didn't even understand what he was talking about when he asked about Lidy or where Izak Hocke's farm was, which Lidy had gone to on Saturday night. Meantime he and the students had not the faintest idea anymore where they were on the polder. They took the people on the lighter to a fifty-foot cutter skippered by a mussel fisherman from Yerseke, who had sailed it through a hole in the dike and anchored there. Day dawned. The wind began to blow from the east and everything on board turned white with frost. He said the cold was so intense that they couldn't think, all they could do was act. They sailed farther into the polder on the off chance of finding something, and came up against the gutters of houses that were in the process of falling apart, with walls that were sometimes thirty or forty degrees out of true. Don't think, said Sjoerd to me, that we were the only ones out on the water that morning. In amongst the oddest small boats there was even a punt from Giethoorn. The skipper, like everyone else, seemed to be aware of a general plan that all these ghost-drivers were following: the little boats gave over their catch to the bigger, mostly fishing, boats, which made sure they either got into harbor or out to the open sea, because the tide was going out. He said you could watch the water go down from one half hour to the next."

Armanda made to open her mouth.

"Of course," Betsy continued hastily, "he kept on asking, no matter what. He told me that he pointlessly questioned a farmer's wife whom he and the students had had the greatest difficulty in persuading to leave her attic. Clutching two jars of preserves, she was sitting under the roof. She only agreed to put her legs over the windowsill after he, Sjoerd, had looked at the roasted rib cuts under their thick layer of fat and told her they could come too. While the students steered toward the outline of a church tower, the woman shook her head in answer to his interrogation, she thought about it carefully but no, said Sjoerd, she'd never in her life heard of anyone named Lidy. So they headed for the tower. Two helicopters were in the process of rescuing some people who had crowded onto the parapet of the hollow circular structure, which was so narrow that you couldn't imagine how there could be a staircase inside. Its sides were full of holes and it could collapse at any moment. Nothing of the church itself remained except the tips of wreckage of wood and brick in a sea that stretched all the way to the horizon. They heaved to and followed the rescue operation. A man, a rescuer in yellow oilskins and a life vest, was calmly— or so it seemed, said Sjoerd—attaching a steel cable that came snaking down from the helicopter to people who lined up one after the other, some of them wearing local costume, and then rose into the air like saints. After the machines had made a sharp dip to the side and flown away, three of the remaining people had decided they would rather board the boat than wait for the pilots to return. This was successfully achieved through a small window halfway up the tower. The most striking thing about these people, said Sjoerd, was their complete lack of fear. They sat disheveled in the deckhouse, breathing a little heavily, but didn't say a word. In the moment when they were saved and the boat was pulling away, and he asked about Lidy, Lidy Blaauw, they apparently looked at him as if he weren't quite right in the head. Finally one of them had opened his mouth. 'Just take us to the Raampartse Dike.' "

Betsy broke off and her face went slack, as if the report had suddenly led her to something else. She turned to Nadine and said unsteadily, "Oh, Mrs. Brouwer . . ."

The latter looked astonished, then showed her understanding of the moment: the silent, awkward turmoil of someone trying to express empathy. She bent forward and closed her hand round the visitor's wrist.

Three. There were three people in the room, plus an animal that hadn't yet been heard from, a neutered yellow tomcat that was sitting on the windowseat looking out. Of the three of them, one had a mouth that had suddenly gone dry, eyes that were suddenly swimming and who felt she was a ghost, lucky to be able to see anything at all. Armanda got to her feet, picked up the teapot, and went into the kitchen to brew a fresh supply.

When she returned with it on a tray that also had a plate of open sandwiches with smoked mackerel and mustard, Betsy was saying something that sounded very like a closing remark.

"By the end of the afternoon, there was nothing more they could do."

"Why?" cried Armanda, coming to a halt in the middle of the room, her voice rising in distress. "Why was there nothing more they could do?"

Betsy stubbed out her cigarette in the full ashtray. It took her some time.

"Because everyone was either saved or drowned."

For a moment it was still. Then Betsy, with an almost placating look at Armanda, said, "Sjoerd said that the professionals have now taken over. The army and the Red Cross."

Armanda set the tray down on the table with the greatest care. "The army," she repeated. "The Red Cross."

She didn't sit down with the other two again. Her hands wrapped around a cup of tea, she walked slowly up and down in the front room as she often did when she was thinking or, as now, pulling back into herself because the world gave her little other choice.

Meanwhile the streetlamps had come on, and Betsy made a move to say good-bye to the lady of the house. She had told almost all there was to tell. In three days her brother would take up the continuation of his report himself. At the same, always semimagical hour of the dusk, he would ring the doorbell of number 77. And Armanda, guessing at once it would be him, would run downstairs and open up.

But for the moment things weren't that far along. For the moment Armanda stood in the darkened front room, almost absent from the other two women, stroking the cat, and thought, as she climbed the first step toward a capacity for empathy, about Lidy. A distant and strange state of being, annotated by the newspaper, presented by the newsreel, and commandeered by the army and the Red Cross. The craziest circumstances, which everyone understood how to report on—except her.

For Nadine and Jan Brouwer had also gone to the southwest this week to search for their daughter. They had managed to reach Schouwen-Duiveland on the boat of a fisherman from what had once been the island of Urk, had learned in the dreadfully damaged little regional capital that their daughter hadn't remained there on the night of the calamity, also learned that everyone without exception who had been rescued from the polders had been evacuated to terra firma, and by afternoon they were on a lugger from Scheveningen overladen with other refugees on their way to Dordrecht and Rotterdam. Jan Brouwer had already started to take medical care of the people crammed into the hold while they were still in the harbor. Then, barely a few miles out from the canal, the ship steered toward the bank again, from which a sloop had set sail. Fifteen minutes later Nadine saw her husband, a small gray figure on the afterdeck, disappear from view in the churning white wake. It was snowing. Aside from a row of pollarded willows, she could see nothing in the pale distance that suggested a village in which the field hospital was supposed to be, which had appealed for a doctor over the radio.

She reached Dordrecht in the early evening. Failing to find any trace of Lidy among the evacuees in schools and churches, she spent the night on the floor of a post office and went on next morning to the Ahoy Halls in Rotterdam. There too she searched for Lidy for hours in the throng of people that seemed to have adapted itself noisily to a world roofed in glass and steel, with row upon row of stretchers on the concrete floors, coverlets, cushions, cardboard boxes tied up with string, prehistoric suitcases, the occasional well-behaved dog, and an army of helpers, mostly extremely nice women of the sort who always knew what to do no matter what the circumstances, making the rounds with coffee and open-face sandwiches. When she came home around dusk, she was too exhausted to speak. But Armanda, who had barely reached the front door herself, because she had been taking care of Nadja, hadn't been able to wait, and wanted to know what her mother had seen.

Was she cold, was Armanda's first question, was she tired? And she had read in her mother's face that Lidy for the moment had been nowhere to be found. After she had guided her into the warm sitting room, led her to the sofa, taken off her shoes, and waited till she had hugged Nadja and kissed her, Armanda stared at her inquiringly.

When nothing was forthcoming: "I've heard there's looting down there, and people have already been shot."

Her mother had looked around the room. "Where's Jacob?"

She hadn't answered. No one in these days was paying attention to the thirteen-year-old. She said: "An entire cowshed with all the cows still tied up inside is said to have been sucked out to sea on the ebb tide."

Armanda saw her mother nod thoughtfully. "I read somewhere," she said, not giving up, "that the atmosphere over some of the islands is so wet that the birds in the air are inhaling water and just drowning on the wing."

To which Nadine replied that she hadn't seen that, but she'd seen plenty else.

"In the Hollands Diep . . ." she began, but then broke off at the sound of the front door closing downstairs. While Jacob came up the stairs whistling a tune, she hastily told Armanda, as if wanting to be done with it as fast as possible, about the flotilla of ships in the snow that had spread out in two directions across the waters, still almost at peak levels.

"And it was so odd," she said, "suddenly"—she turned her eyes to her son, who had just entered the room—"one of these boats climbed right out of the water and went up this really steep dike, and then drove away quite fast on wheels."

"An amphibious vehicle" was Jacob's calm response. "A Detroit United, made by the Americans."

Later that evening, alone in her room, when she thought back to her mother's return home, Armanda could make no connection, not even the beginnings of one, between her own days just past and those of her mother. Small-boned, in the gray roll-necked sweater that was soon too warm for her, her mother had sat on the sofa, right on the edge, as if she had to leave again at any moment, and had talked about seeing a ship near Moerdijk coming toward them from the opposite direction and then passing them, with hundreds of coffins piled on deck.

Downstairs in the hall Betsy put on her cap in front of the mirror.

"He also told us," Armanda heard her say to her mother, "that they spent the night outside the dike. They were allowed to tie up the boat to a fishing smack from Hellevoetsluis that was anchored there with its bow toward the open sea. They were given permission to sleep in the galley, which they did, despite force ten winds, storm gusts, and showers of hail. But shortly after four, the smack tore itself loose as the tide reached its high point, and vanished at high speed, their boat behind it, somewhere on the pitch-dark waters of the Krammer."

8

Missing

Three days later, early in the evening, the doorbell rang. Sjoerd.

"Give me your coat!" said Armanda, who had opened the door to him. But he didn't want to, and upstairs, where the family was already sitting down to dinner, he declined good-naturedly but firmly, when his father-in-law, who had also returned home that afternoon, invited him to stay.

"Sit down, man!"

"Go with him for a little bit, Armanda," said Nadine, when she realized that Sjoerd, after three disturbing days, evidently wanted to have his little daughter back home with him. By which she meant, take bread, fresh milk, cookies, and a decent portion of the casserole that's still in the oven, because of course there won't be anything in the house over there.

Number 36 was dark and cold. But Armanda didn't mind, quite the contrary. It was actually really nice, while Sjoerd lit the oil stove and switched on the lamps, to warm the food, button Nadja into an extra cardigan, take a neatly ironed cornflower-blue cloth out of the cupboard, and lay the table.

After dinner, while Sjoerd was putting Nadja to bed, she sat smoking with her feet up on a stool, looking out of the darkened window. Kindly, with a feeling of being a simple, gentle woman, she thought, No, no coffee for me, I'd rather have something stronger. Yet all through dinner, she and Sjoerd had kept giving each other brief, faintly embarrassed looks, in which each recognized the other's sense of guilt. Perhaps it couldn't have been otherwise, with Lidy in the background the whole time. What had happened to her, where was she? And so they had eaten well and played with the little girl. Would you like something more? Should I heat up a little more of the meat? And of course without really daring to think about it clearly, Armanda from second to second was replaying the party of a full week ago now, and them dancing, and the fact that he had been turned on by her. She liked it that men's bodies responded so openly and spontaneously, despite themselves. And she liked herself for being so sensible, and not having gone home with him to number 36 for a quick drink.

When Sjoerd came back downstairs, Armanda asked, "Is she asleep?" Sjoerd said, "Yes," and next moment they were both sitting on the sofa by the stove, each in a corner, drinking cognac out of shot glasses. Sjoerd began to recount everything he'd seen and done. He took his time and spoke straight ahead, as if he were giving a slide show in a darkened room.

"It was the Raampartse Dike," he said. "A dry stretch of road that was still high enough out of the water. When we tied up, there were at least a hundred freezing people standing there, more were lying on the ground soaked to the skin, you have to imagine that they'd been washed up there for days and the storm was still blowing. And don't think that there was much we could do at this point. The army had arrived at the same time as we did; in those practical amphibious machines they call DUKWs. I stood on the dike and heard a British, a Dutch, and an American officer consulting. It was the American, a short little major, totally calm, who had hit upon the idea of taking the DUKWs and had come chugging up from the Rhineland in short order with an entire collection of emergency assistance teams. And the teams were made up of Germans, former German soldiers, and in less than a minute they were scaling the dikes."

"Whaaat?"

"Yes. And you can bet that the poor half-drowned devils on the dike were happy to see the enemy come marching along in their big boots."

Armanda sank back a little and tucked her legs up under her. Gradually she felt herself slipping into the tentative, trusting frame of mind that she often felt with Lidy when they were talking as if they were both caught up in a dream. It was just like that now, although Sjoerd was the one talking while she only listened, more or less uncomprehendingly, a fact that bothered her as little as it would in such a dream, in which recognition doesn't follow the usual logical patterns. The room was getting warm. Armanda listened to Sjoerd saying how bad it had been when the sky, after the third day of pointless activity, had turned absolutely black again. Nodded sympathetically. And at the same time heard a kind of interior running commentary rubbing her nose in the fact that all the while she had been at home taking care of an adorable two-year-old, reveling in her little fat hands, a doll with her book made of cardboard to read aloud from, and that she had gone shopping and done a little cooking: the usual rhythm of her own usual days. Everything else, everything dramatic, everything large-scale, was as far distant from her as could be, and even as part of the country disappeared from the map, she could almost have been working away peacefully on her diploma thesis, so that she'd be able to hand it in on time in the upcoming week. . . .

And so, as her mind wandered in Now and Back Then, Here and Back There, she suddenly saw herself with utter precision sitting at home in the corner, surrounded by books and notebooks. She *had* in fact been doing exactly that: on Wednesday evening, full of cheer, Armanda had finished her paper on Plot in Shakespeare's Early Plays. Somewhere around midnight she had rubbed her eyes, listened to the wind for a moment, and gone into the bathroom. The water from both taps began to fill the bath rapidly. She had undressed.

Sjoerd stood up. She watched him, trying to work out what he wanted.

"Okay," she said sweetly as he held up the bottle questioningly.

He filled her glass right up, then turned a little farther away from her as he sat down than he had been before.

"Yes?" she said.

A confusing muddle of images. Dream images, but they were real. Trying to find a support, she fixed her eyes on his mouth, which was still talking about their common theme, Lidy; she wanted to know what there was to know. Impressed by the gravity of things, but happy that Sjoerd was talking to her so gently and seriously, she tried to picture Lidy out in the flooded provinces. She could barely manage it. What had to happen, happened, but the evening hour meant that what took absolute priority was her perception of someone else, i.e., herself, Armanda. She, who at midnight last Wednesday had slid into the warm water without so much as a thought for her lost sister, leaving the taps still running, till the bath was full right up to her chin. So as not to veil the sight of her own body with blobs of foam, she didn't lather herself with soap. I think it's really good now, she said to herself. Appreciatively, still caught up in the spell of her own cleverness in finishing her work, she had contemplated her white body as it floated almost weightlessly under the surface of the water in the deep enameled bath.

Sjoerd looked sideways. He was eyeing her in a way that indicated that he was expecting a reaction from her to what he had just reported. Still absorbed in her memories, which were engendering the feeling in her that he must be sharing them, she leaned toward him, radiating warmth.

"Next day I went to a Red Cross station, right behind the streetcar stop. There was a woman there behind a table buried in paper, to talk and answer questions; she was dog tired and her patience was such as to kill all hope."

"And?" said Armanda, while what she was thinking was: Please why don't you move a little closer? Everything imaginable has happened, everything imaginable has gone wrong. Why don't we just embrace each other?

"Yes," he said. And after a little pause that produced a small shift in the mood: "She asked me for Lidy's personal details."

"Lidy's personal details . . ." Armanda began, and stopped, suddenly overwhelmed by the significance of everything around her, pictures lined up together like pictures in a rebus puzzle of which the solution wasn't a word but something far worse. The sofa, the lamp, Sjoerd's body, fragments of dikes, wisps of water, ink-black sky, her own body, absolutely flat, if she was to be honest about it, and—mixed in with it all—Lidy's body, whose details the Red Cross Information lady had noted down precisely on a form.

She sat up and listened now, frowning in concentration.

Sjoerd described how the woman at the table had first entered

Lidy's date of birth and similar details, and had then asked about her hair color.

"Deep chestnut brown," Armanda answered promptly. "Long." She thought for a moment. "Probably in a ponytail."

Sjoerd nodded. "Eyes."

"Emerald green."

"Height."

"Five foot ten."

"Yeah, and then she wanted to know the state of her teeth. I couldn't help her there."

"Well, better than mine. A few fillings, nothing more. But we can check with the dentist."

"She wanted to know if she'd ever broken a leg or anything like that."

"No, never."

"Scars, birthmarks."

"Umm, that little patch on her stomach, you know the one, just below her navel."

"Her clothes. That ash-gray winter coat, as far as I know."

"Yes, the one with the glass buttons."

"Shoes."

"Size nine."

"She was probably wearing that pale blue sweater, I thought. And dark blue trousers with cuffs."

"The sweater belongs to me. Turquoise, angora. It needs to be hand-washed and dried flat on a towel."

"She asked about underwear. Cotton? Silk?"

"Could be either."

"And the make of her bra. I never paid any attention."

"Maidenform."

"What is it?"

"Nothing."

"Really?"

"We . . . we once bought an expensive one, by Triumph."

"Would you like a drink? A little water?"

. . .

"I think I'm going to go now."

II

This Is What They Call Sleep

9

Against a Background of Moonlight, Icy Cold, Night

Squalls of snow battered the windshield, which the wipers could barely keep clear. They had left the town behind them. Izak Hocke had just taken over the driver's seat; Lidy was beside him and Simon Cau in the back. Lidy looked with interest but absolute ignorance out at the pitch-dark road and the overflowing black drainage ditches to either side, which had nothing to do with her.

They were driving northeast.

She had reached her decision without hesitation. When she had been inspired within a couple of seconds to say, "Hang·on, I'm coming with you," it was only a confirmation of her previous decision to embark on this little excursion, which had at first simply attracted her and now had become an essential condition of her life.

She had thrown on her clothes in the blink of an eye. Trousers, the angora sweater that had originally been Armanda's and that she'd worn all day on the way here. Izak Hocke and Simon Cau had waited for her downstairs in the entrance hall by the reception desk. With their heavy coats and headgear—Hocke was wearing a woolen cap—they looked quite different from the way they'd looked at the family gathering, during which she had immediately and quite naturally addressed both Hocke and Jacomina using the familiar form, whereas she had spoken to the charming landowner who was her dinner partner using the more formal turn of phrase. Now both men were standing waiting at reception, their faces expressionless. But she didn't feel awkward in any way.

Why had she wanted to go along too? Why hadn't she just handed over the car keys instead of getting into her winter coat, dark rings under her eyes, and marching after them as if it were the only thing to do?

They had needed a means of transport. The two men, friends and neighbors, had come to the party in Hocke's car, but Hocke had then lent it instead of holding on to it. What Jacomina had told Lidy in a rush at the bedroom door was that Simon had had an urgent call and needed to get to a dike on the other side of the island and Izak Hocke should have been back home with his old mother long since in this terrible weather. Whereupon she had offered them the Citroën. With the greatest pleasure, of course. And when she said—just like that, because it seemed self-evident to her—that she would drive, the two men accepted with distant politeness. Only Jacomina still asked, "Do you really want to do this?"

"Yes."

"Not go back to your nice warm bed?"

"No." And with the bedroom door still open, she was already unbuttoning her pajama jacket.

So this was her situation. Straightforward, nice, and it was fine with the Hockes and Simon Cau. Which of them could have known what was coming at them? The land was used to storms and bad omens. And besides, Lidy was a girl with a taste for adventure, for whom finding a second bed out in the polder tonight was not an alarming thought in the least. As she stepped out onto the deserted street behind the men, all she felt, fleetingly, was that her father's car, there at the curb, stuck out as very much something from home.

"Nice car," said Hocke.

"Yes," she replied, "but it's hard to start."

But she knew how to do it; the first time the engine turned over you gave it a little gas, and the second time you immediately gave it more. The wind was making so much noise that she had to do it by feel this time, not by ear. It worked on the second try. The lights went on, and the three of them drove off. The windshield was steamed up; Hocke wiped it clear and gave her directions.

"Turn right at the end. Now there's a sharp curve. The Nobelpoort is just past the corner. Why don't you switch on the windshield wipers?"

It was around 2 a.m. The town was asleep, and elsewhere on the island, which lay far below sea level, most people were asleep too, the way they sleep when the wind sweeps over the roof on a Saturday night. Just here and there, things were beginning to happen. A few people in a house near the New Harbor had got up to make themselves a cup of tea, because even the wallpaper on the walls was moving. And at the flood fence that blocked the access road to the quay, the mayor, wrapped in his fur coat, was looking in amazement at the waters of the harbor on the other side, which had almost reached the topmost plank and therefore were simply going to overflow it. Someone in his entourage had immediately signaled that something had to be done, and at lightning speed: namely, go fetch the carpenter who lived a hundred yards down the street. At the very moment when the latter, screaming into the wind, was beginning to explain that the ramshackle props couldn't take one more nail, even a decorative one, the Citroën, with Lidy still at the wheel, was clearing the Korte Nobelstraat on its way to the town gate at the other end.

And afterward, it was absolute madness for anyone who had no experience to be trying to hold a car on the road. Once you were out beyond the houses, it really came home to you what a force-11 gale actually was. But before Lidy could panic, Izak Hocke turned to her and said calmly in her ear, "Pull over."

He got out, the interior light went on; she grasped immediately, got out too; he had already gone round the car past the headlights and held the door as she hurried past him in the insane wind. Switching drivers only took a moment, but as she slid back into the car next to Izak Hocke, she was out of breath, said, "My God" several times over, and realized that what she was sharing with her two companions was something enormous. She tried to look over her shoulder, seeking agreement, but Simon Cau, his face gray and sunken, was sitting hunched over in the middle of the backseat, his eyes going from the road to her and back again, no smile to be seen.

So the three of them were a group portrait.

The car drove off again at once. Izak Hocke searched for the lever to push the seat back farther. "It's here," said Lidy, noticing how hard and impatient his hand was. What a night, she thought. The kind of night that would stick in the memory as a sort of dream.

The straits formed a funnel through which the flood came pouring in, thundering against the coastal ramparts in an ever-rising tide. On the south side of the island these coastal defenses were lower and in a great deal more wretched condition than those in the north, where the unceasing northwest winds ensured that the sea was taken seriously.

The Citroën meanwhile was driving north. Lidy, now over her sleepiness and her initial confusion, saw that Izak Hocke knew exactly where he was going and, with the wind blowing at them head-on, was focused entirely on the driving. She felt his concentration, without any sense of anxiety or panic. But he was in a hurry, as was Simon Cau: you can tell something like that even when you can't see your hand in front of your face. Which is to say: exasperation when the car suddenly had to stop. The engine died. Curses from Hocke. An electric pole was lying right across the road, along with all sorts of drifting debris, including a piece of reddish-orange tarpaulin that had got caught up in it.

Pity, just when we're almost there, she thought.

Glistening harshly in the headlights, the tarpaulin sprang toward them. Like a dog on a chain. She stared into the chaos. She knew that somewhere behind it, maybe twenty or thirty yards from here, were two farms diagonally across from each other. To the left, Simon Cau's, though neither the farmhouse nor the outbuildings were visible, but to the right of the road, where Izak Hocke lived with his wife and children and his mother, she could see light. An upstairs window showed that the old lady, alone in the house, was still awake.

She leaned toward the man sitting beside her, but before she could ask anything, he was already out of the car, and Simon Cau with him.

What can they do? she wondered. The two figures stood at the barrier after some futile tugging and had a discussion. Simon Cau turned his face toward her and nodded, while Hocke, head forward with the cap pulled right down, spread his arms wide and shrugged.

She switched off the windshield wipers. It was hardly raining anymore. Curious, her eyes wandered to the distant little illuminated rectangle, and suddenly she knew: he would rather leave the car standing in the middle of the road than leave her alone for another five minutes.

From that moment on, she sensed that she was in danger.

She had watched Izak Hocke climb over the barricade and disappear into the bottomless darkness on the other side without so much as a backward glance. Simon Cau came back to the car, crawled behind the steering wheel, started the engine, and as it sprang to life, shifted awkwardly into reverse.

"Now what?" asked Lidy, who was thinking the storm had suddenly intensified.

"We're going to drive along behind the unloading docks. We turn right there, and then on the other side we'll get to where we're going."

"How long will it take?"

She didn't get an answer right away. It wasn't easy navigating a road that was underwater and had ditches on both sides.

"Ten, twelve minutes."

Lidy glanced sideways. An almost unrecognizable figure. Simon Cau, her only link now to the putative bed that was waiting for her somewhere in all this violence, and was beckoning her to come to sleep in ten, twelve minutes, all warm and snuggled in.

An almost black landscape under breaking clouds. Here and there an obstacle, a house or a barn. Lidy, still believing in the bed, hadn't lost her mind. All around here, people were sleeping securely, although they knew, indeed took as given, that this was a region of ancient and thus deep-lying polders. The older the dikes, the lower the land. Rationally or irrationally, over the course of many generations, people in this area had developed the unshakable conviction that whoever lived in this waterlogged, self-created terrarium made their homes here by inalienable right and would never leave. Very close to here, during the night, the sea dike would collapse in several places. Lidy, who was a stranger here, was not the only one who had no premonition of this. This was land that had been pushing itself outward for centuries, changing its shape constantly and sometimes drastically, because it lay embedded between two arms of the sea that did what arms usually do: they move. That their villages and hamlets were in some way impermanent, as was the sea itself, was not a perception held by the inhabitants. Unwaveringly they drew the common boundaries of their polders far out beyond the sea dike. They counted eddies, shallows, and barely navigable channels as part of their living space just as they counted drowned church towers, windmills, farms, and livestock sheds on the sea floor.

The detour that Simon Cau was taking now led directly to the sea dike, where a few little harbors used to ship farm produce lay in a bay of the Grevelingen. Lidy, who had lost any idea of where she was some time ago, along with any sense of time, straightened herself up at a certain point: on the left-hand side of the road she thought she was seeing some kind of ghostly apparition running toward them in the beam of the headlights. Simon Cau braked. He knew exactly where he was, he also knew the boy lurching at them, yet he brought the car to a halt in a kind of trance.

"The water's *coming*!"

It was his nephew, Marien Cau, who was poking his windblown head through the open car window. The boy had studied advanced agricultural economy, but the only thing that counted for his widowed, childless uncle was that he had proved himself to be perfect with horses.

"Are you heading for the stables?"

"Yes."

The two of them consulted for a moment, while Cau, prey to some wild, rising impatience, kept peering through the windshield in the direction of the dike, which here, right in the Grevelingen, rose a good twenty feet above the official Normal Amsterdam Water Level. The boy, they agreed, should continue to his uncle's farm without delay, where the animal quotient consisted of not just the ten horses that were the pride and joy of both uncle and nephew but also thirty cows. It was almost two thirty in the morning, it was not yet high tide, and neither Simon nor Marien Cau had yet seen the water come right over the dike. Nevertheless, they agreed that the boy should untie the cows for safety's sake. The cowshed was low-lying. The road, and the inner dike, ran approximately five feet higher. It was an impulsive thought, and not illogical, but neither of them had ever tested it as an emergency measure. This night Marien would indeed herd the cows out up onto the dike, and his uncle, unable to reach the farm any-more, would be able to watch from a window on the other side of the road to see it being done. But the cows, all thirty of them, would be found some weeks later by a group of men nicknamed the cadaver team, their bloated bodies dragged up out of the mud. The cowshed being the only thing they knew, they had swum back to it in the dark-ness. The horses . . .

Horses are something else. It is certain that Simon Cau told his nephew and chosen successor to get to the horses first, as soon as he reached the farm, to talk to them, calm them down, and watch over them till his uncle returned from his mission. But nothing happened that way. Two of the horses, the heaviest and most handsome, were photographed some days later by a journalist in a boat. They had been standing for more than fifty hours in water by then, up to their nostrils at first, then even up to their withers as time went on. The photo, intended to be a prize shot, was for the next day's paper. Two horses, about sixty feet between them, turned away from the camera lens in a gray-white rectangle of endless sea. That they had been intelligent enough to remain on the dike can be seen from some things sticking up from the water in front of them, and the parapet of a bridge. The two horses seem to find themselves in some mysterious harmony with their hopeless situation. In exactly the same poses, heads turned a little to the left in the direction of the wind, they stare at the water, each moved independently by the same feeling of deep sadness that they are the only creatures surviving on earth.

"Back soon, back soon!"

As the Citroën drove on, nothing in the atmosphere inside sug-gested an intention to make for home and bed as soon as possible. The car heading for the unloading docks was being driven by a man who was feverishly preoccupied with practical things. Beside him was a young woman who, once again, had no role here. However, even she felt the strange—or perhaps not so much strange as concen-trated—aura of danger in which people know that something has to be done. After about five minutes the dike appeared, a hunchbacked silhouette against the moonlight. Turn right here and a half mile farther on you came to the loading docks, which were no more than a mooring place where, in accordance with regulations, the passage through the dike to the quay had to be closed at high tide with flood fencing.

But the car braked and stopped right here. After a moment, Simon Cau bent over and ran for the dike, to try to climb it on hands and knees. An unreal sight. What was he trying to do, grabbing onto the weeds to pull himself up the pitiful structure, which had been built as steep as possible to save money? Sinking down continually into the waterlogged mole tunnels that riddled the entire edifice, he reached the crown. It was impossible to stand upright on this arched crest, barely twenty inches across, in the teeth of the hurricane. Cau pressed his stomach to the ground, held on to his cap with both hands, and lifted his head, drenched with flying water, a fraction. What are visions of terror? Unreal things against an unreal backdrop? Simon Cau drew in his breath with a loud gasp. What he was looking at, almost at eye level, was an oncoming mass of water that had no end.

Lidy too got out for a moment. She stood there beside the embankment, which was echoing from inside with a sonorous, throbbing roar audible through the wind. She listened without knowing what was causing the throbbing: a mountain of sand coated with a thin layer of clay, which after years of seawater washing over it was useless. On the very narrow crown, a few little walls erected here and there after the flood of 1906, with spaces to let the sheep through. The inner side was already so cracked even back then that it is a miracle that it had held until tonight before crumbling in the space of an hour and a half under the enormous hydraulic pressure on the outer side, foundering into the ditch of the inner dike. The outer side, undermined, will withstand the sea for a further fifteen minutes before finally collapsing.

Lidy tugged her feet out of the mud and ran back to the car. Even on the reinforced road, the ground was shaking perceptibly.

10

Seeing Her

April had begun with rain, but since yesterday you could smell spring. Armanda was taking a stroll along the Kloveniersburgwal, after spending the entire afternoon in lectures. The sun was shining in her face, and she'd unbuttoned her coat. The weather report in De Bilt had forecast a moderate west wind, but instead it turned from northeast to southeast and slackened to the point where the flags outside the Hotel de L'Europe hung down limp.

From the Amstel bridge she saw Sjoerd coming from the direction of the Muntplein, which was no surprise, since the bank he worked in was on the Rokin. She raised her arm, saw that he spotted her, and waited. Nothing was more logical than that they should walk home together. It was Monday. During the week, Sjoerd Blaauw ate dinner with the Brouwers, his in-laws, who had also taken in his two-year-old daughter, full of affection for her and totally understanding that she would spend weekends at home with her father. Armanda, the way things worked out, also tended to spend some time there too.

She watched him approach with long strides, looking toward her without even the hint of a smile. Her books in a bag pressed against her hip, she stood still as other people walked on past her to either side; there was a lot of traffic at this hour. Without an idea of how they would or should behave toward each other, she waited for her brother-in-law at the corner of the bridge. She would just let things happen. What was the alternative? For some time now things had been awkward between her and Sjoerd. Would there be the same iciness between them today as there had been yesterday?

She thought about how suddenly his mood had changed as he stared into her face in a way that wasn't pleasant. And she had stared back. Widower . . . the word pushed its way up into her mind without her being able to suppress it. Widower, but his dead wife had still not been found.

That had been yesterday in number 36. Sunday afternoon, the doors to the little balcony at the front had stood open, and fresh air from the park came streaming in through the wrought-iron grille. Inside the sun-filled room Nadja was thundering across the room on a red wooden horse with wheels, working her way busily toward her by pushing off with both feet at once. Sjoerd and she had talked over the racket.

"She's still somewhere," he had said after a moment's silence.

She had wanted to reach for his hand, but he pushed away from her, changed the way he was sitting, and looked around. In the sumptuous sunlight the furniture, mostly old family pieces, looked a little shabby, and in the corner by the sliding doors, motes of dust were dancing above the piano in a fan of light. She followed his gaze and felt that he knew in his heart what her eyes could see: Wherever she is, she's not *here*.

But she had nodded. "Yes." And afterward, to say something that would comfort both of them: "She certainly hasn't just vanished from her house and her life without a trace."

Did he hear what she said? Remarks, thoughts, remarks, thoughts, it doesn't take long to put miles between them.

Expressionlessly, almost formally, he had repeated, "She's still somewhere." But as he turned toward Armanda and searched her face with his eyes, as if trying to find something, his words changed, though they were the same words, and suddenly they sounded a second meaning, icy, hostile, as if what he'd wanted to say was: scandalous, unforgivable, my sister-in-law, how much you look like her!

Now she waited for him at the corner of the bridge, and knew, as he came toward her in a straight line, that yesterday's conversation was still ongoing. She smiled—what could be more natural than that?

Less natural, perhaps, was that she *saw* herself smiling, saw herself in her wide blue coat smiling out at him from under her bangs, with the rest of her smooth dark hair hanging down on either side of her face.

They greeted each other. "Hello!" And said, as they continued on their way: "How was it today?" Good, good. They crossed the road.

"Lovely day," she said a few minutes later.

He didn't react.

A bit farther along the Amstel, the street got noticeably quieter. The river glistened like a band of silver.

"Shall we take a little walk?"

Relieved, she said, "Yes, why don't we!"

They went along the Keizersgracht. To break the silence, she asked, "Do you have any news? Did you get another call?"

She was alluding to the identification. Lidy's identification, for the sake of which Sjoerd had already traveled several times into the disaster zone, an undertaking that struck Armanda as spookier and more abstract with every day that passed. Lidy was one of hundreds of the missing who were still being searched for. Sjoerd made calls and was called. He, the husband, was the contact person. But gradually the calls from the Red Cross to come and check the morgues in Goes, Zieriksee, or Dordrecht became more and more infrequent, and it was also a rarity if he got a message from the police to please come look at a photo. The faces of the dead who were still being washed up or surfacing out of the mud were no longer fit to be photographed.

Close together they walked along the narrow, crumbling sidewalk in front of the houses, then over a wooden footbridge and through underneath a landing stage, and finally down the middle of the street. The canal under the canopy of the new green leaves looked very welcoming in the sun.

She glanced sideways. He seemed to be sunk in thought. Would she ever appear out of the water? Did that ever happen? Hastily she began to talk.

"When you asked me last week about that pullover . . ."

He immediately said, "Lidy's pullover."

"Well, actually, mine."

She saw him shrug uncomfortably. "In the end it didn't belong to either of you."

Last week they'd called him again. An investigator had told him about the body of a young woman whose physical description included a blue roll-neck pullover made of thin fleecy wool. The collar and sleeves were edged in a decorative pattern in paler blue, and one of the helpers, who was a keen knitter herself, recognized the pattern from *Woman and Home* magazine.

"Decorative pattern? *Woman and Home?*" Armanda repeated, when Sjoerd relayed the details to her. "Our pullover was only the one color. Made of angora. I bought it at Vos."

Now she said, "Maybe you'll think this is crazy, but it really did me good to talk, well, so normally about the pullover that Lidy swiped."

He grabbed her arm hard. She was shocked. "Do you think it's crazy?" she asked hastily.

They had reached the spot where a little arched bridge leads over from one canal to the next. They stopped at the balustrade. His grip on her arm became so tight that she looked at him.

"She has to come back to me," he said. "It's possible, you know that."

She could hear that he was talking like a madman, but she too, as she realized, was listening to him like a madwoman as well, as he said, "I want to hold her tight again, hold her in my arms. Does that make sense?"

She looked at him unflinchingly.

"It makes absolute sense, Armanda. Think about it. Her and me. Our whole lives are still ahead of us!"

She turned away, confused. When he let go of her, there was an unpleasant tension between them. A barge appeared under the bridge. She watched as it traversed the crossing of the two canals, where trees and houses were reflected in the water, and continued toward the inner city. Was there any place he hadn't been in the last months? she wondered. What had he seen? She knew any number of small things about him, the everyday routine, the rhythm of things in number 36 and number 77, but what about the big things? When he returned home from one of his trips, none of them at home knew how to deal with the combination of his grief and their own. Her mother would hastily lay another place at the table, her father would offer him a cigarette, and Jacob would steal glances at his face, lit up by the flame from the lighter. As far as they were concerned, words were unnecessary. "No." A shake of the head. "Nothing."

To break the ice between them, she said, "Listen, Sjoerd." And asked him if she could maybe hear some more details about these journeys into hell. He looked at her for a moment, as if wondering where she found the courage to do that, then an odd weary look came into his eyes, as if he were getting ready to tell a story.

"Shall we go over the Amstelveld?" he suggested.

They were in warehouses, schools, the wholesale fish market in Yerseke. The morgues at the cemeteries were mostly too small for the number of dead who were recovered in the first two weeks. Because a large number of those drowned in Schouwen-Duiveland had been washed right across the Oosterschelde to Beveland, it made sense to at least take a look in the Great Church in Goes. There were things he'd had to get used to. He had been in a nursery school somewhere out on the Vierbannen polder where someone had lifted a cloth to show him the mortal remains of a young woman, still unidentified, underneath. The filth that was all that was left of a village, and the stinking horse lying on its side in the mud as if it had been poured into it, had prepared him for what he saw. It wasn't her. Long, dark hair, age between twenty and thirty, teeth complete except for the two molars at the back: she would be identified during the course of the week by her husband, a tenant farmer in Capelle, by her clothing.

"You'll receive word as soon as we hear anything new."

So a day later he found himself in the church in Goes. A town that had survived unscathed, and a space dedicated to the Lord in which an immensely long row of corpses was laid out. Washed and wrapped in shrouds, they were awaiting identification and burial by their relatives. He arrived at around four o'clock. A buzz of voices; he was by no means the only one going round and searching. Shortly beforehand a Red Cross helper had shown him a national police report signed by the state attorney in Middelburg. Nails and toes well taken care of, he had read, skin color white, chin round, no calluses on hands. In consternation, he had nodded. Even the clothing seemed right, though he hesitated. Blue pullover, dark gray trousers with a zipper on the left-hand side, white underpants, white undershirt, pink shirt, gray men's kneesocks. The Red Cross helper lifted a cloth from one of the tables that stood at the head of each bier. There lay the clothes and other objects as described to him. And when he said nothing, only nodded carefully, she pulled the cloth back farther so that he could see the face.

He screamed, "No!" and began to tremble violently.

Who has such a thing on their conscience?

Pointless question, which nonetheless kept running through his head as he made his way out of the nave by way of the transept that was dedicated to prayer but now was echoing with the stuttering cries of the eighteen-year-old girl who had recognized not just her parents but, totally unexpectedly, the boy she had been going out with, the murmuring of women with lists of names in their heads, the whispering of the man who had broken down at the sight of three blond children, in a row, their little muzzles completely eroded, and confirmed that yes, that was them, yes, yes, the three youngest of his four children. He had already pushed open the door of the vestibule when he heard, off to the right, the cheerful sound of men discussing a job. He looked over with something like relief. About eighteen or twenty feet away, through the open door, he saw a room, probably the presbytery, with a large number of coffins piled every which way on top of one another. On some of the coffins men were sitting in their work clothes, smoking and talking.

Out to the street! Cars, passersby, he looked upward. Was he trying to refer the nightmare to the heavens? He was more closely related to the men on the coffins, the excavators, the poachers, than he realized. For they were the ones who had been found by the health officials and the police to pull the bodies out from under the driftwood, fish them out of the water with pickaxes or their bare hands, and so it followed that they were also the ones who had pulled the woman he had viewed today out of the barbed wire. *Nails and toes well taken care of.* Once again, it hadn't been her, no. But for a second, in the face with the empty eye sockets, he had seen Lidy's features.

Weeks went by. Then there was a call from Zierikzee. The local body squad had found a woman, still young, whom the state identification team could describe only in the vaguest terms, clothing almost disintegrated, hair color no longer identifiable, left arm missing, feet approximately size nine. He borrowed a car from a friend and went to the cemetery. Hopeful, yes, as always. Come to look at the victim's ring. Lidy had got married in a bright green silk suit; in the church on the Amstelveld he had slipped a ring with a little ruby onto her finger. Without paying attention to the graves, he went to the morgue, situated to the side of a path covered in tire tracks at the edge of a mudhole.

Late morning. He had already spent a short time with Jacomina Hocke, who was still living in her parents' hotel with the three children. In the lounge, packed to bursting with officials, soldiers, and journalists, he had sat opposite a woman about whom all he knew was that she had lost her husband, which didn't interest him. After a brief conversation she had fetched Lidy's little suitcase from upstairs and set it on the table in front of him. Oddly shy, he had searched for the lock with his fingers and then looked up at Jacomina for a moment as if to ask for her blessing. Then: a moment of overwhelming, ignominious happiness. There were her clothes! No possible doubt. Her tight skirt, her petticoat with the narrow straps, her nylon stockings, her shoes, size nine, that she called "Queenies," her good-little-girl pajamas made of pink and blue striped flannel. What else is there to do at such a moment than to take a very deep breath?

The scent of L'Air du Temps had stayed with him all the way through the accursed town and along the path between the gravestones till he entered the Lysol-saturated morgue, where a very young girl showed him a bucket with a couple of pathetic objects floating in it.

"Knitted woolen undershirt," the child read out from a piece of paper. "Knitted pullover, color no longer identifiable."

Then she showed him a box with some smaller objects in it, standing ready on the table.

"Ring with red stone."

He bent down over it. Half dreaming, distracted, he stared for a while at the touching piece of jewelry. Sweet, he thought, small, for a narrow fine finger. And then, his mind clouded by the chemical stench in the room: dammit, now can I finally find out what happened before all this?!

As he turned round, he found himself looking straight into the eyes of a man who had just that minute walked in. Powerfully built, red-faced, he wore overalls, a green slicker, and rubber boots. A farmer, Sjoerd assumed, and looked at him for a long second in wild supplication.

It was the leader of the body squad, a preacher, who had just driven a small truck full of new human remains onto the grounds. They were pulling out two, at most three, new corpses a day, using the engineers' boats, always with someone from one of the old shipbuilding families on board, because they knew the places to look. If they spotted a screaming flock of seagulls somewhere fluttering over the brown water rising and falling with the tide, then they didn't need anyone to point it out to them, they already knew themselves what it meant. The trips with the corpses became fewer over time, but grislier. Some of the watchers on the Steinernen Dike, where the boats moored, spread unsparing descriptions of the bodily remains that were brought onto land, they couldn't leave it alone, and said they would never eat eels again as long as they lived.

The red-faced man didn't say why he had come, but held his cigarettes out to Sjoerd. As the latter said, "It wasn't her," the man nodded and suggested they go out into the fresh air. They talked for a while in front of the little building. Sjoerd indicated the gravestones with his head. "So that's where you buried her." The other man understood that he meant the woman who wasn't Lidy.

"No. The mass grave here is full. And we always take the unknowns to the emergency burial ground farther away on the island."

To their left, by the small truck, some workers from the body squad had begun to unload something. In the brief exchange that followed, Sjoerd said, "I don't know how you can do this."

The other man didn't answer at first, and seemed to recognize that it didn't matter whether he said anything or not. On Sunday he would preach an ingenious but truly comforting sermon on a text from Isaiah: "Behold, I will do a new thing; now it shall spring forth" that came to him with mysterious ease after or even during the filthy work, but for now, all he could see was what the other man saw.

"Damn mud," he said.

No reply.

Then, "To begin with, the only way we could get through it was with gin; man, we drank, sometimes we were completely loaded. But now we do it stone-cold sober."

The emergency cemetery was not far from the harbor at Zijpe, close by the marshaling yards for the streetcars. Because the ferry to St. Philipsland wouldn't leave for another hour, Sjoerd had had time to pay a brief visit. He got out and was immediately stunned by the panorama, which had the bleak power to bury the onlooker in memories of horror, whether the memories were real or not. In the foreground were two rows of hastily but professionally piled up mounds of earth with the approximate dimensions of a prone body, and slightly higher behind these the streetcar rails, in the curve a row of wet black freight cars, and behind them, in the distance, scarcely distinguishable from the sky, the line made by the bank of the Zijpe, where the afternoon mist was already lying low over the water. He walked down the row of grave mounds. Read the inscriptions on the tarred wooden crosses stuck at angles into the earth. Unknown man, number 121. Unknown girl, number 108. Unknown woman, number 77. He didn't know whether he abhorred them or was grateful to them in his heart as he thought, From now on they're her relatives, and imagined them waiting there, cold, wet, unidentifiable, until she joined them for good.

They crossed the Amstelveld. Children were playing between the parked cars. The sun had disappeared behind the houses, and Armanda did up the buttons on her coat. Sjoerd walked beside her, silent for some time now, and smoking, but she sensed that it wasn't calming him. Where *is* he? she wondered. He's wandering around somewhere where I can't follow him, even with the best will in the world. Mourning my deeply loved, woefully missed sister. *She* would have known how to fathom his mood. If you know how a man is when he makes love, when he drops all restraint, can you also know how it is with his other passions? I think so.

Unable to change anything, she suddenly thought irritably: You look pale, brother-in-law, and hollow-eyed. And before she knew what she was doing, she began to scold. "Shouldn't you start to let go of her? She's out there and she's going to stay out there. You can't reach her anymore—it's impossible!"

Odd, the way her words found their own direction, took on their own force as they revealed something in her that had turned from gentle to angry. She felt Sjoerd look at her, stunned. As she was about to carry on in the same rough tone of voice, he cut her off.

"Don't say that! They're still working flat-out! Aside from this phone call about the pullover, I was also summoned to the police last week. The station at Kloveniersburgwal!"

He had picked up on her fiery tone. For some reason, this pleased her.

"They had received another photo for me to look at, God knows why," he said.

He had stopped. She looked at him intransigently.

"And?"

"It was the face of a middle-aged woman," he said. "You know, a motherly type with dark curly hair, all stuck together, and a double chin. You could see that they'd set her on a ladder when they found her, as a sort of stretcher, and that's how they photographed her, with her head against the rungs. She looked nothing like Lidy, nothing at all, but as I stood there with the photo in my hand and it looked back at me for a while, I don't know, every face of Lidy's that I knew was gone, I couldn't recall any of them, I didn't even try. I liked the woman. Her head seemed to me to be caught a little between the rungs, but the expression on the face was peaceful, although one cheek was very creased and much more bloated than the other. The eyes weren't quite closed, her little pupils stared brokenly but kindly into the distance, dead. So I stood there holding the photo, which was as foreign to me as it was familiar, while the policeman behind his desk waited for me to be finally ready to say yes or no. I think I must have tried his patience. You'll probably find this strange, but somehow I couldn't bring myself to hand him back the woman's face, which didn't really look like Lidy's but still was her, at least a little bit."

He threw his cigarette butt into the canal.

"Of course you won't understand."

I understand very well, thought Armanda, and lowered her eyes. The red paving stones were cracked and old. She ran her foot over them. A moment devoid of rational thought, a moment when her mind stood still. But she had pictures in her head. Fragments, faces, all signaling death. As if knotted on a rope, they told their story, one that was made up, as every story is, of its gaps and dark holes. Holy God, thought Armanda, and envisioned a last photo in the police station at the Kloveniersburgwal, that was neither of Lidy nor of the poor woman on the ladder. It was a friendly image of death itself, which may have different expressions in each individual snapshot, but the subject is always the same.

She stood for a moment, lost in her own broodings, but was distracted when Sjoerd seized her arm again, and her light-headedness changed to a chaos of emotions.

He was staring at her.

"Please don't look so angry!" he begged. "Don't clench your lips like that."

As she obeyed, he took hold of her hair with an innocent, absent-minded movement of his hand, played with it for a moment, then let it go again.

11

At the Harbor

Ten minutes later. Simon Cau's destination, to which he had been hurrying them with increased urgency, was suddenly reached. The road ended. The car stopped next to a pitiful little crane on wheels, overturned, the wooden cabin smashed to pieces. They got out. She, Lidy, was a mere figment of herself, but Cau too, who seemed to have forgotten altogether that she was there, looked in the soft violet light of the moon as though he no longer belonged among the living.

About sixty feet away stood a small group of people, lost in the thundering surroundings of the dike embankment, the sky, the ragged clouds, and the black land at their backs. It was icy cold, the temperature around zero. The northwest wind was blowing straight at the bay and at the little arbitrary jumble of people, villagers, dike workers, six in all, who had thought it better to leave their beds to check on the water. You had to know there was a tiny harbor here at all, a mere mooring-place for the flat-bottomed barges that came and went in fall during the beet harvest. It was invisible, because both the quay and the landing stage were under water, and the opening in the dike through which one normally gained access to the quay was blocked off by a kind of barricade up to shoulder height. They both looked at it as they headed down across the sand. Even Lidy knew instinctively that the first thing they had to check was the five old beams, one above the other, pushed into two slots to build a sort of plank fence, and only after that to look at what was behind it. In this she was behaving in exactly the same way as everyone else here.

As night fell, the structure of the flood planks had been put in place by two workmen—Simon Cau was now hurrying guiltily in their direction—with much cursing and groaning. With the dike sheriff nowhere to be seen, they had come here on their own initiative with a tractor and a cartful of sand. It had been a struggle, and during all their trudging and messing around the dowels—there must have been forty-nine of them—had regurgitated themselves as they dragged the things out of the shed for the last time, nor was there any remaining trace of the chalk marks that had been left on them the previous time.

Simon Cau greeted the two men with a nod, as they stood crouched over behind the flood planks and smoked.

"So?" asked Cau.

The men didn't answer. What was the point? Because the concrete roadbed leading to the quay had no slots in it, never had, they had laid some sandbags against the lowest beam, but the sea was already spraying a little water through them again.

"Very high," said Cau, pointing with his chin toward the water. "I've never seen it so high here in my life."

The two workmen nodded, but they weren't pulling long faces the way the dike sheriff was; they took a brief look at the young woman who had fetched up here, didn't recognize her, and then straightened up to look over the timbers of the barrier at the unholy blue-tinged expanse behind. High. That was certainly the word for it. The sea, never in their experience so far inland, looked to them like a mad-dened beast penned in behind their shoulders.

"Another four inches," said one of them, turning back again, "and it's going to be coming over."

Simon Cau looked at the other man silently, glanced sideways again as if trying to persuade himself that the half-rotted wood, already bowing forward under the pressure from the other side, would certainly hold, and said, "Going to be like this for another two hours. Won't be high tide till then."

He had spoken in a formal way, unsure of himself in his role as officer-very-late-arriving-on-duty, but the men both signaled their solidarity in a way that implied "Right." And one of them said, "Not much we can do, is there?"

A couple of the other bystanders joined them. Slightly in disarray thanks to the howling of the wind and the interruption of their sleep, they chimed in with their own ideas of what could happen next. The sea dike here at the harbor suddenly dipped more than six feet below its height farther away. No one paid much attention to Lidy; the circumstances were too unusual, and the very fact that she was here at this impossible time of night made her one of them, half-awake, half-asleep, half-focused, half-calm, with the sly cunning of the mad who know that reality is what it is, and must be accommodated.

So she was freezing now. Scarf pulled down over her forehead. Hands deep in the pockets of a dark gray winter coat. As she looked over at Cau and heard him pronounce that it was impossible for things to come out well, he struck her as sounding sharp, indeed very suspicious. And, far from being capable of seeing the despair that in some people resembles pugnacity, far from being capable of registering the shame, the appalling remorse of a man who knows he has committed the misjudgment of a lifetime, the error that will define him until his death, she didn't understand him anymore. His cheeks made two deep vertical furrows on either side of his mouth.

"What does the bürgermeister say?" he barked, after a pause.

Alert, very dependable. One would have to know him well to know that his loyalty was rooted in a single passion that had long been concealed from the outside world. A man can love a farm every bit as much as he loves a woman.

On June 14, 1947, at the open auction for the Gabriëllina property, when Simon Cau had learned that his was the highest bid, his knuckles went white. More than a year before, he had buried his wife, a farm wife, who had understood the force of his will over the years and had only occasionally, on sleepless nights, reminded him that *this* was his life and there was no point waiting for another one, she hadn't given him children. The latter argument was no argument at all. With or without heirs, Simon Cau signed on the dotted line, and the business, which he and his now dead brothers had leased twenty-five years before, became his property for the contractual sum of 37,000 guilders. And yes, a different life, with the same summers, winters, meadows, fields, drainage ditches, and weather reports, began! It makes quite a difference whether one is a farmer's tenant or the big farmer oneself. When he received the letter with the request from the polder authorities, he was not surprised. No one else knew more about the drainage on the polders than he did.

He wrote his reply that same evening with great seriousness. "I would like to accept this appointment and I promise you to engage all my skills in the care of the dike and the polder." So it was that from then on, when there were storms, he sometimes went to the dike and sometimes not, depending on when it crossed his mind, to check whether flood timbers needed to be brought or sand required; in such matters the dike sheriff is his own authority. And at the meetings of the dike association he was always a most amiable leader of the company, and soon came to terms with the fact that no matter how one pleaded or haggled with the royal authorities or the local ones, there was no money for the dikes so soon after the war, though everyone knew that they were a joke with regard to a storm that was certainly in the general calculations but that unfortunately came too soon.

Snowflakes stuck to her cheeks. The wind sometimes brought moonlight with it, and sometimes icy precipitation. So there she stood on this winter night on a muddy landing stage, a sliver of ground by the Grevelingen, which was an arm of the North Sea piling toward land under the force of tempest and spring tides but held back by five ancient timbers in a fence, and she felt no fear. Of course she saw the danger, she wasn't crazy, like all the others she could see very well that no power on earth could hold back the biblical flood, but it still seemed a beautiful thing to her that one could have such a close-up view of the situation and know that one had done everything that could be done.

Meantime it escaped no one that Simon Cau was cracking up. When he asked the two workmen what the bürgermeister's view of things was, his voice was harsh and his face looked furious. The two of them looked back both somberly and obsequiously, and shrugged.

"We couldn't wake him."

To which Cau, even more angrily, replied, "Did you hammer on the door?"

They had.

"Yelled? Threw stones at the bedroom window?"

That too. And they'd also telephoned twice, unsuccessfully, from a farmhouse on the Krabbenhoeksweg.

"That's the limit!"

Very nervous. Was he the only one to understand that they were faced with an enormity? The two men he was addressing nonetheless stayed calm. They simply asked themselves if they shouldn't be going home. Lidy asked herself nothing. She waited for them to finally set off in the car again. Where to was a mystery, but she'd stopped caring.

Cau was about to say something crude about the bürgermeister when his attention was so distracted that everyone turned round to look. Two girls were pedaling toward them in the darkness from the direction of the village. Silvery blond hair was blowing in every direction from under the caps they wore pulled down tight over their heads. Although the others here had also come the same way, they had pushed their bikes for most of the distance. The girls were lurching along yard by yard and didn't dismount till they reached the group.

"Horrible weather," they said breathlessly. "You can barely move."

It was the Hin sisters, daughters of the tavernkeeper and owner of the gas station, who lived with his family at the three-branched fork in the inner dike that was known as the Gallows. They must have been eighteen or nineteen years old; faces white with cold, they were wearing their nightdresses with a winter coat over the top, and high boots. Their father, they reported, had sent them off with instructions to reach a couple of the outlying houses and tell people they'd be better off coming to the tavern tonight because it was on higher ground. He himself had mounted his motorbike and had gone with his son to the inner lock on the Anna-Sabina polder, where the gate was so rusted after many years that it probably couldn't be closed, but it was worth a try.

The girls looked away from the circle of faces toward the other side of the open expanse, where somewhere in the darkness was the little house they wanted to make their last call.

"We must get going," they said.

But Simon Cau was looking in the opposite direction and then back at the dike workers. While the girls were talking about their father and brother—who were certainly trying in vain at this very moment to cope with an immovable piece of scrap metal—Cau must have come to the realization that he had failed to take care of the two inner sluices in his own polder. Both were reasonably well-maintained mechanisms, built of cast iron in a casing of plastered stone. At high tide he usually lowered them, one of the standard measures that nobody ever thought about. The dike-enclosed inner polder didn't draw its excess water off into the sea but into the ditches of the neighboring Louise polder, which then took it across the Vrouw Jansz polder to the pumping station at the docks for agricultural produce on the Grevelingen. If one closed the sluices of the inner dike at high tide, the polder, should the sea dike give way farther along, would also be protected from direct contact with the sea.

Simon Cau shook his head swiftly several times, like a man trying to stir up something in his memory. In an accusatory way, not making eye contact, he reminded the dike workers about the Dirk sluice and the sluice at Draiideich.

"Get going! Now!"

Yes, chief, and they were already on their way. The two dike workers ran with deliberately long strides, so as not to slip on the muddy ground, toward the tractor, which was still hitched to the cart with the last of the sand. Meanwhile the handful of people who had come out of curiosity started back to the village. "Look at that," said one of them, pointing to the left side of the dike, apparently feeling that the vision in the moonlight rendered him and all the others now setting off home something close to sleepwalkers. A tongue of foam, followed by a swell of black water, licked over the crown of the dike.

As his companions all moved away, Cau, as if nailed to the spot, stared at the gobs of foam shooting past him. The advance guard of the floodwater was pouring in a glistening stream down over the dike. But surely the water came up over the protective barriers somewhere on this island almost every year? Somewhere this island was always underwater. And it was well known that in 1944, when the Germans, who feared an invasion, left the sluices in the delta open, the land was flooded without raising any surprise. People here were really used to water, but tonight the situation was obviously scaring Simon Cau. As Lidy headed for the car and the Hin sisters began to push their bikes through the sand to the road, Cau hesitated and stood still, leaning against the wind. He moved his lips and made a face, as if he were assessing the massed weight of what was behind the dike and preparing, if possible, to take it on his own head, neck, and shoulders.

She had driven with Cau and the Hin girls to the last address on the pair's list. She sat in the backseat with one sister, while the other, in front, gave Cau directions. They had come along because Simon Cau, desperate to appear to be in charge at the dock, had ordered them to leave their bikes; they could come back for them tomorrow, he would drive them. They reached the little house. Quick now! Cau kept the engine running. One sister leapt out of the car with Lidy, and both of them ran immediately to the windowpanes, but these were already making such a noise in the wind that their hammering did no good, and everything inside stayed dark. So they went around the house, through the vegetable garden, already underwater, to the back, where they banged on a crooked side door that had a little window at eye level. Meanwhile Cau, waiting on the road, must have felt the pressure of time to be unbearable.

Suddenly the wind was drowned out by the heavy blast of a horn.

Lidy froze. In the pitch dark, without a conscious memory, she was called to order. A signal from home. Loud, long, three notes. The cramp that ran all the way into her fingertips was like an electric shock. For a long moment, shocked awake as if from an anesthetic, she was back in her own life, along with everything that belonged in it, father, mother, sister, husband, child, and then just as swiftly, just as she registered all this, it was gone again. Behind the door a dog had begun to bark.

The little window opened. A vague face had showed itself.

Now they were on their way again, between pollarded willows bent over at odd angles. Lidy's legs were wet only to the knees; the girl beside her was soaked to the waist. Because the road was underwater, they had failed to notice the hollow filled with spurting water as they raced back to the car. Lidy had suddenly seen the girl sink, and had grabbed for her reflexively. It wasn't clear why, but the Hin girls were now insisting on taking part in the next stage as well.

The village, in which every inhabitant had crawled under the covers.

The sleep of the simple minded: on the other side of the island, ten miles farther south, with a sound of thunder like the end of the world, the sea dike had just given way. The fourteen-ton front of a lock was lifted out of its colossal iron joints. The windows in the lockkeeper's house were blown out by the pressure, even before the building was flattened by the water, and everything in the surrounding area rocked as if under bombardment. From a place named Simonskerkerinlaag after the village that had drowned there hundreds of years before, the Oosterschelde poured in a torrent over the polder.

They were driving straight for the village on an unpaved road. Cau pointed at the church tower and ordered them to begin by ringing the warning bells.

"But they're rung electrically now," said one of the girls, as if she knew that the current was about to fail or had already failed.

"Electrically or with a rope, I don't care."

Lidy took her eyes off the road to look at the glowing tip of Cau's cigarette. Twenty hours and an awkward excursion had been sufficient to exchange the familiar bright reality of everyone she had lived with until now for these traveling companions.

Between them and the oncoming tidal wave were still two inner dikes.

12

Dreams and Ghosts

It was a day in late February 1954, a month with so little sun that De Bilt was talking about it as the second-darkest month of the century. In contrast with the year before, there hadn't been much wind. De Bilt said that not since records had started being kept in 1848 had there been a February with so little wind.

As Armanda, rolled umbrella in hand, opened the door to the hair salon, at exactly the moment when the shop's bell rang, a harsh ray of sunlight shone in like a path of trick light of the kind that appears when the sun is hidden behind fast-moving rain clouds. She said hello to no one in particular, hung her coat on the stand, and went to one of the seats covered in fake leather in front of the row of mirrors. It was quiet in the salon, Tuesday afternoon, two o'clock. Armanda, who wasn't planning to have any changes made to her haircut, stretched out her legs. She had come to be cheered up by the sight of the flacons, the brushes, and the hair dryers, and to look at herself in the mirror.

The hairdresser, an Indonesian of indeterminable age, his neck outstretched in an attitude of permanent devotion, positioned himself behind her chair. Their eyes met in the mirror, smiling in understanding, and then they both looked at her reflection in the brightly lit glass.

"Wash? Trim the ends?" Experienced fingers were already lifting her hair and tying a cape around her neck.

"Yes, but no more than a quarter of an inch."

The hairdresser moved a washbasin behind her head and went off to get something. Armanda kept looking forward, pale, with rings under her eyes. Although she and Lidy had always been good sleepers and loved the way dreams did such a beautiful job of mixing up everything that had happened in real life with things that hadn't happened yet but could happen at any moment, Armanda was sleeping very badly these days. If she thought at all about Lidy during the night, she simply felt a distressing distance, quite different from the normal, actually quite comforting sadness of her days. Irritating. Moving her legs restlessly, she would stare into the darkness. And force herself not to go into the deep sleep she and Lidy had enjoyed since they were children and in which it didn't matter whether this dreaming girl corresponded with the woman she would certainly one day become.

This kind of thing is likely to mean that one doesn't feel quite all there on the following day. Because look—the sun, which had disappeared into the clouds, came out again, casting a cone-shaped beam of light that seemed to be almost religious; she was lying with her head back on a washbasin on wheels, while the hairdresser's hands ran through her foaming hair, then came warm rushing water, then a towel, and then suddenly she sat up: there went a camel! In the mirror she was seeing a camel walking down the rather narrow street that led to the bridge. She stared. Camels, she thought, remembering involuntarily a book about the zoo that they had at home, are slow-moving, patient ruminants approximately ten feet tall. Approximately ten feet tall . . . she mentally persevered even as she observed the actual smallish, skinny, maybe one-year-old creature from the Orient, stretching its long neck and emitting strange cries as it passed the window of the Amsterdam hair salon.

"What's that?!" she burst out, not able to believe her own eyes. She turned to look out directly, to where the vision of the camel with its pathetic little tail over its hindquarters was fast dissolving again into the daylight, leaving a large crowd of children behind it.

"That'll be that camel," drawled the hairdresser.

He waited, a large comb in hand, for her to be nice enough to face front again. Responding to her quizzical look, he explained that the children of Amsterdam had written twice to Prime Minister Nehru of India to remind him how much damage had been done to the city zoo during the war. Although they had been thrilled with the baby ele-phant he had already sent them as a present, they were now hoping for a camel as well, because, as they had explained to Nehru in a little poem, no camel in a northern city means no soul and that's a pity. That was all. Nehru had answered in the affirmative, and it was his answer, received with great acclaim, that they had just seen striding past.

"Camels?" she murmured. "Are there camels in India?"

"Oh yes," said the hairdresser in a way that implied this was com-mon knowledge. "There are camels in North Africa and Arabia, and also some in northern India, though not so many."

Convinced all over again that there was a great wild world out there, just beyond arm's length, that she couldn't grasp at all, or only in miniaturized fashion, as if through the wrong end of a telescope, Armanda decided to keep silent. The velvety brown humps still an image on her retinas, she felt the comb pulling the tangles out of her wet hair. An apprentice, a well-meaning little thing, brought her a cup of tea slopping over in its saucer. She nodded and thought, Just put it down, child, yes, this is my life. Small, quotidian, all of it as much like the old one as possible. A noisy dryer was pushed down over her head. Her hands in her lap, Armanda thought first about the shopping list in her purse for a moment, and then about herself.

Oldest daughter in the family now. The one now who had to make conversation with all the aunts and uncles on her parents' birthdays without her sister to support her. A memory came to her. Last year, the middle of November. Her mother's birthday. In the big room upstairs at number 77, about twenty guests, relatives and friends, all knowing in advance that the hospitality will be splendid and that the conversation, despite the fact that a daughter is being mourned here, will be light and quite lively. She, Armanda, is wearing an old but still very beautiful blouse of violet-blue silk. Carrying a tray full of coffee cups, she maneuvers past the guests from the sliding doors to the cor-ner of the room.

It was not unexpected that conversation at a certain point should turn to the uncompromising and generous Dutch people who found themselves, so to speak, in a war again.

"Over here!" a young uncle had called to Betsy, who was following Armanda with a bowl of cookies. He raised his eyebrows, stretched out a hand, looked at Betsy emphatically, and continued to make his remarks to nobody in particular.

"Ships' warehouses full! And there are about half a million people living in this area. They reckon you could clothe eight million people from head to foot with what's there!"

Armanda saw that Betsy didn't yet understand what this was about, but she herself did. In the disaster zone of Zeeland and South Holland, people had already been driven mad with the sheer quantity of clothing in the first weeks, donated by a nation possessed. With a knowing look she glanced from Uncle Leo, her mother's youngest brother, to Uncle Bart, also a Langjouw, sitting next to him, and jumped into the conversation.

"There were evening capes in there, and swimsuits, and streetcar conductor's uniforms."

Her eyes slid past them, and as she moved on she said, "Wildervank sent a whole batch of chef's hats."

As she and Betsy handed round the coffee and cookies, always the boring bit at such a party, she heard the uncles continue.

"Be quiet," said Bart.

"I swear it." Leo had been the envoy-on-the-spot of the City of Amsterdam, which had taken on special responsibility for Schouwen-Duiveland. "Shoes lying everywhere. In the square in front of the church, in the streets, all of them in the mud. There was barely a living soul left to be seen in the village, everyone had been evacuated, it all looked absolutely tragic."

"Really," said Bart.

"Yes. One of those donations. Thousands and thousands of pairs of shoes. Out of sheer despair, because every warehouse on the island was already overflowing with clothes, so they threw them at the first fishing village they came to."

The other man snorted.

"In Bruinisse the stuff was stacked to the ceiling in a school with big high windows, there was so much of it not a single ray of light could get through. I saw how people can get drunk on the sheer availability of a huge quantity of stuff, it doesn't matter what the stuff is. The ones who came to find something didn't just take what they needed, they began to carry on like voles or crazed moles, tunneling through it all. Honest. Do you know that the Red Cross is being almost bankrupted by the storage costs? Someone told me that recently they had a hundred thousand cubic yards of clothing that they didn't even distribute, just shunted it down the line like that, free gratis and for nothing."

"How about a cigar?"

On the living room table diagonally opposite them was an opened box of Sumatras.

"Yes, give me one. Some of it went to the rag merchants, and some of it to all our faithful Indonesian immigrants."

A few minutes later, when Armanda came back to sit with them again, the conversation had become more general. She followed it with a cup of coffee in her hand and a plate with a slice of pie on her lap, but didn't join in. In the circle across from her sat her father and her mother. With the forbearing, slightly astonished expressions that were so typical of both of them and sometimes made them in some remarkable way the spitting image of each other, they listened to these anecdotes that were circulating through every Dutch living room right now, and which their guests were telling one another the way people tell jokes. In Zieriksee the entire population had been forcibly evacuated by the authorities. Nobody wanted to leave, everyone had to. And as a result the workers, yes, it's true, who had the necessary knowledge to work on the dikes, were suddenly sitting parceled out with host families in Arnhem, Hilversum, Aerdenhout, and so on, and most of them had never even been away from home before. But because the work still had to be done, every single road worker and anyone who could hold a shovel were herded together by the officials of all the city engineering departments across the country and billeted in emergency barracks behind the Stone Dike.

Armanda saw her father's fingers tapping quietly on the arms of his chair. Uneasily, she felt the impulse to go sit on one of the arms and put her hand in his. All men, the conversation went on, young unmarried men and fathers of households with withdrawal symptoms, basically they were expected to wait. But it wasn't for long. A holiday bus from Leiden swept festively into the old marketplace, where it disgorged its passengers in front of a well-known small hotel. It was almost evening. The entire waterfront street was full as the girls, roughly twenty of them, climbed out, laughing and waving at the men, to get rooms.

Smiles all round. A very strange atmosphere, Armanda remembered later, without a single drop of anything high-proof doing the rounds. A cousin, the daughter of a certain Aunt Noor, had burst out laughing loudly, but then checked her laughter to tell a quick story about her fiancé, who had spent the summer with a colleague from the national police in one of these half-drowned villages. The girl, a rather brainless creature, gave some totally tactless details about her fiancé's summer. Beautiful weather. At high tide you could sail through an opening in the sea dike to the highest point of the village, where it rose up out of the water, and you could moor behind the pastor's house. Residence permits were almost never granted to the actual inhabitants of the village, not even if someone's house was still standing and they absolutely wanted to return. The only people there were a rescue team, a tavernkeeper with an ancient mother on whom they, the fiancé and his colleague, could unload entire boxes full of cats they'd fished up, and a few boys who collected the machinery from the farms and set it out to dry in the sun. The two policemen had their hands full. Even late at night they would sometimes be awakened by the approaching buzzing of a motorboat with a troop of merry thieves on board, who assumed the village was totally abandoned. All in all, a terrific time: driving around, hilarious evenings in the tavern, fish to catch by the pound just by lowering a net in front of the opening by the dike, idiotic games with a pig that was running around, the *Handelsblad* sent a crate of oranges, and naturally going swimming, jumping into the water, which they did right from . . .

The cousin, a little uncertain now, had begun to pull at her lip.

"Oh, I'm boring you."

"Not at all! Which they did right from . . . yes?"

Armanda had already stopped looking at the storyteller some time ago, but as the account began to pull her in, she had turned her eyes toward her father, her mother, and her brother. She saw her father pick up a matchbox and examine it carefully, while her mother bent forward with a lifeless smile to pour some cream into Jacob's coffee. In the meantime she heard, as did her parents, how the cousin's fiancé and his colleague had jumped right off the makeshift landing behind the pastor's house to go for a swim. Of course, only when the water was as clear as glass, and with their eyes open, because as her fiancé had said, man, you had no idea what was floating around down there!

At that very moment everyone looked up, laughing and saying hello. Sjoerd had come in, a little late, he'd had some things to do in the city after dinner. Armanda, who had hardly been able to move for the last fifteen minutes, felt a surge of relief go through her. With a sense of everything's-okay-now she got to her feet to take the empty coffee cups into the kitchen, knowing that Sjoerd would take up his duties as son-in-law at the sideboard in the back room where the bottles and glasses were standing ready. As the two of them did the rounds shortly afterward with wine, vermouth, egg liqueur, and gin, most of the guests barely detected any difference between this and earlier parties here in the house, and after the first glasses nobody saw any difference at all.

Shortly after eleven the door to the living room opened. A little barefoot creature with dark sleepy eyes came toddling in: Nadja. The entire assembled company immediately stopped all conversations, looked at the child, laughed and cooed, and in general presented a picture that would make anyone wonder what kind of spooky effect it would have on a stone-sober almost-three-year-old. But—at this moment the little one discovered the face of her mother and steered for a pair of open arms.

Nothing special. Armanda, who had been called Mama by Nadja for so long already that she'd forgotten it had ever been otherwise, kissed the copper-red curls on the head of the toddler now sitting on her lap. Then, contented, as she looked around the room, where conversation had started up again, she realized that Betsy was trying to meet her eyes, and looking acutely interested. It was the look of a friend from a far corner of the room, but so penetrating that her inner ear could pick up the whispered arguments that came with it.

"Sweetheart, fate has certainly intervened in your life, hasn't it?"

Calm, persuasive. Armanda stared back.

"A little effort on your part, and my brother, shall we say, gets his wife, whom he misses, back again. But à propos, do tell me why you behaved so impossibly to him after the movies last week."

Without dropping her gaze, Armanda had carefully picked up her glass from the occasional table and taken a sip. Then, with Nadja's hot little head resting against her neck, she had telegraphed back: "Dear Betsy, I do understand—you want to see your half brother and his family settled with a competent woman to run the house again. I myself am conscious of certain powers that sometimes encourage this, and sometimes suddenly rule it out altogether. When the three of us went to the Rialto last week to see *La Città Dolente*, to begin with I liked it that you arranged things so that Sjoerd sat in the middle and I could feel his shoulder against mine as soon as the lights went down. When afterward you wanted to excuse yourself quickly so that Sjoerd and I could spend a few minutes in the rosy dimness of the foyer talking a little about the really moving story of the man who got left at the North Pole, I was already ahead of you. Two quick kisses for each of you, then I beat it. And now you want an explanation. All I'm going to say is that because of the short that ran before the main film, I didn't register a single thing about the North Pole business. It was about Schouwen-Duiveland. Do you remember? The weekly newsreel once again was delivering the most heroic report, and in the most heroic voice: all forces had been deployed to close the last breach in the dike in Zeeland, near Ouwerkerk. Why this had to be done in night and fog was a mystery, but here were the pictures: the black expanse of water, sections of the dike, cranes, and on the foredeck of a ship the queen, a beret on her head, standing among the workers chewing her lip, because this job has already been done once, and failed miserably. But this time it works. Incredibly impressive, all these lights at night! The gap in the dike at Ouwerkerk is enormous, and four huge concrete caissons have to be pulled into it by tugs and then lowered. Three of the things are already in place, tonight it's the turn of number four. The tugs have brought it into position as the tide goes out, and now, one and a half hours later, it comes to rest on the sea bottom, precisely placed to the inch. How diligent we are today. From now on, no more tides turning right there between the houses. All over the island, which I've long thought of as Lidy's island now, bells begin to ring out in the night. Major celebrations. I kept hearing them, Betsy, in fragments, all through the other film about that man at the North Pole."

They had both laughed out loud. Betsy had stuck out a knee and filched a cigarette from the glass on the table.

13

Let's Crawl Under the Covers

When she was finished at the hairdresser, Armanda took care of a couple of errands, then went home. Surgery hours were still in progress on the first floor, her father's patients came and went, but upstairs she bumped into no one. So I'll just pop over to number 36, she thought with the feeling of happy relief that she had come to associate with this idea. She liked going to Lidy's house. She really loved to keep it running in apple pie order.

When she got there, there were a couple of letters lying on the mat. As she picked them up and checked to whom they were addressed and who had sent them, her raincoat dragged on the floor. "Mrs. L. Blaauw," she murmured on the stairs, realized it sounded strange, got a lump in her throat, and went, as soon as she got upstairs, to the garbage can that lived in a deep cupboard next to the kitchen. A short time later the unopened mailing from the perfumery to its customers was buried under the chrysanthemums that had been there all week. She also emptied the ashtrays.

The light was already fading as she looked around the living room. No need to dust today. So I'll iron a couple of shirts. A few minutes later she was doing this, one flight up. The ironing board had its allotted place in the hall, with a lamp above it, and she spread out the ironed shirts on the bed in the master bedroom next door.

Inhaling the smell of steam and almost singed cotton that Lidy always said made her feel faint, she was just getting a dress iron out of the cupboard when she heard the front door close downstairs. She jumped, and looked at the time. He's early today, she thought, and then did something that just came over her. She hurried to the dressing table set at an angle in the corner, ran a brush through her hair, and pulled her sweater nice and tight over her breasts. Then she switched off the overhead light, and lit a floor lamp, cast a glance at the curtains but decided to leave them open so that Sjoerd, whom she could already hear on the third tread of the stair, would find her bathed in ocher light, very much to her advantage, with a mysterious reflection in the window behind her.

He stood in the doorway. Pausing for a moment to take in the situation, he came over to her with the same decisiveness, she realized in a flash, with which he must have stopped work half an hour before. And they started to kiss, immediately, greedily. Moving one arm behind her back, he had already succeeded in closing the curtains.

It was not their first embrace, far from it. For more than a year now, Armanda had been going around the house at the oddest hours for a woman. And Sjoerd had quite often reached out in the dark hallways or by the stove in the kitchen to pull her close. But contrary to what might be assumed, the more time went on, the more she began to be coy, pushing him away from her when he pressed her against a wall, his desire for her declaring itself openly as he went hard against her stomach. One time she had interrupted their playful wrestling and said, "I won't do it till I've seen my sister's dead body."

Did those words come out of my mouth? she had thought immediately, and was relieved when he reacted so casually, even quite heartlessly.

"Anyone who still surfaces these days is put straight into a closed coffin. You'll never get to see it now."

So today it looked as if Armanda had pushed her reservations aside. When Sjoerd said, "Be my wife," whispering, as if someone could hear him, she found it wonderful that his fingers, which never had a problem anyway, had already located the hooks on her bra.

Armanda returned his embrace, pulled her sweater over her head, let him undo the zipper on her skirt, climbed out of it eagerly, and searched at once for his warm mouth again. Then she simply couldn't find anything amiss in her behavior, as she fell back with him onto the bed covered in carefully ironed shirts, first she was on top, then he was. In that moment Armanda was already far away in her head. The only signal her thoughts gave off was in a certain look, yearning, utterly honest, that a man would recognize as declaring that she was his love, and yes, she was willing.

Then, at a moment that was totally inconvenient, erotically speaking, Armanda, who was still a virgin—this requires saying, because these things are relevant—started a conversation. And its opening theme was the undeniable fact that legally speaking, Lidy was still alive.

"Ridiculous," said Sjoerd in the same tone of voice he had just used to whisper something sweet in her ear. "You know as well as I do."

"Maybe," she said, and told him right to his stunned face that in this moment she could feel not only her sister's ghostly eyes on her but, to tell him the truth, his as well. Together they were watching to see if she did everything the right, well-tested way. "Am I right, or not?"

"No."

"And while I remember it, why did you just say 'be my wife' and not, for example, 'be my love' or, just as good, 'let's crawl under the covers'?"

He began to laugh. Before she knew what was happening to her, he slid out of bed, switched off the lamp, and took her in his arms again in the pitch darkness.

"Nobody can watch you now," he said in the same sweet whisper, but then his voice changed. As if he found himself in a discussion with her at a point where only the most powerful arguments could hope to prevail, Sjoerd told Armanda how much he loved her and how beautiful she was. Not a night went by, he said, in which he didn't spend time thinking about her—and she should know that thinking meant more than just thinking—as he saw her face and her perfect round mouth and emerald green eyes always in front of him, no different from now, along with her long dark brown hair, and the most magnificent naked breasts that a lonely man could imagine, and if it came to that, would be able to recognize at once and prefer to a thousand other pairs of breasts!

At this point his voice sank again, as Armanda buried him in kisses.

And everything would have run its normal course if the front door-bell had not rung at that very moment.

Armanda flinched, horrified.

"There's someone at the door. Someone wants to come in!"

"No, no," murmured Sjoerd, who actually hadn't heard a thing, since the sound of the doorbell sometimes didn't reach this high up in the house.

But it was true. In number 77 the table had been laid ready for some time now. Grandpa Brouwer and Nadja had taken a little walk and come to fetch the two lovebirds home to supper.

The bell rang again softly.

Up on the fourth floor the bedroom was already bathed in lamp-light. With Sjoerd's cold, tired eyes looking at her from the bed, Armanda was slipping hastily into her clothes.

14

In the Village

This is what they call sleep. . . .

As she stumped through the puddles of an anonymous street in an anonymous village at half past three in the morning, she was alone with the storm for the first time. To left and right were low houses, and not a light to be seen anywhere. Simon Cau had dispatched her and the two daughters of the tavernkeeper to different parts of the village to drum the inhabitants awake.

"Wake them," she had had time to ask quickly, "and then what?" They had climbed out of the car at the church. The sky had begun to rain large hailstones. Simon Cau had wanted to start ringing the storm bell immediately, but although the church door stood open, they discovered by the light of a match that the door to the tower was locked. Back outside, as they stood in the moonlight that had somehow found its way through to them, Lidy had looked into Simon Cau's face. And seen that he had no belief in his own orders, but didn't know what else to do.

"Wake them!"

She did what she was told. It wasn't easy. It was obvious that nobody here had any wish to interrupt their sleep. Embarrassed, she stood between doors and windows that remained closed to her hammering. Everything was calm and secure in the world behind them, she could feel it; buried in their bedclothes, legs curled up, men, women, and children slept with slow heartbeats. Inhaling the warm breath of their sleeping companions, they placed their trust in the strength of their inadequate imaginations and let her muddle on in the storm that was just a storm, that swooped down into the narrow street and howled through it as if through a fallen chimneypot.

She looked around. Nothing but this bedlam of noise. Suddenly it occurred to her that absolutely nobody knew she was here. With a new kind of unease she crossed the street, decided on the door to a small shop, and banged, palms out, on its upper portion. Unreal village, she thought, with the fearfulness of someone who knows herself to be overlooked by an oblivious God and her oblivious fellow men. If nobody has any idea where you are and cannot form any image of it, do you exist? Her eyes slid over the white letters, carefully painted in italics on the dull glass pane above the shop door: *Baked Goods.*

Someone had awakened in the apartment at the back. An alert, elderly lady who heard noises in her sleep that her ears couldn't identify as a normal part of foul weather like this. She felt her way blindly into her bedroom slippers. The light wasn't working, so she lit a candle. She was about to go directly to answer the drumming on the front door when she noticed a faint roar from somewhere in the house that demanded her more urgent attention. A moment later she was standing in amazement in the toilet, where the water was spouting up out of the pan as if from a spring. She turned around, hurried through the shop, and opened the door.

"Come look at this," she said, and Lidy followed her.

It was one of those lavatories that had been carpentered together out of planks and sheet metal against the outside wall at some point in the past, capturing every bad smell forever. Now it had a white porcelain toilet bowl and a lacquered cistern above it with a chain. Lidy and the old woman, who had survived most of her life without electricity and had possessed this beautiful WC with its connection to the sewage system for only the last four years, which made it still a daily enchantment, looked first at the high-spurting column of water and then at each other.

Their reactions were almost simultaneous.

"The light's out too."

"The water's up over the sea dike already, I've seen it myself."

The woman in her white nightgown turned round, because someone was coming through the hall, lantern in hand.

"Nothing's working anymore," she complained loudly but patiently to the man whom she didn't yet recognize but took to be a neighbor.

She couldn't know how right she was. For at this moment elsewhere on the island the first telephone poles were coming down. The total isolation had begun. There were, it is true, a few telephone operators at their posts in some of the slumbering villages, attentive employees who had gone to work in the belief that the need to make an emergency call to the provincial or even the national authorities tonight might not be just the product of an overzealous sense of duty. But none of them got through. In some places the telephone switchboard was an old-fashioned operation, run by hand with a generator that produced its own power, and it happened a couple of times that the operator, totally concentrated on the alarm call even as the floodwaters poured into the building, received an electric shock as the water reached the height of his chair and the stool supporting the equipment with its worn but indestructible parts. This was a lost island. It would be submerged completely, without the outside world lifting a finger or even noticing, because as chance would have it, this confluence of the position of the moon and the endless wind happened during a weekend.

Nonetheless: *one* extraordinary exception.

Very early in the morning, a post office employee was still trying. At the last moment, shortly before the technical equipment gave up the ghost and the last shutters on the telephone exchange fell off, he managed to dial the number of a fairly high official. He reached him personally.

"Yes?"

The chief engineer of the Royal Hydraulic Engineering Authorities was three-quarters asleep. The phone operator had to repeat his request twice, in different formulations. "I'm calling you in desperation, something's got to happen."

"Yes, well, but what can I . . ." the chief engineer began, then said, "Good, I'll order the necessary measures." He hung up again, looked at the clock, yawned, shook his head—the bright green hands were pointing to ten past four—and crawled back under the covers. But he kept his word. When he dared to rouse the queen's commissioner from his Sunday-morning sleep with a 7 a.m. phone call, in the village under discussion the flotsam and jetsam was already thundering against the house walls and there were corpses floating everywhere.

Having to die is everyman's excusable fear, and in a region such as this, death by drowning rapidly becomes the most particular fear of all. Lidy, who had now been traveling for eighteen hours, found herself on the street with a handful of villagers who were arguing with one another. The storm had increased to force 12, i.e., a hurricane. People were wearing coats over nightclothes, and kept to the shelter of their houses; two or three of them were carrying torches. Universal darkness. Going by their faces, none of them seemed overly concerned; what was occupying each of them was what the others were making of the spectacle.

Bad weather. And not good that the water was coming over the dike out there. Everyone knew that at ebb tide that evening, the water-depth gauge at the Laurens sluice hadn't gone down by even a quarter of an inch. And where there had been no ebb, they had projected that there would be no high tide, because this logic had held true all their lives. A young man who had been down to the harbor to take a look tonight said he'd seen the farmer at the entrance to the village hastily hitching his horses to the wagon not fifteen minutes before, with his best cows in tow, to move himself, his wife, his children, and all his worldly goods, farther inland.

The people standing around in the darkness let their eyes slide wishfully leftward, away from the silhouette of the church tower, inland, away from the sea.

Living in a dangerous place leads inevitably to a kind of deaf-and-blindness to the elements of that danger. Every single person in the street, Lidy included, knew that yes this was a village, but it was also one tiny point in a landscape given over entirely to the moon, the sea, and the wind. Water is the heaviest element in existence—that was also known. Whoever lived here was descended from generations who had centuries of experience that in long-drawn-out storms, the sea exercises a counterpressure and then rises on one side. Oceanographers had done the calculations to prove that the height of this lopsided rise is in inverse proportion to the depth of the sea—but people here had known this forever and understood it. Every person here in the street had grown up with eerie tales of monstrous hands of water reaching abruptly out of the arms of the North Sea, whose floor rises toward the coast of this country like a chute.

Lidy glanced to the side. The old woman had nudged her.

"I think I'd better carry some things upstairs."

"I'd do the same," replied Lidy, and thought: I'll give the woman a hand for a few minutes.

Other people, too, were giving one another meaningful looks. The group in the street broke up. Shutters and attic windows had already been made fast that afternoon. There was nothing on any of the farms still standing around loose. Now they went to fetch their children out of bed, taking all the covers with them, and to settle them back down in attics, along with buckets of water, camping stoves, supplies, matches, and even perhaps the most valuable thing in the house, the black sewing machine with the cast-iron treadle.

Permission to stay granted, and best not to think too much. Another way of fighting back against the impossibility of nature. It is true that most of the houses in this street were little buildings put up for farmworkers, with walls thrown up using not cement but a pitiful mixture of sand and plaster. But they were their dwellings, and they wanted to feel safe in them. For the time being they wanted to have the interval between one sleep and the next preserve as much of the order of their everyday lives as possible.

Lidy went back into the little shop. The old woman walked resolutely ahead of her through the dark. Behind an intervening door the candle was still burning.

A few seconds later: "Here, you take these."

She had two large biscuit tins pushed into her arms.

"There."

A cash box.

Filled with the same dreamlike sense of closeness she'd experienced a few hours earlier at the family dinner, Lidy climbed a ladder to a peaked attic where she couldn't stand upright. In the circular glow cast by a tealight she saw her feet encased in muddy shoes. A person must have two or three different people inside them, she thought, as she stood at the top of the ladder to receive a cushion, parts of a kapok mattress, a chamber pot, a coverlet, and then another.

"Got it?"

"Yes."

She set the things on the floor, pushing aside with her foot what was lying there. The shrieking night outside and the sea, which she'd seen with her own eyes at the crest of the dike, had been shrunk again to something less enormous in this creaking, groaning little hut. As the other woman worked her way up through the trapdoor, now wearing a hairy brown coat, she looked at her crumpled old face, lit from below. Enough? Everything the way you want it? And imagined herself and the old lady, when dawn came a few hours later, carrying the whole lot back down and making coffee in the kitchen behind the shop.

"Quiet!"

The old woman turned her head toward the din raging a hand's breadth over their heads. Then Lidy heard it too. Laboriously, at intervals, yet unmistakable, the sound of a bell was making itself heard in the wind.

So he managed it, she thought.

And immediately thereafter she felt, more than she saw, the old woman's eyes fix themselves on her, huge and dark with anxious recognition.

"Fire!"

Simon Cau hadn't been able to get the key to the bell tower. It was no help at all that he knew where the sexton—a good carpenter and also the commandant of the fire brigade—lived. Neither ringing the doorbell nor banging a stick against a windowpane had succeeded in waking the man, who as he slept had one ear cocked only for the sound of the telephone. After some time a blacksmith had got out of bed in a neighboring house. It wasn't long thereafter before the hinges of the door to the church tower gave way under the blows of a sledgehammer, and Cau and the blacksmith climbed the stairs by the light of an oil lamp. At first they were barely able to coax a sound from the bell. The failed electrical mechanism gave off sparks when they tried it with a rope. So Cau had run back down and fetched the sledgehammer.

When Lidy and one of the Hin daughters wanted to attract the attention of the men a short time later, they found it hard to do. The two of them had met outside the church: Lidy sent out by the old woman to find out what was going on, and the tavernkeeper's daughter to spread some reassuring news.

"The water's going down again already," the girl said.

It was no easy task to bring the good news up into the tower. Lidy and the tavernkeeper's daughter stood in the stairwell with their fingers in their ears, looking up at the two men who were going at it as if possessed. The blacksmith, hanging onto the rope with all his weight, managed to keep the bell swinging in the correct rhythm while Simon Cau, who clearly didn't find the heavy booming sufficient, struck the sledgehammer against the rim, which produced an additional high-pitched clang. Eventually they noticed the two young women.

"Impossible" was Cau's first exclamation after the bell had stopped moving. "Absolutely impossible!" Without straightening up, he stood there panting, the heavy hammer in his hand.

But the tavernkeeper's daughter was certain. She named the names of several boatmen who had just returned from the harbor and whom she had met in the village.

"They said it happened very quickly. In just a few minutes they saw the water go down by whole yards!"

Speechlessly, Cau handed the blacksmith his sledgehammer. Wrapping his scarf around his neck, and looking angry, he reached for the lamp, which was smoking in the downdraft under one of the louvers that let out the sound.

As the little group got downstairs, there were more people in the street, including the tavernkeeper's other daughter. Everyone had just heard that the water situation wasn't so serious, and feeling somewhat light-headed because of the alarm bells and the strange hour, they were having little chats about it all. Relieved, naturally. And again, all too naturally, drawing only those conclusions that made sense to them from the reality in which unwittingly they found themselves: the night, the wind, the wet, and the salt in the air.

Let's go, quick, back to our featherbeds!

Soon the car was bumping its way over the water-filled potholes out of the village again, where peace had descended once more, and only the occasional dog refused to stop barking.

Was Cau thinking perhaps that he'd be held up as a fool?

Or what?

When he drove back by way of the harbor with the three girls again, it was a needless stop, and one that bored the three of them to distraction. Nevertheless they all got out, went to the barricade in the dike, and there was a brief discussion. Cau, to sum up, didn't want to believe his eyes, while the three others just wanted to go to bed.

"The timbers really held up well!"

"Till now!"

"God I'm tired."

"It's . . . it's impossible!"

"Well, anyhow, the water's down more than six feet!"

"It can't go down!"

"Shall we go?"

"It can't go down, high tide isn't for another hour!"

"Nonetheless, shall we go?"

Cau couldn't get the engine to start, so Lidy tried it her way. After a few attempts it worked, whereupon she set off confidently along the bend in the road as if she knew the darkness here like the back of her hand. Five minutes later they were at the three-way fork in the dike, and the little tavern, a hut, appeared. Vague silhouettes, vague light behind steamed-up windows. The two tavernkeeper's daughters leapt out of the car. Lidy watched as they stumbled up the steps to their parents' house, blew the horn by way of a farewell, and set off on the last part of the detour to Izak Hocke's farm, where they were, she assumed, expecting her.

Cau was silent now. Lidy was wide awake and, remarkably perhaps, still felt no fear or anything similar. Her instincts corresponded in no way with what was bearing down on her. Where was the awareness, however minimal, of those moments that precede reality, and yet are themselves their own reality?

While out in the southwest polders the inner dikes were crumbling and one sea was joining with the other, Lidy was struggling in the blasts of wind to keep the car on the road. As she reached a very dark spot, she took her foot off the gas and leaned over to her traveling companion. Which muddy road should she now take—the left or the right? There was a growl from Cau, but it hardly registered with her in her eagerness to reach the end of her winter journey. Nearby, more than half a mile northeast, where the mouth of the Grevelingen opened into the bay, this was the moment when the masses of water forced their way through the sea dike in three places, filling the polders behind it at such speed that the water-level gauge in the little harbor dropped briefly but powerfully by almost seven feet. But Lidy steered back on course again and thought, Ah, there they are, the two farms, diagonally opposite each other, and I can see a light in each of them behind a window.

Finally she parks the car squarely in the yard in front of the part of the building that is the Hockes' house. She and Cau get out. They go to the front door to see if it's been left open. The cold is even icier now. Lidy takes a quick look at the rather high-stepped gable end and the adjacent barn, its shutters closed with crossbars. She knows there's endless flat land to right and left. There's a little moonlight, but on the southern horizon it's as if the night fields are being faintly lit by a glow that comes out of the earth itself. Okay, the front door is open. Just as she's about to say good-night to Cau before he goes across to his own house, Lidy realizes that he's gone rigid and is listening for something. She catches his eye, registers that he's frightened, then she hears it too. The noise to begin with is abstract. A kind of rushing sound, getting louder. For a moment she's seized by the image of a plague of locusts, then of an army of a thousand men marching toward her at top speed from the other side of the island. She has no time to be terrified. The entire view disappears. A horrifying wave of black water comes towering out of nowhere and rolls down on them.

III

There's Always Weather

15

The Meteorologist

In the Netherlands, the radio stopped broadcasting at midnight on the dot. At one minute to midnight, Hilversum One and Two played a lively brass-band version of the national anthem, and after that the country, radio-wise, was put to bed. As Simon Cau and Lidy Blaauw flew into the house and heard the water break against the outside of the door that they were holding shut with the full weight of their bodies, someone in the weather bureau of the Royal Netherlands Meteorological Institute at De Bilt was still awake.

A meteorologist, who was under no official obligation to be on duty at this hour, was standing at the window high up in the building, looking from the telephone on his desk to the outside and then back to his desktop again, where a couple of weather charts were spread out. He was wearing a good suit. After accompanying his wife to a concert, he couldn't get back quickly enough to his post, from which he could keep an eye on the storm. Its howl was deafening. The meteorological institute, a relatively slender six-story building topped with a roof terrace, was in a little park in the midst of flat meadows that stretched all the way to Utrecht.

What could he do?

He ran his fingers over his lower jaw and listened to the storm, which he not only felt he understood better than anyone else but also regarded as his absolute personal property. During the concert he had totally ignored the oscillations of the musical sound waves, focusing instead on those of the gusts of wind, which he estimated at close to sixty knots, if not higher, against the walls and windows of the hall. As he did so, he had mentally reviewed with razor sharpness the weather maps of 6 a.m. and 12 a.m., Greenwich Mean Time—large hand-drawn charts, on which he himself had penciled in the contours of air pressure over northwestern Europe, erased them again several times after receiving updated information, and drawn them in again: the isobars were lying more and more alarmingly close together. Hunched over the paper, he had studied the warm and cold fronts, drawn in red and blue, and the violet lines showing the areas in which the cold following behind would dissipate the warm air over the earth's surface, and the harsh green shading filled in with the pencil held flat to indicate the zones of rainfall surrounding the fronts.

This was the view, the true heavens of the RNMI that the meteorologist had held fixed in his mind's eye right through the Brahms. And which that eye, trained to measure barometers, thermometers, wind, and rain, had read all too clearly.

The areas of low pressure. He'd been following them since the beginning of the week as they formed over Iceland, Labrador, the Azores. And here, the trough with very large varieties of pressure that started developing northwest of Scotland at 6 a.m. One can know an enormous number of facts, and still the 12 noon chart will be made up of countless details that are already in the process of escaping their own diagram at the bidding of some force unknown to us. The trough had moved ineluctably to the east coast of Scotland. Look what was bearing down on us! From this time on, the meteorologist had kept promptly demanding updated figures. At 3 p.m. he had received a transmission from an English lightship about a sharp drop in air pressure, followed by another at 6 p.m. Almost immediately thereafter, shortly before he was relieved by a colleague, because he had to get home to change for the concert, he had taken another look at the measurements from Den Helder and Vlissingen: the difference in pressure between the north and the south coasts of the country was now more than 13 millibars. The prognosis was certain—it was going to be quite something!

And so he had sat motionless in the parterre of the warm concert hall next to his equally motionless wife. Although he, like she, had his eyes closed, he was still looking, being a bird like all meteorologists. His element, the air; his perspective, the earth. Surrounded by the music, increasingly restless, increasingly impatient, he made a mental picture of the weather chart he had had on his desk today. Nothing but fleeting visual snapshots, which had already changed considerably by now. As he followed the storm in his head as it veered northwest, his mind was drawing the new map, which showed with utter precision that the area of low pressure was moving into the German Bight, in the direction of Hamburg. The storm field accompanying it now took up the entire North Sea west of the fifth degree of longitude.

He was right. Around 10:30 p.m., after the meteorologist had hurriedly delivered his wife back home and gone to his colleagues in the weather bureau, he saw that the storm had indeed developed according to the scientific predictions. He bent over a message that had come in by telex from the *Goeree*, a lightship positioned some miles off the coast of Zeeland. Given the breaking waves and the behavior of the short but mountainously steep seas all around the ship, the crew had relayed an estimated wind speed of sixty-three knots, which was the equivalent of almost force 12 on the Beaufort scale. A hurricane. The meteorologist had looked at his colleagues and received very dark looks in return. Then he looked at the clock.

Hilversum was still on the air.

The telephone made the most terrible crackling noises. First there was a woman's voice, then a defensive male voice. "*Who* is this?"

The meteorologist presented his proposal that they keep the radio transmission going tonight so that news updates and warnings could continue to be passed on, confidently at first, then merely impatiently, as he could already tell from the silence on the line what the other man was going to say.

"It's not my decision to make!"

More silence on the line. The meteorologist waited, drumming his fingers, till he heard something again.

"Office of the Director of Programming," sighed a three-quarters-asleep or bored man.

With authority, but without expectations, the meteorologist asked Hilversum again to keep the transmitter open tonight.

"Given the weather conditions, it is my opinion that you would be justified."

He squeezed his eyes shut, felt a second go by as he listened to the windows groan under a wild pressure, and received his answer.

"What are you thinking of? The last newscast here is and always has been eleven p.m., and we're past that now."

The meteorologist heard the radio employee take his time to stifle a sneeze and blow his nose.

"Besides which, I'm unwell."

Midnight had passed. His colleague went home, he stayed. At first the meteorologist followed every bulletin that came in, but as night wore on, he lost interest in charts and numbers. He sat stiffly in his place, the left-hand desk in front of the window, getting to his feet only once, to fetch a telescope from the bottom compartment of a cupboard where all the useless junk was kept, and then trained it directly against the windowpane to spy into the blackness outside. Naturally there was nothing to be seen. It was simply a storm that had reached its top speed and was racing unchecked, whistling and screaming. As he looked farther, to where the darkness dissolved into a pale, transparent heaving motion, he felt everything downstairs being upended. He put down the telescope, took his seat again as if in an abandoned theater, and imagined the appalling devastation, images of derailed freight trains, torn-off roofs, uprooted trees, tangled power lines. He also thought of the chaos out at sea and the helpless ships in distress.

But his mind was not capable of imagining real flooding.

The state of dikes and coastal defenses was not his area of expertise. Nonetheless he would always remember these hours, later, as hours when he had had to sit with his hands in his lap, watching, as the sea rolled over Capelle, Stavenisse, and 's-Gravendeel, as Kortgene, Bath, and Battenoord found themselves directly in the path of a mountain of water being driven into the narrows, as the dike southwest of Numansdorp collapsed in nine places and neighboring Schuring, no more than a little road, disappeared from one moment to the next. Oude-Tonge, pitiful site of a storm flood that attacked it from three sides at once. Ouwekerk, Nieuwerkerk, villages that were, mind you, right in the middle of the island, he saw them go under without any warning from him in the northwesterly storm whose charts at this very moment were right under his nose.

The weatherman stared out into the night. The northwesterly storm, whose eye, he knew, was now moving toward Berlin, would be forever in his memory: 4 a.m., when people everywhere began to attempt to flee, in carts, in trucks, in a bus, most of them on foot. And everywhere on that first February night in the icy wind, people were to be found in small groups on the overflowing dikes. Shuffling over the ground to try to avoid being seized and dragged away by the current, they linked arms tightly, heading toward a village on higher ground or the red or yellow lights of a distant car, till they were captured by the pillar of water that came in pursuit out of the utter darkness, the little clusters disappearing in a flash into the wave as it broke and they were sucked under into the storm that was emitting a sound that none of the refugees had ever heard a storm make before—a long-drawn-out, deep bellowing, the noise that cows make when they're swimming in circles in blind panic, before they give up, quicker than horses do.

The three of them looked at it from the attic window. Lidy, Simon Cau, and Gerarda Hocke, who had waited for them up on the stairs, while the water at the bottom tore out part of the side wall. The old lady of the house was wearing the costume of Duiveland, black, with a white bonnet that fitted tight around the face, and what was amazing was that the first thing Lidy had noticed as she rushed toward the farmer's wife was the two gold pins to either side of the bonnet; they seemed to her to be ancient, probably heirlooms.

Now all three of them were staring out of the only window on the top floor of the house, built with its narrow side to the street. Gray moonlight shone down on a wild surge of water in which wood, straw, and large dark shapes were floating around, some of which made movements now and again. They saw one of the cows swimming to and fro like a dog, striking at the water with its forelegs. Roughly twenty yards away, to the right, they could see the pointed gables of the attic floor of the Gabriëllina farmhouse poking up out of the swell, a light inside still burning. The first to look away was Cau. As the farmer's wife asked him if he would like a cigarette, he patted his coat and said, "Got my own." She pushed a glass of cognac into his hand. Lidy got one too, and a cigarette, dry socks, and a pair of black shoes with laces. The attic was as large as a church. A coachman's lantern threw a weak blue light on the things that were stored here, among them two featherbeds with accessories and a bed frame with a mattress, all of which would soon come in handy. Lying peacefully on a small rug were a dog and one of the six geese from the coop in the orchard next to the street, which, like the shed alongside it, and the beehives and the bees, no longer existed.

Izak Hocke, his mother told them, had set off more than an hour ago with the big wagon hitched to the tractor.

16

Low Barometer in Amsterdam

The last week in June finally brought summer with it. The wind blew from the southeast, bringing a heat to the city that was very pleasant to begin with but had turned humid and oppressive today. The people assembled in the Amstel church for Lidy's memorial service felt it too. The wooden church, originally built as a barn church and then rebuilt in the Gothic Revival style, was extremely dilapidated, which added an extra touch of the tragic to the consecrated atmosphere.

Armanda sat in the first pew between her mother and Jacob. She glanced from the place where the coffin should have been up to the three pointed windows high in the façade, from which white sunlight, as damp as steam, was slanting down. Lidy, where are you, she murmured inside her head, and wiped off her sticky hands on the black worsted skirt that she was wearing for the second time this month and in which she felt miserable for the second time, because the skirt, which was unlined, was the kind that works its way up your legs when you walk. Ten days before, she had gone with Betsy and Sjoerd to Schouwen-Duiveland, where the congregation of Ouwerkerk was burying its dead once more in the cemetery that had reemerged from the floodwaters. There had been coffins beyond number that time; now just a single was jarring by its absence. She fixed her eyes on the flagstones that had formed the floor of the church since the seventeenth century.

It was suffocatingly hot. Her mother's light perfume, very faint but typical Nadine, was the only counterweight to the atmosphere of depression and overt grief that filled the church. No flower arrangement, not a single burning candle. Instead a pastor, corpulent, short, who began to declaim something mournful. Behind her she suddenly heard the labored sniffs of a man trying to choke back his sobs. Probably Sjoerd's father, an elegant banker, nice man, who had just come for a month from New York with his second wife. She had to force herself not to turn round in sympathetic curiosity.

God knows this isn't a normal memorial service, she brooded. And all these people, all the relatives, friends, Father's colleagues and patients, neighbors, fellow students of mine and Lidy's, they all know that those of us here in the first two rows aren't a normal family, we're one that's been stood on its head. And I, the surviving sister, who can certainly say I'm the personification of us both, have spent the last year and a half occupying a horribly ambivalent position in this family.

Jacob and she were sitting shoulder to shoulder in the pew. It occurred to her that her brother was listening, stock stiff, not leaning against her. She glanced at his face, far too weary for his age. It seemed as if the voice of the pastor, who knew how to make it echo right up into the roof of the wooden building, had put him in a trance. She nudged him, asked, "Peppermint?" raised her shoulder to grope in her jacket pocket, saw his gratitude as she held out the bonbon to him, and lifted her head again.

The voice meanwhile seemed to her to be using a normal way of speaking, but from the beginning, during the first prayer, it had turned her to stone. Stern, almost peremptory in his direct conversation with the Almighty, this preacher had used no euphemisms in stating the essential. "You know where she is, we don't."

Oh yes, that is how it is. Amen. That is the situation.

After which the pastor, who might be small but radiated authority, began to beg for help and comfort. He managed to weave Lidy's name into every new subject. Lidy here and Lidy there, but whether it was Armanda's fault or not, as the service went on, Lidy, rather than coming closer, began to retreat further and more finally into her absence. Until Armanda finally grasped that this was his intention.

"As for man, his days are as grass." So it's not so terrible, you're dead, or at least that's what we're assuming for now, we too will be dead soon enough, but not yet! The organ started to play, with full vibrato. Armanda, who could feel the deepening bass notes vibrating in her chest, noticed that the general state of feelings about Lidy was slowly changing, secretly at first but then more and more openly, from tenderness to sheer hard-heartedness.

Clear them out of the way, your precious dead, otherwise you will never get free of them!

Yes, Armanda sobbed inwardly, bury their physical remains, give them peace, these ghosts who arouse our sympathy but are intent on our warm, living blood. And as she did so, she was acutely aware that the poeticizing, insincere tone of her lament fitted perfectly with the tenor of the psalms and hymns, whose melancholy certainly wasn't aimed at *them* but at the sighing, panting attendees of the memorial service here in the church. Bury her, yes, but what, when there's nothing to bury?

Impulsively she bent forward a little and turned her head to look for Sjoerd. Surreptitiously, of course, because as a member of the immediate family, you're supposed to be sitting still, in silent sorrow. She spied along the row. In a passing glance, she saw that her parents, to her left, were holding hands. Jan and Nadine Brouwer were sitting, alert, with goodwill in their faces, but totally focused, when it came down to it, on what the two of them shared to the exclusion of all else as they listened.

Sjoerd sat in the place of honor due to him as the widower, in the end seat on the other side of the aisle. She saw him wipe his brow with a folded white handkerchief; he was perspiring freely. With literally every minute that passed, it was getting muggier. The color of the light falling through the three windows was turning to gray. You could feel that throughout the city the atmospheric pressure was dropping under a high, heavy cloud of powerful dimensions and carrying an increasing electrical charge.

He's much less together than he was in Ouwerkerk ten days ago, she thought, even as she noticed how carefully he'd combed his thick, blond hair. Does he feel he's finally, before God and the world, becoming the widower he's allowed to be after eighteen months? The legitimate survivor of his wife? What terrible weather, she remembered, when he and Betsy and she had stayed on after the ceremony in the churchyard at Ouwerkerk to ask one of the gravediggers working around the graves for help. For they had seen that seven or eight places had been staked out for missing people from the village whose bodies hadn't been found. These, too, like the proper graves, had been covered with flowers.

Drizzle. Empty grayness all the way to the dike on the horizon.

Was it because of the absolute contrast in the state of the weather that this entire spectacle was coming back to her like something from a foggy past? And that the three of them, under close inspection, had been in much worse shape than they had actually felt?

They had stood there after all the local survivors had left to go to the reception in the town hall and the cars for the mourners and the trucks were heading back to their garages. The gravediggers, aided by a work detail from the city Board of Works, were hard at work shoveling earth on top of the more than fifty coffins that had been interred, and bringing a little order to the ocean of flowers. A dredger had stood in the expanse of mud behind them. Looking over in that direction, it was not hard to imagine that a hound of hell was standing there, bony, gigantic, dazed by today's sudden influx into his kingdom of grief of more than fifty dead in a single procession.

"Should we ask?" said Betsy suddenly.

All three knew that each of them had been thinking about the seven or eight still-empty places in the wet, salt-saturated ground. So they went to the workman who struck them as being the leader, and their first question was what was going to happen with the graves that had merely been numbered with a little metal shield stuck into the soil.

"They'll be getting gray concrete memorial slabs," the man replied, without raising his head from a worn notebook he was holding. "Fifteen by twenty." The foreman scribbled something down, paused for thought, and then, as if announcing the result of this meditation, said, "And then they'll be getting black lettering with the personal details of the dead. Name, place, and date of birth, date and place of death."

Then Sjoerd asked about the still-unoccupied graves.

The digger had looked at him with a certain kindness in his eyes. "They get a stone too."

And after a moment, as if he heard their unspoken question, he nodded and said, "Absolutely. With their own inscription too, though of course in these cases the date of death and the fact of death itself aren't one hundred percent certain."

The three of them kept looking at him.

"So to be safe, we'll add the word *missing* to the inscription."

As they walked away down the narrow, trampled paths, it had suddenly started to rain much harder. They began to hurry. Armanda took a last look around the pathetic burial ground, which she couldn't ever imagine looking like a normal, friendly churchyard. Those gravestones for the invisible dead. Why not inscribe *presumed dead* on them instead of *missing*?

They were in the train heading for Rotterdam when the idea came to them about a memorial service for Lidy, a farewell that now, ten days later, was taking place in the Amstel church, where the weather was making the air insufferably sticky, and Armanda had started to cry openly, her tears streaming down her cheeks as the individual details being cited in the ongoing words went through her head again.

A snack cart had come by. Hungry, she'd asked for coffee and rolls. Staring through the rain-soaked window at the fields, she'd then thought out loud, "Once we're home, we ought to do something for Lidy. What do you think, something in her memory or . . ."

As she looked away from the landscape again, she saw that Betsy and Sjoerd, sitting opposite her, were nodding in agreement, almost delighted.

"Good idea," said Sjoerd, biting into his roll. "Yes, why should we wait for the endless legal procedures to drag themselves out?"

But then, chewing quickly and swallowing, he had given her another look, so openly that she had immediately understood his question had not been a question at all but a bitter male reproach. They had still not gone to bed together. Oh God, she had thought. What a torture, for me but most of all for him. For she was not so naïve as not to know that any man would consider it a scandal and a crying injustice for a woman living more or less continuously under his roof, who had made clear more than once that she had nothing against being kissed and fondled by him, nonetheless to keep suddenly pulling away each time like an awkward bride, an unbearable tease.

In recent days she'd been trying whenever possible to avoid spending time with him in number 36.

She had looked down. The rumble of the train was intoxicating. Sjoerd and his half sister began to discuss the process that would soon allow Lidy, as everyone hoped, to be finally declared legally dead. Armanda leaned back, her body language indicating that she had switched off. It had always been difficult, she knew, to obtain a death certificate for someone who had clearly gone missing. Ten years had to elapse before a declaration of probable death could be wrung from a court, after which the heirs could raise specific but very modest claims and a surviving spouse would be permitted to marry again. Armanda heard them quietly touch on the law of 1949, which had allowed more than one hundred thousand of those missing in the war to be reclassified as dead and entered into the register of deaths in the local government offices nearest their former homes. They talked very dispassionately and matter-of-factly, perhaps because Betsy, who was Jewish on her mother's side, had already had her own dealings with this law and its macabre stipulations. This tragic law, the result of intensive efforts by the state, soon had to stand as also valid for a new list of missing persons, shorter than the original one, but still encompassing more than eight hundred names.

"All that's needed is a stamp," she heard Sjoerd say, "and then they can immediately apply the wording to anyone living in the provinces of Noord-Holland, Zuid-Holland, Noord-Brabant, and Zeeland between January thirty-first and February tenth, and *for whom no further proof of existence could be found.*"

She was weeping uncontrollably now. Her mother passed her a handkerchief. This gesture by her gentle, innocent-looking mother shamed her in a way she couldn't define, and she became even more upset. She felt as if the conversation in the train was now echoing through the entire church, its bone-dry words transformed into something quite different in this heavy atmosphere, exposing their true meaning for everyone to hear.

Lidy's farewell was also her, Armanda's, engagement party. The sister is dead, long live the sister.

Armanda rubbed the palms of her hands across her face, licked the teardrops from her lips—I miss you, Lidy, you know that, oh no, Lidy, don't let it be true, be alive again—and who knows what further display her distress would have prompted, had she not been jolted back to life by the force of a new text.

"The wormwood and the gall! My soul dwells on them and is cast down."

God! Armanda's eyes turned to the preacher up in the pulpit, who was looking extremely imposing. How do you mean us to take this? Leaning perilously far forward, here was someone engaged in reiterating Jeremiah's song of sorrow, working it, expertly tailoring it to today's occasion. What I mean is, it's about time for you to stop all this. How? thinks Armanda cunningly. You know perfectly well. Wormwood and gall, all the wretched thoughts that do not make any soul more magnanimous, including yours. And think of the little one who stayed at home this morning! Nadja! Yes, precisely. Should she have to grow up in such misery-ridden surroundings? God has taken your sister from us, and it is according to His plan. Stop. Pay attention. God's cruelty is a great taboo. Let go of your narrow-minded outrage and reflect that His ways are not your ways. God encompasses even those of us who are of unsound mind. And today He is giving you His simple commandment. Let her go. Live your life.

How? she moaned. Just tell me, man . . .

Even in the church it could be felt that not the slightest breeze was stirring outside. Breathing in was still feasible, but breathing out was measurably more difficult. All of a sudden the daylight vanished. Then, just before the final blessing, as if the one God had been unable to wait until the other God had finished speaking, there was a deafening crash of the kind that makes your heart jump into your throat, and the thunder broke. The family in their two front rows got to their feet, shocked.

After that an unceremonious procession formed. Armanda didn't wait around. Green eyes glittering feverishly, drops of sweat on her nose, smooth fringe glued to her forehead, the spitting image of her sister. They're all looking at me, she thought, naïvely perhaps but not wrong, and she looked with them. Look, look . . . all she could see was an image of herself. To the terrible din of the organ, overridden by cannon shots of thunder, she steered carefully, like a drunk, for the exit.

A few yards to one side of the porch the funeral cars were waiting. Everyone ran to them through the downpour. Armanda jumped into the first one she came to and let herself fall into the backseat. One of the Brouwer aunts slid hastily sideways and a Langjouw uncle, Leo, leapt in after her. "A beer!" he cried, as the car started moving, and Armanda answered, "Oh, God, yes please!"

17

Moon in Its Apogee

Lidy was the only one still at the window of a farmhouse that, strangely, no longer stood in the middle of fields or meadows but in an ocean current. For an inundation was no longer the word for it, what was out there on the other side of the window, the swells, was part of the sea. High tide of the North Sea with the moon in its apogee. Up in the attic of the farmhouse were now, in total, two animals and three humans. They were all absolutely still, as creatures are when they encounter something utterly unexpected that defies description. Simon Cau, a man transformed by the decision to go to a birthday party instead of checking, however quickly, on the Willems, Galge, and Westwaartse dikes, was sitting on a stool, or rather a little footstool. Because it was placed under the roof that sloped steeply down to the floor, he had had to tuck himself in, forearms on his knees, hands hanging down loosely. Gerarda Hocke was no longer making an effort to take care of him, let alone ask him to give her a hand in some fashion. In what was still the house in which she had been born and in which she intended to die, she tugged at the mattresses, held a match to the kerosene stove, adjusted the mantel, and turned off the flame again. Downstairs in the living room, tables and chairs were floating around and banging against the walls.

Lidy stood there and looked out. Very early on Sunday morning, February 1. Since waking some hours ago in a strange bed, she had never felt for a moment that she knew where she was, stuck between waking and dreaming, her memory being shuffled like playing cards between a stranger's hands. Suddenly one of life's most normal accompaniments, the weather, had pushed its way into the foreground in demented fashion. Was the water still rising? In her head, the wind was already blowing in longer gusts like a now familiar, deafening dream, but what about the water, which was flooding into and out of the house four or five feet below her? She thought she felt the floor sway gently under her feet. Out there, to the left along the road, was the barricade, wasn't it, where she had had to turn around in the Citroën tonight? Impossible to tell whether any remnants of it were still poking up out of the water; the cloud cover had closed itself again to a jagged edge tinged with violet and pink, and sky and water were almost indistinguishable from each other. Yet she remained where she was, and looked. A wind from hell! she thought vaguely, lethargically. But the cows were now quiet. Through a fog of anxiety and weariness, Lidy marveled at the general destruction, as if she were an onlooker not a participant, trying to figure out how it had come about that yesterday's trip to the seaside had got so out of hand.

Astonishing circumstances, or rather, fairly normal circumstances that had shed their skin tonight in a most astonishing fashion. These big northwesterly storms cropped up along this latitude in western Europe several times a year, after all, and spring tides were two a penny.

But tonight all this had been swept away. The visitor, snowed in here by chance, was not the only one who was bewildered. The entire delta of southwest Holland, which was always a puzzlement, was in the same predicament. Were they on one of the outlying sandbanks here that normally stayed above water off the coast of Brabant? Or were they in a real honest-to-god province, on solid ground, through which the Rhine, the Maas, and the Schelde empty themselves in an orderly fashion into the sea just as the Nile, the Seine, and the Thames do elsewhere on the planet, even when the arms of the sea reach greedily back at them along currents and channels? Not now— it would be days before the Netherlands could even believe it—but later, people would know the answer to the question of how it could possibly be that the Wester and Oosterschelde, the Grevelingen, and the Haringvliet, along with the inshore waters behind them, would flood over the islands like a plague from heaven, sweeping away 1,836 people, 120,000 animals, and 772 square miles of land at one stroke. Was this scientifically possible? Lidy stood looking until her eyes were out on stalks, her pale young face lifted above the collar of her thick coat. Scientists some years before had used a ruler to divide the North Sea that was now catapulting itself toward her into three precise sectors.

North sector, south sector, channel. Three figments of the imagination which affected Lidy tonight, like everyone else here, in the most personal way, whether she knew anything about them or not. Even the north sector, the absolutely straight line between Scandinavia and Scotland where the North Sea is still connected with the Atlantic Ocean and is also fairly deep, was something thought up by others, but frighteningly real, and that had a place in her life story. The wind had already created a modest mountain of water there hours before.

A shallow sea offers a larger spectacle: the south sector, the triangle drawn between the coasts of England, Denmark, and the Netherlands. Lidy sees a violet-tinged mountain range of water, the waves in it making peaks and valleys that cannot be underestimated, bearing down on her from all sides. Can anyone see such a thing and not be dumbfounded? And yet it is fundamentally normal, for even when there's the lightest wind, the surface of the water begins to ruffle, the gentle push that is the beginning of every wave. But tonight the *Goeree* and the *Noordhinder* have already reported wind speeds of sixty-three knots off the coast. So: waves, enormous waves, that the eye can measure only above sea level, like icebergs, but whose main force to a fantastic degree is exercised below the surface of the water. When they encounter a shallow seabed, they get shorter but do not lose a significant amount of energy. They pile up, higher and steeper, the longer the wind blows, at the southernmost point of the south sector, where the seabed rises quickly to meet the Dutch coastline, ending at a row of dunes and an antiquated system of coastal defenses, locks, barriers, and pumping stations. Halted finally in sector three, the channel, where after more than sixteen hours of storm there's a sort of traffic jam at the narrow bottleneck, the flood, the depth of its line of attack now stretching back more than a thousand miles, will burst unchecked into the sea arms of Zuid-Holland and Zeeland. From there it will force an exit to achieve what every liquid *must* achieve: its own level.

Something was coming. She pressed her forehead to the glass. To the right of the farm, something seemed to be approaching. A monster, with a light leading it. Was this Izak Hocke returning? The closer the 28-horsepower Ferguson and its trailer got, the more clearly Lidy thought she recognized him. Strange. Because the sky right now was so overcast that she could hear the water storming, but could barely see it. The slowly approaching vehicle with a man slumped down in the driver's seat looked more like a hallucination than something out of the land of the living.

Somewhere there was a full moon, or, more accurately, it was two days after the full moon, the time when the spring tide is at its highest. But by chance tonight the moon was exercising relatively little pull; astronomically speaking, it was ebb tide. Moon and sun, aligned on the same axis, were indeed both drawing the water table upward, but the moon had just reached its farthest point on its elliptical path around the earth, the apogee, in which the forces it exerts on the tides are particularly weak. It has no relevance for the movement of light, and so this aspect of the moon's disc during the night was fully present—cool, pale, and undiminished in its capacity from somewhere behind the cloud cover to cast its unshadowed spotlight, like the one in which Lidy now saw the tractor struggling through the water.

In the trailer behind it was a handful of people.

The wind hurled a piece of wrought iron like a curved sword into the room through the windowpane. Everyone flinched. There was a momentary but powerful wave of pressure, the shutter was wrenched out of the back wall of the house, the lamp flared up. Simon Cau had clearly become the kind of man who could just sit there motionless at a time like this, as if he were all alone, but Lidy and the old woman pressed themselves against the wall next to the window, to see what was going on out there. With your arms up shielding your face, wind gusts of more than seventy-five miles an hour feel like glass splinters in your hands and eyes. The old woman, who had cataracts, was relying on the observations of her visitor.

"Make sure you take a good look!" As if she didn't totally trust the reports of the girl she was already inclined to regard as a daughter or daughter-in-law. Such connections are quick to form in certain circumstances.

The girl kept looking. "It's him. Hocke."

They both flashed a glance for help at Simon Cau, but his back was turned, so they looked out of the window again. About a hundred yards away, the trailer, now almost entirely invisible underwater, was transporting a little group of people who could still be seen above the swells and who would have to find a place in the house here. Aside from Hocke she counted seven of them, survivors of a group of families who had lived a few miles from here in a hamlet on a protected island formed of silt where the ditch surrounding the polder divided into two arms—one contained a lock that had been rusted shut for years, and the second ran on until it met the main drainage system at Grevelingen.

Hocke gestured and yelled something that was unintelligible from the window. He had maneuvered the tractor into position right opposite the house and was now apparently trying to figure out how far he could still advance along the road that sloped downward under the water. Meanwhile the travelers he had brought waited, their faces set and cold. They looked as if they had appeared out of the void, resurrected perhaps, but without any idea of where they'd come from, or any expectation that they'd ever find out. Yet the massive current pouring from the north swept past them, carrying entire collections of their random household possessions, from clog boxes, doors, and roof gutters to smaller objects like beds, scales, tobacco jars, birdcages, shoes, a set of false teeth, a baking pan, an edition of *Donald Duck*. They looked out over it all, not so much blank as unburdened of everything their eyes had known before.

Eight little houses. The wall of water had come at them from one side at the exact moment when Hocke on the other side was trying to get down to them by driving alongside the drainage ditch. The families of two of his farmhands and several day laborers didn't know which they heard first, the breathless honking of the tractor horn or the bomb that split open their house walls and tore off the roofs. The energy of a hurricane when transferred into water is a mad force in any space that presents obstacles to that force. Shearing its way with razor sharpness along the collapsing dikes, turning, forcing its way to the side, and then streaming back, the flood wave was carrying a pressure of dozens of tons per square meter as it reached the first eight houses on the Naweg and landed on them like a wrecking ball. Most of the inhabitants made it just as far as the ladder in the stairwell. What followed was something that no human being was there to witness.

A fourteen-year-old boy and his father hack a way through the roof tiles with a chisel, pull themselves up hand-over-hand to the ridge beam, hang over it; the next minute a vertical tongue of water sweeps upward, the father drowns immediately, the boy thrashes around in the water, struggling desperately. Another house: a fifteen-year-old girl squeezes herself against the chimney, the roof is torn off, nothing around her but a force-12 wind and the floor heaving under her feet. Her forty-year-old mother, extremely pregnant, lands in a floating laundry cupboard as the house wall collapses outward; she's been having cramps all night but now they stop. The current will carry her by chance right past the tractor, she will manage to make it, at least to begin with, as does her eight-year-old son, whom Hocke fishes out of a hedge of whitethorn. As the girl falls backward, along with the chimney and everything else, she gives a deafening scream and clutches empty air. It's pitch black. The sea pushes on from the north with huge force, only to crash into the constricted waters of the Oosterschelde on the south side of the island. The inhabitants try to grab onto whatever they bump up against in the water. Not one of the flimsy houses held together with little more than whitewash withstands the enormous churning movement of the waters triggered by waves that are now breaking under their own weight. A man and two children in striped pajamas are standing on the rear part of a shed that is already sinking. As they land in the water, the man manages to pull them onto a rafter, which immediately shoots away like a torpedo.

Lord have mercy—but the man is astounded to find himself groping the road embankment a minute later and crawls up it under the lights of the tractor. It's snowing. A young married couple and child have been pulling themselves forward along the hedge that lines the road. The man, who's very strong, is holding his two-year-old daughter above water by her clothing, switching from his right hand to his left. He's also using his teeth. Hocke, who hears them calling through the darkness, comes to their aid and pulls them onto the wagon. The mother takes the child, who's been plunged right under the water twice, in her freezing arms. Extraordinarily, the rumble of the Ferguson engine can be heard even through the howling storm. Six or seven rats have popped up out of the water next to the trailer and are climbing onto the tailgate. There's still room on the trailer, but if they don't get away from there now, up the gently sloping road, there'll be no point in trying.

"We're going!"

He knew the lay of the land around here. Hocke took his bearings from the electric poles and the wind-bowed picket lines of willows and poplars planted after the deliberate inundation by the Germans in 1944. The absolutely critical thing for him was to stay on the road, which laid an underwater trail to his house if indeed it still existed. Working his way forward on an imaginary path, taking an imaginary curve, everything done by guesswork. It was after about ten minutes that Hocke, the one in charge, the only one with a thought in his head, stopped and peered over his shoulder.

At first there was nothing to see but waves crashing and crisscrossing one another in fountains of spray and general chaos. Then suddenly something was yelling and coming toward them, a dot that soon grew until it became a living thing clamped to a bale of hay. Hocke looked, as did the others.

It was a boy, a child, who as the hay bale raced alongside them in the current, slid into the water at the exact right moment, also contriving with considerable skill to dodge the driftwood that was hurtling past as well. Coughing and bleeding—one of the rats landed on him as people pulled him in over the tailgate—he joined the little group, who reached the farmhouse shortly thereafter. The boy's name was Cornelius Jaeger, he was twelve years old but would soon make an everlasting impression up in the Hockes' attic because of his deformity—he was a hunchback—and he came from Dreischor. Vague things, the kind one doesn't notice consciously, but that still led Lidy to the assumption that none of the others knew where this child came from or what his name was.

18

When the Wind Roars and the Shutters Bang

"Mister Cau!"

She couldn't recognize his face. She had no idea what was driving him. Madness? A despairing soul? It didn't interest her. She bent down as if approaching a trained animal and touched his arm. He seemed to understand, to decode it at once: a woman with her hair down loose and hanging over her shoulders in strands, a voice that still addressed him in a formal way but nonetheless was in command. She was holding a tangle of flax rope in her hands.

A moment later Lidy and the man were standing at the west window.

No thought of home, not one. Only the question: Will we manage it? The ease with which one self takes a step back, allowing another to take precedence. Not twenty-four hours before, she had been the wife of a future banker and mother of a future primary school pupil, high school pupil, student . . . now the only thing that interested her was the Stygian panorama of sea and sky—both in motion, south- ward, chasing desperately past the house. Izak Hocke's diesel tractor was drowning in them. How in God's name to get these little figures, ten, twenty yards away, into the house? They were wedging a large piece of driftwood against the side of the trailer. They had managed to make themselves heard over the howl of the wind, screaming that they needed a rope to save them. Following the farmer's wife's direc- tions, she had gone searching for one in the middle of a heap of the most unlikely things—never before had she seen a schoolbag made of wood.

Lidy. Cau. However the relationship between the two of them had been formed, it was stable enough for her to know what tasks belonged to each of them. She pulled the window inward till it was wide open and held it firm with both hands. He was short and no longer young, but he had the strength of two men; he paused for a few moments to assess the situation and then slung the rope, which he'd fastened at one end to a roof beam, out into the night. The old woman was also standing by.

Of course, no. Doesn't happen that way. The three of them at the window realized this as clearly as the people in the trailer with the water foaming as it climbed its sides; they had been freezing for so long already that they had forgotten their own terror. The rope sank. While they were hauling it back in again, Cau and Lidy saw a small, stocky figure stand up, arms wide.

It was the crippled boy. He leapt into the water and plowed his way thrashing toward the house. Lidy laid the last tiny remnant of her detached carelessness on ice. From now until the moment they could pull him up over the windowsill, all she could think of was, would the boy make it?

A troll! was the first thought that came to her mind as the boy stood before them, dripping wet.

They had pulled him out of the water, yet to her it seemed as if he had abruptly pushed his way into the house by himself, his entire character expressing itself in his arms and legs. Light and shadow played over his face, which was scratched and bleeding and reminded Lidy of something very familiar, whether out of her own life story or not. When one feels at home with something one encounters, a certain gentleness, then one loves that gentleness, and it becomes one's own. Life is no longer life without it. She was not thinking for a moment of her own child, this tiny signal from a faraway place. *Here and now* she wanted to dab carefully at this battered face with a cloth, the hair too, and press a kiss against it.

Without looking up, he pushed her hand away.

"Onto my belt, now," he instructed, teeth chattering, chin down to his chest.

A child's voice, she heard. He and Cau wrapped the rescue line around his waist and he insisted that they also tie it to his belt with a loop, for safety's sake.

"Are you sure? Can you really do it again?" asked Lidy, who was no longer trying to meet the boy's eyes, noticing only that his whole body was trembling.

He looked sideways for a moment. Irritated? Or was he merely half-blinded by the stinging water in his eyes? She took his hand and stroked it, waiting for him to pull back, but he didn't right away.

"We'll hold tight to you with the rope."

A smile, as if she had said something idiotic.

They paid out the line. For the first few yards she could still see him, then he seemed to vanish under the flotsam and jetsam, then, if she wasn't mistaken, she saw his head break the surface of the water again. Relief. Then nothing more. Nothing but the passing minutes that seemed to go very slowly. The present can push itself so far into the foreground that everything that has happened before, the entire story, becomes a hallucination that lacks all conviction.

19

Sunny Day I

Weddings often suddenly bring together two families who do not know each other, but when Sjoerd and Armanda got married, intimate bonds already existed between their relatives. Nonetheless something occurred that frequently happens at large family parties, particularly weddings: a deepening of mutual feelings and the real confidence that these will endure.

It was a sunny afternoon in May. Flecks of light danced off the blue damask tablecloth, a wedding present. The doors to the little balcony on the street were open. On the narrow side of the oval table Armanda was laying out photographs and sorting them, barefoot, wearing a dress of checked muslin that had belonged to Lidy. She had pulled the garment quickly out of a cupboard and slipped it on, because the sun on the windowpanes was making the house warmer and warmer; the photos were waiting on the table. That very particular starting-today-everything-is-different mood of the wedding guests soon fades for most people, but not everyone. Armanda lifted her head. The kettle on the stove in the kitchen at the end of the hall began to sing. She was expecting her mother. Armanda went into the kitchen, rinsed out the teapot with boiling water, poured the rest of the water onto the tea leaves, put the cups and some cookies on the tray, and encountered in all these little routines what was new in herself, the mysterious thing that most people around her had a word for, whether spoken innocently or ironically: *wife*. The doorbell rang.

"Wonderful!" said Nadine Brouwer a few minutes later. "Gorgeous, oh, and look at that one!" She laid her hand against her neck and glanced from the photos, each of which she picked up for a moment, to her daughter and back again. She looked fresh and rested in a bright red dress in a dotted material that set off her still-girlish figure. Her upswept hair, ash-brown, showed no hint of gray.

Armanda, sitting beside her mother at the table, took another look at her wedding photographs. Her mother's profile, with its fine lines, and her candid blue eyes, radiated a delight beyond words onto the photographs and also of course onto the day that they commemorated, May 3, 1955. Yes, thought Armanda initially, my wedding day, my wedding day, what a celebration, look, here we are at the town hall, here we are at the church, and she had the urge to relive it all with her mother.

A virgin as she left her parents' house to begin a marriage. In white, yes of course, anyone could have told her that, why not, in a beautiful white dress, therefore, but maybe better not to have a long one, and with a little white hat, no veil, and of course no traditional entrance on the arm of her father: five years before, Lidy and Sjoerd had walked into the Amstel church arm in arm, she in a lime-green suit with a loose jacket that came down over her stomach, to enjoy the organ playing and God's blessing simply because they were so festive. It had been a beautiful June day, Armanda remembered. Clear sunless weather without a breath of wind, the kind that never shows up in photographs.

"Look, Uncle Leo's in this one, nice."

"Yes, and here he is again with Betsy."

"If you ask me, the two of them really hit it off!"

Armanda felt her thoughts wander off, as often happened, even as she was talking. With some people you can have really interesting conversations, she'd noticed, but they stop your thoughts. Others, and her mother was one of them, leave your private self in peace and yet always manage to latch onto wherever your mind has landed up.

"Everyone was in a good mood, absolutely everyone," said her mother at a certain point.

Armanda had been quiet for a while.

"Yes," she murmured, stretching out her hand, and drank her now lukewarm tea at one go. The sun was now shining straight into the room. She stood up to partway close the curtain. "But Mother . . ."

Armanda saw her mother look up with an expression that can only be described as "knowing." Knowing that her daughter's high spirits had left her, and also knowing why.

". . . but something about the day was, was . . . dreadful!"

The answer came at once. Fully formed, as if she'd already heard this remark before and had thought it through.

"Child, please don't say that." Her mother frowned for a moment. Then she glanced at her watch. In a moment, at four o'clock, she would collect Nadja from play school, as they had arranged, and take her to number 77, and only bring her back at bedtime. "And please don't think it either."

"Can I tell you something?" Armanda looked at her mother defiantly, and let her wait for a moment. "All day long what I was secretly thinking was: This isn't my wedding!"

But her mother immediately shook her head. Oh no, don't talk like that, you're just imagining things!

And she was right. In reality, the entire day had run its course for Armanda in a kind of haze. The slight sense of strain to begin with, then the emotion, and then finally the happiness all around her had created a ringing in her ears like a confused blur of voices. Almost like an anesthetic. Now, by contrast, it broke up into clearly identifiable individual voices: this wonderful celebration is really a continuation of that other wonderful celebration, a little course correction between then and now. The bride is wearing a mask. By chance it's her own face.

"Don't spoil it for yourself in hindsight."

Like a hand being stroked over her hair. An exercise of maternal influence that Armanda was glad to heed. She reached out and began to push the photographs together, but there was one thought she couldn't suppress: Will I ever be able to remember who or what *I* was back then? One of the photos wouldn't align itself and slipped out of the stack. Her mother set her finger on it.

"Ah!"

Armanda looked too. Her mother's favorite brother.

"Uncle Bart," she said briskly. And then, "My God, Mother!"

The crumpled-looking man with the gray buzz cut and spectacles perched on the end of his small nose had made a long speech at the end of the wedding feast. Deep in his cups, breaking out repeatedly in tears, he had spoken to the guests about Lidy, whom they must never, never forget. Shortly before his voice broke, he had even managed to ask the company for a minute of silence.

"I spent the whole time staring at the napkin next to his plate," said Armanda. "I could still draw you every little fold in it."

Her mother nodded, as if to say, yes, maybe he shouldn't have done it, but Bart is a good man, through and through.

The minute of silence was not entirely silent, naturally enough. Nonetheless each of them, a little dazed, a little painfully, had thought of Lidy, whose name today had been entered for exactly the past three weeks in the official Register of Deaths at the local government offices. The date and place of death were made up.

Died in the environs of Zierikzee on Schouwen-Duiveland on February 1, 1953.

Finally. Finally there had been someone—the minister of justice, in fact—with the legal authority to pronounce the death of Lidy Blaauw-Brouwer, along with more than eight hundred other victims of drowning. According to the rules of the state courts it had been a fairly quick process, completed already in July 1954, to expand the law originally written to cover only those deemed missing from the Second World War to those missing in the storm flood. Three months after January 13, 1955, the day when, following an enormous amount of work in the files, the mass listing had been officially published in the *Nederlandse Staatscourant*, the survivors were allowed to make applications to the various town halls. On April 13, at two thirty in the afternoon, Sjoerd drove in the first car he had ever owned, a used Skoda, to the town hall on the Oudezijds Voorburgwal. He was shown to a small office and handed a copy of the certificate, a rather unusual document even for the official who had prepared it.

"Please would you check to see that everything's correct?" the man had asked.

"Yes, thank you," said Sjoerd, cleared his throat and began to read: "Article Two of the Law . . ." and then, after he'd read to the end, said, "Thank you" again.

The official looked at him with reddened eyes, as if he'd had a sleepless night.

"My deepest condolences, Mr. Blaauw."

That was a Wednesday. On Friday, Armanda and Sjoerd posted the notice of their intended marriage.

A painful moment! While the bridal couple had intended to slip away quietly at this point, here was this uncle insisting on making a speech! The wedding guests had made faces like a group of miscreants who are perfectly aware of what they're doing and aren't really sorry about it.

And one of them naturally pulled himself together sufficiently to say, "To the bride!"

Silence. Mother and daughter were each thinking their own thoughts. The sun meantime had moved on around until it was shining into the room through the curtain again. Now it was Armanda who checked the time. It was time to pick Nadja up from play school.

"Oh," said her mother, getting to her feet and looking for her purse. "Bart is a sweetheart. He meant well."

Armanda went downstairs ahead of her mother. The stairwell was dark except for a bright ceiling light that shone down onto the middle of the first step. At the very moment she was suddenly struck by the conviction that she and her mother had just been conducting a conversation that was totally mad on both their parts, Armanda saw two huge shadows swaying across the wall.

They said good-bye in the sun-flooded front doorway. Intending to finally tidy herself up and change her clothes, as Sjoerd would be home in an hour, Armanda was about to close the door behind her when she heard, "Wait! Wait! Armanda!"

Oh, please, she thought, no!

And, before she knew what was happening, she was back in the living room next to a panting Betsy, who had called out, "Only a moment, just to say hello," but had now discovered the photos on the table and was bent over them, stirring them to life again.

Armanda followed. Still barefoot, she followed the glance of her friend, who quickly pulled out a photo of the adorable Nadja. The child had been a bridesmaid.

"Do you remember?" asked Betsy, glancing sideways surreptitiously, with a curious expression.

Of course. Armanda nodded in a slightly sleepy way, but she remembered everything. She relived the whole incident, seeing it more precisely now than she had the first time around. After the ceremony in the church there had been no reception, better not to, but a formal banquet in an old house on the Geldersekade, a property that could be rented with its own staff for private parties. After the main course, when everyone was swapping places or running around a little, and she, Armanda, was sitting under a palm tree adjusting something on her dress, Nadja came up to her newly married mother. Somewhere in the background an accordionist and two violinists were playing.

"How pretty she looks." Betsy said.

Armanda cocked her head to one side and looked at the photo, slightly confused. Suddenly she felt the memory of herself with the little girl come flooding over her.

"Oh, my sweetie pie . . ." She stopped short.

Extremely elegant, as only a four-and-a-half-year-old bridesmaid can be, Nadja had walked all the way across the room, hopped and skipped a couple of times, never once blinking her large pale green eyes, till she jumped with outstretched little hands onto Armanda, smiling under her palm tree. A little game. Definitely. A little act of aggression, like a cat that forgets what it's doing for a moment because it's been blissfully stroked for too long. Suddenly a smack from the little hand landed unhappily on Armanda's outstretched cheek, and little fingers clutched at the pearls on one of her earrings, which got torn off. Inadvertent, really not intended. Can happen. But the little girl in her white dress, with the copper-red hair, knew nothing, absolutely nothing about the fact that before her mother there had been another mother, as nobody in the first chaotic days had wanted to talk to her about it and afterward it just hadn't happened; and the little girl stood there looking at the blood welling out of Armanda's ear, as if this stream of red was the very thing she had wanted to see on this memorable day. Armanda had risen to her feet. She had bent down, taken Nadja by the hand, and pulled her along.

And while several of the guests got onto their knees to search for the pearl, Armanda and Nadja spun round in a merry circle to one of the Viennese waltzes being played at top speed by the three musicians. Whenever her feet left the floor entirely, the little one crowed with laughter. At one moment Armanda felt a stab of a compulsion—which would only grow stronger between the time of the party and the session with the photos—both to hug her small dance partner and to join her in bursting into tears.

A little cough. Betsy was watching her discreetly out of the corner of her eye, as she could feel. Oh, Nadja, she thought. Oh, such a pitiable little creature, who first of all has no real mother, only a substitute, in a world in which you can expire in thunder and lightning like a heroine in a tragedy, but in which you can also be granted the freedom to live a totally banal life from one day to the next, with no greater mystery to struggle with than one you've inherited from someone else. Oh, poor little half-orphan!

"You know," she said to Betsy, "maybe you'll think I'm crazy for saying this, and even crazier for saying it to you of all people, so please don't take it badly, but in some way I feel like a half-orphan."

They stared at each other for a moment, each of them unfathomable, and Armanda said quickly, "I mean, a half-orphan as regards my own life. Everyone has a past and a future, which sounds really banal, you'll say, but I don't care, that's how it is."

Betsy, up for more, kept quiet.

"Yes, really, everyone has a past, a run-up to the present, and that's your youth, at least for normal mortals, in which you were already fully the creature that you are now, it wouldn't be possible any other way, would it, but mostly it first took the form of a promise. I know, nice story, my run-up to today isn't to be found in my past, it's . . . *tsch* . . . it's in my dead sister. So let's . . ." She turned around, reached for the tea things, and stared crossly at the photos of the most beautiful day of her life. "Just call my past what it really is: a step-past."

Betsy, who had promised only to stay a minute and didn't want to offer the slightest excuse for more tea to be brewed, started making hasty, spur-of-the-moment remarks about starting a new life, which were meant to cheer her up. She, Armanda, she said, was herself, Armanda, and absolutely nothing could prevent her from choosing her own path through life and making it a great success. Finish your studies first, you hear me? Get your hair cut. Paint the doors and stairs in your house blue or green. Buy yourself a ficus tree. . . .

But Armanda kept shaking her head thoughtfully as Betsy, all excited, came to the end of her long list with: "Love your husband!" And gave a merry look as she brought up the night at the school play; she and Lidy had got the giggles when the leading actor, who was seriously drunk, said, "*If* you're on the planet, it's a fact that you've got a no-account job in nowheresville."

"Well, Betsy, don't misunderstand me, but how does this sound? '*If* I'm on the planet, it's a fact that strictly speaking I'm my elder sister.' "

Armanda chose a cookie, a café noir, Betsy did the same, and for a moment the two of them stood there nibbling, first with a grin, then expressionlessly, but quite peacefully; for their conjoint nibbling was actually an echo of Lidy and Armanda as sisters, since everyone always said they were exactly alike.

"Absolutely not," Armanda suddenly said unexpectedly. "We distinguished between the two of us the way only sisters can. We knew it. If you live that close together, if you grow up minute by minute in a world that's almost yours, but by a hair's breadth not quite, then you register the tiniest things about each other that are different."

Her face was animated now. Had she not at that moment heard the front door opening and closing downstairs, she would have been able to chatter with her beloved visitor. For however odd, even mad, her conversation with her mother had seemed a short while ago, she had felt that she was being completely rational in the other conversation that had just followed it. "Fundamentally different!" she had said again. "Brothers always want to be the opposite of brothers, and sisters of sisters. Oppositeness is at the root of the brother or sister relationship. I'm pretty certain that's the case. So now that my past has been exchanged for hers, while her future has passed to me, there's this veil of bottomless sadness, though naturally I try to ignore it."

That is roughly the kind of thing she might have said, slightly breathlessly but in a heartfelt way, if she hadn't heard someone coming up the stairs.

She blushed.

20

Sunny Day II

Sjoerd and Armanda Blaauw-Brouwer. Married couple.

They too took a brief look at the photographs together, why is not clear, for the two of them were focused on something else entirely; Sjoerd had just thrown the jacket of his beautiful light gray suit onto a chair. He was now in his late twenties, a tall, slender man with carefully combed blond hair and a face that was beginning to show the open, straightforward, intelligent qualities that are valued in the world of money and business. With an arm around Armanda's hips, he bent loyally over the photos. It's well known that when a newly married couple first sees their wedding portrait, the bride looks only at the bride and the bridegroom does the same. One could switch bridegrooms in the darkroom for fun, but never brides.

"Beautiful," murmured Sjoerd, without the faintest astonishment over the snow-white dress lifting away from the neck and the little hat, perched at an angle to set off the beloved little face, and the bouquet held up under the chin, that he must know from a previous photo, already glued into the album, in the same always-flattering three-quarter pose. His eyes were already elsewhere. He turned around purposefully and felt Armanda's whole body respond immediately, as he had expected, with a yes! yes! During this afternoon's meeting with the administrative department of the Capital Investment Committee of Mees & Hope, he had felt as miserable as a dog, almost ill with sheer repressed impatience to get home. It was his first

week back at work after his ten-day honeymoon, the first three days
of which had been extremely peculiar, because after so much hesitation, he and Armanda had felt no desire for each other at all.

Neither of them had been able to understand it.

The wedding banquet in the Geldersekade was still going on when
they escaped at around five thirty. After they had changed clothes at
number 36 and number 77 respectively, they put their luggage in the
trunk of the Skoda and began their honeymoon journey to Nor-
mandy. First stopping point was a village near Rotterdam, a surprise
for Armanda, just like the beautiful hotel there where Sjoerd had
made reservations. They arrived at around eight. Along the way they
had still been talking about the party at first, then, when the car left
the main road, Armanda, showing her surprise, had gamely read out
the place-names of the little towns they passed through, Alblasser-
dam, Ridderkerk, while the bright blue sky turned slowly to a deeper
blue. She awoke on her husband's shoulder in front of the hotel, it
was still light, but there was a thin layer of mist over the flagstones
and the surrounding area. They dealt with the formalities at reception, took the elevator, walked down a long, brilliantly lit corridor,
and came to their room, outside which the porter was just lifting their
suitcases off a gold-colored luggage cart.

It was idiotic, but the moment the door closed, neither of them
knew how to deal with the sudden proximity of the other. Okay, go
and stand close. Armanda was happy that he immediately threw his
arms around her; she cuddled up to him, kissed him somewhere on
the face, now I must be happy, she probably thought, and probably
that's what he thought too. Free at last! At last we can do and not do
whatever we want! Meantime they avoided looking directly at each
other, Armanda even kept her eyes closed and found herself thinking,
whether she wanted to or not, about her suitcase with its tightly
packed, freshly ironed clothes, some of which she ought to hang up
right away. Sjoerd, over her shoulder, looked out of the window.

He left her standing there.

"Take a look, see what it's like outside."

Of course she followed him. "Beautiful," she said as she slipped off
her shoes and felt how small she was next to him on the soft carpet.
They leaned side by side on the window bench. Dusk was falling, the

sky turned yellow, and they were looking at a rolling countryside, meadows, trees, with a broad stream of water running through it, flat and pale in the mist, and on the other bank a row of eight or nine windmills. What was there to say about it? It was nature, the windmills included, as they stood there in a pensive row, their vanes motionless despite the weak to middling northwest wind, fixed, the sails rolled up. A few minutes later, when they were lying in each other's arms in bed, cheek to cheek, Sjoerd still saw the windmills in his mind's eye, and Armanda was realizing that there were two, three dresses and a blouse that she really had to hang up right away.

"Just a moment," she said and rolled away from him.

Without paying any further attention to him, as if she were alone in the room, Armanda opened her suitcase and began carefully to unfold several pieces of clothing at the shoulders, to inspect them and then hang them up. Sjoerd listened to the hangers being pushed this way and that, heard bathwater running a little later, and dozed off in a scent of soap and perfume. The next thing that happened was a naked Armanda tiptoeing to the bed, and then an Armanda in a nightshirt tiptoeing to the bed again. To take a good, long look.

All he had taken off was his shirt, which she picked up off the floor. Then she began to fumble with his shoelaces. It is perfectly possible to undress a sleeping man without his noticing, but as soon as you pull down his pants, he will wake up for a moment unless he's dead drunk. Sjoerd, without a moment's thought, crawled under the covers and sank back happily into a deep sleep. Armanda went round the room switching off the lamps, then slipped into bed on her side. She dropped off to sleep too, a heavy, abandoned sleep, though with interruptions. The first time she awoke, she lay there, surrounded by a glowing warmth, in the pitch darkness, and began to actually pant when she realized that Sjoerd was starting to caress her the way he had once a long time before, in the bedroom at number 36, when an oh-so-unemphatic ring at the doorbell had interrupted them. To heighten her desire, she thought back to it in detail, to this postponement, intending, with superstitious naïveté, to have everything from back then happen all over again, this time with a happy ending. When she opened her eyes for the second time, she knew immediately that she was alone in bed. There was tobacco smoke in the room, and it was still dark, but not completely. As she allowed her mind to dawdle peacefully over the fact that what was supposed to happen had happened, she heard the wind, strong now and blowing from the west, whistle against the wall of the building, and she turned her head away.

He was standing at the window with his back to her. Ground mist, mist on the water, and a row of water mills, their lower parts invisible, their vanes with the white starched sails spinning madly, joyously, in circles. What effect does such an image have on a young woman who has just woken up? If she saw the tip of his cigarette glow from time to time and then disappear again, she was lucky.

For three days they felt almost no desire for each other, and Armanda found herself ugly. Then she noticed that whether the moment was suitable or not, her eyes would linger whenever she looked at him.

"Come with me," he said on the fourth day, when for a moment she found herself unable to utter another word. They were already in a hotel in the Strandboulevard in Houlgate and had made love on all three nights.

She came to his side, he took her hand, and they climbed the path through the dunes and up to their room.

How is that possible, she wondered some time later.

The bedroom revealed a certain customary disorder in the middle of the afternoon, and through the window you could hear the sea. She liked hearing her husband snoring on her shoulder with an innocent face. How is it possible? she thought, by which she meant: Three days, it's only three days, two days before yesterday, the day before yesterday, then yesterday, I've never heard or read anywhere that as time elapses, it exposes each of us to its manipulations and its unmistakable side effects, though we have no idea where these come from and how they work. The way we kissed first! Then took off our clothes so uninhibitedly, so fast, so urgently!

On the floor a man's shirt, a top-quality pair of light gray trousers, men's shoes—no, no women's shoes—and a pair of panties, obviously toe-kicked right over into the corner behind the vanity, where they would have to be searched for later; the long shadow of a tree outside in the inner courtyard; inside, another piece of clothing, a worn checked dress that carried some vague memory, but one that wasn't damaging to anybody. In bed the pair of lovers who belonged to these belongings.

Armanda: for the first time in her life as a married woman, experiencing the long pang of what is also known as *la petite mort.*

21

By Chance, a Low High Tide

Years later, when Lidy had been long dead, the experts were united about one thing: it could have been worse. Had the moon, for example, been close to the earth, as it had been two weeks earlier on January 18, then the astronomical high tide could have used its pull to rise almost another two feet. An absolutely exceptional spring tide would then have been a possibility.

The possibility that did occur during this night was the following. A farm, between Zierikzee and Dreischor. The sea, that had risen to within three feet of the attic floor. Moonlight, ear-deadening noise, a wind now blowing in short blasts, that seemed to temper the movement of the waves in the deeper water over the fields even as it reinforced the speed of the current coming over the road. The great mass of the water pounded against the sides and back of the trailer, which miraculously had not yet cracked to pieces. Inside the house, Cau, Lidy, and Gerarda Hocke were asking themselves if it might be possible for these people to ferry themselves across using a door to one of the stalls that was floating around as a makeshift raft.

And indeed, something seemed to be separating itself from the wagon. Ignoring the rumbling of the furniture down below them, they watched the little load approach. It was managing to keep on course with the help of the rope slung around a roof beam at this end and attached to something else at the other. It didn't take that long. Dragged in over the windowsill dripping wet, three of the four passengers stood there for a long minute, gasping for air. Lidy noticed that they brought with them a heavy stench of putrefaction. And somewhat later, as she and Gerarda Hocke stripped off their sodden clothes, wiped away the greasy mud as best they could, and offered them bedding and safety on the ice-cold floor, she had a sudden image of them as a gaggle of newborn babies. The trio consisted of a tall man with a thick shock of hair, an extremely pregnant woman, not his wife, as was later established, and a little boy of about eight, her son. Number four had stayed behind on the raft.

As Lidy ran to the window to see how he was getting on, he was already halfway across on the return journey. She watched as the boy, down on his knees, kept moving his hands along the rope and pulling.

Water usually follows wind by a matter of two or three hours. Later, oceanographers would calculate that the whipping up of the waters could have been significantly worse. For the hurricane, which achieved maximum strength on the coast of Scotland, had weakened a little to the south over the North Sea, as the flood was reaching its height on the coasts of the provinces of Zeeland and Holland. Wind speeds can moderate over land due to friction, but over water they do what these winds did. It would have been possible, people reckoned later, for the pronounced trough of low pressure that moved that night from Scotland over the German Bight and on southeast to deviate a little from its course. Had it done so, the Scottish wind speeds and the Dutch northwest storm would have combined with truly fatal results.

The hunchbacked boy had succeeded in making fast to the wagon again. At that moment two seas broke over it, one of them carrying a piece of debris on its crest. It cut deep into Izak Hocke's forehead, the trailer tipped over, but stayed hitched. Shortly before the tractor sank, the last five drowning people made it onto the raft; the rope that had been hanging slack was pulled tight by those in the house. It worked, but everyone was at the end of their strength now; the door was too small for five people and too big to be maneuvered with such a load on it.

Hocke crawled quickly to the other side, and Cornelius Jaeger let himself drop into the water, water that tonight was seventeen feet above Normal Amsterdam Water Level, but that according to experts later on could easily have risen by another seven feet if a third factor had not helpfully intervened. The water level in this area is determined not only by the sea that comes thundering eastward against the coast but also by the rivers that flow continuously west. December and January that year had been unusually dry in the Alps and in the Vosges. If the precipitation in the upper reaches of the Rhine, the Maas, and the Schelde had been typical for the time of year, then, adding to the already devastating situation, there would have been a catastrophe in the estuaries of literally fantastic proportions.

A man had half climbed, half fallen through the window. He immediately got to his feet and turned around, waving his arms, to yell something to his wife, who was still out in the full grip of the wind. She hadn't dared to give him her little daughter, who had turned two in November and was huddled under her sodden coat. Beside him, Simon Cau and the man, who had already managed to climb into the attic, were also holding out their arms. A true reception committee to whom she could have handed the little thing.

No. A hopeless situation that seemed to go on for an eternity.

In reality ten, twelve seconds at most elapsed until the young woman on the door that was now banging against the gable lifted her head and saw another young woman leaning far out of the window. The two looked at each other, sharing the knowledge for one despairing second that if she couldn't keep holding tight to her tiny freezing burden out there in the cold . . .

"Give her here!" screamed Lidy.

The other woman obeyed.

"Have you got her?"

"Yes."

They were all inside. The family complete. Izak Hocke and the hunchbacked boy, who was still trembling all over his body, were already busy with wire, wood, and fiberboard, making a makeshift replacement for the shutter in the back gable end. The newly arrived woman put up no resistance. A woolen jacket was held out to her and she pushed her arms into it willingly. Her eyes fixed on the shadows moving on the sheathing under the steep roof in front of her, she waited to see what was expected of her. Lidy meantime seized a chair that was standing in a corner and lifted the apathetic little girl into her lap. *Eia popeia*, nice and quiet now, rocking comes naturally. Between a natural catastrophe involving 1,836 dead and the fate of this one child, Dina van de Velde, lay countless newspaper articles, newsreels, Red Cross lists, and a five-volume report by the Delta Commission years later.

22

There's Always Weather

When the child was finally picked up, the weather had changed and there was a cold drizzle. One of the fruit sellers from the Albert Cuyp market had seen her walking along the side of the river and over the Amstel dike, leading toward the Berlage bridge. It was around five, and almost dark already. He was on his delivery bike and had turned at the church and was headed for Van Ostadestraat, where he lived, when he saw her trudging along the opposite side past the soaring bulk of the *Generaal Praag*, a decommissioned coal ship that had been moored here for years. "She said she was on the way to Rotterdam," the fruit seller reported to Armanda and Nadine sometime later; they were in no condition at that moment to wonder about it.

He had braked. Nadja was wearing a little white teddy-bear coat. The fruit seller, who would have bet his life that something wasn't right, pushed his cap back on his head and crossed the street. Where are you off to? Nadja had had no objection to climbing up and sitting in there with the Jonathan apples to ride along with him for a bit with the rain and the wind in her face. Right around the corner was a street of dark tall houses with little shops at ground level, but mainly she was interested in the man who bent way down to the left or right each time he pushed on the pedals. In the little tin shed where the delivery bicycle was kept in its place between crates and sacks, Nadja confided in the fruit seller where she lived. "Number Thirty-six *and* Number Seventy-seven?" Calm nods from her. About ten minutes later,

Nadine Brouwer, anxiously keeping watch outside her front door, saw her granddaughter arrive perched on the bicycle carrier of an unknown individual. The picture this made seemed quite unreal to her, the more so perhaps because of the yellow lamplight shining down on the two of them and the wintry vegetation in the park.

Now something occurred that could best be described as a little competition between Nadja and her mother.

For Armanda too had seen her daughter sitting on the carrier. From the moment Nadja had refused to come out from behind her tree or whatever it was, she had been running around the park, calling and searching in between the bushes, and had gone out onto the Ceintuurbaan to ask everyone she met if they'd seen her. Now she was standing distraught by the drinking fountain at the north entrance to the park, diagonally opposite her parents' house. Her cry sounded like a ghost crying in a dream even to her own ears, totally muffled, but the man on the bicycle heard it and set his foot on the ground. At this moment Betsy came waddling out of Tweede Jan Steenstraat, very fat, fatter than is normal in the seventh month of pregnancy, and saw Nadja running fast, and managing to evade Armanda as she leapt into her granny's arms on the front steps of number 77.

"You're really wrong," said Betsy that evening to her husband. "It was dry all afternoon."

Leo had told her he was astonished that Nadja and her playmates had been allowed out into the park in this weather. He jerked his head toward the rain and the third-floor window at the beginning of the almost pitch-dark Prinsengracht, bare elms, black ruffled water.

"Which wasn't in the forecast," Betsy continued, as she followed his glance from her position slumped on the sofa with her swollen feet up on a cushion. "It was supposed to be unsettled. Rain showers, cold air coming in from the east, possibility of snow. But the children were determined that it was dry and way above freezing."

So they had wanted to go outdoors, right after the cake with its six little candles in a layer of frosting. But mother and aunt, who was acting as her assistant, proposed hide-and-seek. It must have been shortly before three when Armanda, standing under the bust of Samuel Sarphati with her hands over her face, began to count, eeny, meeny, miny, mo, while Betsy, also gamely keeping her eyes shut, and wrapped in a warm coat on a park bench, listened and checked that the children had disappeared before the rhyme, a warning now, came to an end.

"I'm coming!"

It's strange that they didn't find each other quite quickly. To start with, Nadja was just crouching in a rhododendron bush behind the first gravel path. Soft earth under her feet, she looked down at it absentmindedly, completely focused on not being seen, and didn't allow herself to notice until some time later that everyone was calling for her, which wasn't part of the game.

The first thing that not being seen involves, as everyone knows, is not looking, either. Nadja moved backward, her head down against her chest, tripped over a small twig, rolled down a sand hill for several yards, and at some point found a new hiding place in a shallow hollow. Next to it was an old oak tree. That's where the decision was finally made that had been coming for some time, and the argument that clinched it began with *B* as in beetle or *F* as in fly or *M* as in moth. She didn't bother to work out which forms of life were now twinkling like a giant handful of precious stones at her feet and moving in some mysterious way. The winter had been mild up till now. Last night De Bilt had recorded the warmest temperature of the century: fifty-two degrees. In any case, it had been raining for days. The enormous insect nest and the bit of the hollow tree it had been in could have fallen down only in the last few months, for the overwintering beetles, flies, bees, and moths had just decided they needed to move on, crawling cautiously at first, then hopping wildly or flying. Oh, marvelous! Astonished, Nadja followed the rainbow-colored creatures, blue, green, some of them even fire red, which were suddenly disappearing as if by magic. Some of them flew up on their transparent tiny wings and hovered in the air so close to her nose that she could see their glittering eyes, and then suddenly—gone. Others crawled around with mysterious single-mindedness, not panicked, quite comfortably, showing her their powerful back legs, their faces elongated into little snouts, their hard, smooth bodies, some of them with stingers, and then suddenly . . . oh, where did they go? Darkness had already fallen when Nadja, at peace with her decision, went up the Van Woustraat and then down again, and then turned right at the corner where the green neon light was, toward the Amstel dike.

"I just don't understand," said Sjoerd that evening after the visitors had gone. Grandpa Brouwer and Uncle Jacob had given the birthday girl a last surprise with a set of tiddlywinks and a Little Black Sambo doll before she went to bed, and Grandma Brouwer, who had already been there during the day, had come back with them for a short moment, to drink a toast to the little monkey. "Absolutely not!" Leaning back from the dining room table balanced on the two back legs of his chair, he looked at Armanda pacing up and down the room with a glass of rosé in her hand. When the child had been missing for more than an hour and a half, she had called him in the office. Pale, his hair standing up every which way, he was in the car turning in to their street when he too saw Nadja jump off the bike, flinch away from her mother, and run. And then leap into the arms of Grandma Nadine, who had squatted down to catch her.

Nadja must have seen herself surrounded by a ring of wet, distraught faces. And from all sides, a slew of questions, which she answered with a smile. It had turned very cold. Everything pointed to a lot more rain or even snow.

IV

Family Novel

23

The Birth

The birth took ruthless precedence. It took precedence first over the darkness; the pains had started, quietly to begin with, in the early hours of the morning, but now they were serious and could no longer be concealed, and dawn was breaking. When the enormously pregnant woman had arrived in the attic, where the strangest atmosphere reigned—a combination of imminent rescue and the awareness that death was just around the corner—she had been helped by many hands to lie down on a mattress laid on a bed frame. They had covered her with a horse blanket. A woman, whose accent defined her as being a stranger to this area, had spread a heavy coat over the bed by way of addition, then laid herself down beside her, shoes and all: "Come close, it'll warm you up!" The woman had obeyed. While the other one dropped off to sleep almost instantly, she—her name was Cathrien Padmos, born Clement—had felt the cold retreat and transform itself into a sensation that she was descending a stone staircase, step by step, into a comfortably warm cave. Then everything started again. Uncontrollable now, in its own rhythm that made no allowances for the weather.

It was coming up on 9 a.m. The attic stank of mud, wet clothes, animal dung, probably rat droppings too, and the bucket behind the door to the staircase. The temperature couldn't have been much above freezing. The west window, one side of which was nailed shut with boards, admitted a first light of a leaden greenish tinge perfectly in keeping with the general aura of death and destruction. Everyone here, whether asleep or awake, dazed or fully conscious, felt the swaying of the house walls and knew that the undiminished power of the storm was close to tearing off the roof. In the bed, which had been pushed deep under the eaves to protect from drafts, forty-year-old Cathrien Padmos began to breathe heavily for the third time in her married life, or to put it more precisely, the cervix was in its last stages of dilation. To her left, a powerfully built man, Albert Zesgever, who had crawled in with the rest of them, seemed not to notice anything yet.

On the other hand, her bedmate on the right grasped the situation. Lidy raised her head. Where am I, she thought for a moment, then she saw, next to her, a sweat-drenched face that almost instantly took on the dull look that she remembered in herself, whether she had registered it or not at the time, with no choice or will of her own. "How often are they coming?" she asked, as she saw the face soften.

"One behind the other. There's no pause now," the other one said, before she threw herself onto her side.

"Oh, then you're already quite far along!"

Humoring her with false cheer.

This one and that one were now awakening in the attic, and the most unbelievable proof of it was that the air began to smell gloriously of coffee. In a corner, on a sort of improvised dresser made of some cabin trunks with flat lids, the old lady had set up a single-burner camping stove and on it a percolator, a kind of pot with a spout, and a little glass dome that lets you see the coffee bubbling up inside. As she watched her son drive off in the storm the previous night, a tiny mound of humanity perched on enormous tires, Gerarda Hocke had made good use of her fear by carrying every possible thing upstairs. An intelligent old woman, certainly, who remembered one thing above all about a birth, which was that there had to be boiling water. She took the coffee off the flame and poured half of a four-quart milk can of tap water into an enamel pail. Everyday, ordinary actions that tamped down the extremes of the morning. In the daylight this randomly assembled collection of people, who had been as unprepared for the high spring flood as they would have been for war or plague, began to form themselves into a group. Utterly disoriented, they got up off the mattresses or off the floor. For the first time they could now see where they were and who were their companions. The dog, large and brown, his head on his paws and staring straight ahead of him, was giving a not unpleasant imitation of being at peace. Some of them were aware that the goose hadn't left the heels of the farmer's wife from the first moment on, others now noticed her, white, with brilliant orange feet, as she stood for a moment then hunkered down again. The first to take up his post by the window again was Cornelius Jaeger. Soon the rest of the grown men were standing there with him. Fundamentally it was the imminent birth that was imposing a certain order on this household.

And obviously it took priority over death and despair. Although Cathrien Padmos must know that her husband and her five-year-old daughter had already drowned, she wasn't thinking of them. She could feel none of the terrible grief that must be there inside her, only a very particular pain that unlike all others is not the harbinger of death. Only now, as it announced itself again, did she remember it from eight years ago.

She had married early, a boy from the next village, when she was only sixteen. An intimation of this had come to her on July 3, 1930. As she was cycling that evening to Dreischor in the low last light of the glowing red sunset, she had suddenly had the unsettling thought that tonight, at the weekly choir practice of Soli Deo Gloria, she might meet her future husband. And indeed, as became apparent, there was a new voice among the baritones. Age: twenty. Profession: ordinary worker on the farm of Anthonie Hocke, Izak's father. His name: Johan Padmos. Cathrien Clement was strongly built and dark blond (her hair the same color as the coats of the farm dogs around her)—a girl of the kind who knows what she wants—to get married and then get pregnant as soon as possible. When that didn't happen, not after the first month of marriage, not after the first year and not after the second, third, or fourth, it became clear to her that she was facing the most important decision of her life. Unhappiness or happiness. The farm girl, who worked as a day laborer, determined to make happiness her calling in the most emphatic way, and was supported in it by her husband, even-tempered by nature, who identified totally with his work and his status on a famous farm where he soon succeeded in becoming one of the six permanent farmworkers. In August, when she rode into the farmyard at vespers on her bike, she saw her husband's work team laboring under the black cloud of smoke of the colossal five-foot reaping-and-binding machine. They were stacking the sheaves in the German manner, crosswise by fours, and then putting three on top with the ears of the wheat pointing downward. Not a communicative man, her husband, but in the evenings, if the wind was blowing with unexpected force, he would say, "Not the faintest chance," and she would know what he meant, and would have an image of the same landscape as he did. Black sky, a path with extensive meadows to either side, and farther down, the stubbled fields covered with the sheaves of wheat stacked in this fashion, laughing off the attacks of the strong-to-stormy northwest wind. To their mutual astonishment, after eight years with her husband, who had now risen to become foreman, she found herself pregnant. Seven years after that, pregnant again.

No, nobody was thinking of that anymore. But they were thinking about the boy sitting half-concealed behind one of the roof beams. Someone had put a pair of thick socks on his feet, and Hocke had squatted down once beside him to say something nice that ended with "lady apple," did he want one from the basket where they were stored here in winter, but he shook his head and went to use the bucket for the second time. Adriaan Padmos had just turned eight. Such a child is sometimes quick to recognize what is familiar in strange things, and squats there with an unreadable expression, all hunched up, his knees under his chin, and looks at his socks.

Nobody, on the other hand, was paying attention to the van de Velde girl anymore. She was dead, and they had laid the little body in the space between two cupboards stuffed full of old clothes which were now coming in incredibly handy. Work gear made of napped cotton flannel underneath, summer skirt with flowers on it over the top. Better this way, yes? Last night the girl had been brought this far by the superhuman efforts of her parents, and bringing her any farther was beyond human capacity. For the moment there was nothing more to be done. The father, Nico van de Velde, stood with the others at the dirty window, outside which dirty things were happening. He and Zesgever were smoking, sharing one of the available cigarettes, which were being strictly rationed. The mother was attending the birth.

Lethargically, but like a night insect drawn to the light behind a kitchen windowpane, Laurina van de Velde had come closer, and was now looking apologetically, perhaps because she was trembling and making no attempt to stop it, at the mounded thing on the wide bed. She knew, had she been capable of thought, that she'd been through something similar, but the event, the actual image of it, where was it? For a moment she caught Lidy's eye, as Lidy stretched her back against the headboard. Did Lidy want to say something? She had had her child, who would be her only one, at the age of twenty-one.

It had been in fall, a beautiful sunny fall day. They had sent word to Nico in the field at Hocke's when things were that far along. He had left the Smythe, a chunky English mechanical sower with an unworkable operating width of six feet, standing. You boys keep going with the winter wheat. What you sow, you reap at the appointed time, I'm off. Nico was an agile, well-set man who was often able to rouse his wife, who was inclined to melancholy, with his abruptness. "Be a little more cheerful, kiddo," he'd say when he got home, saw her looking absentminded, and took her face with the sky-blue eyes he'd fallen in love with in his hands, or again: "Stop thinking so much! Both feet on the floor, that's it!"

"Where? Here? On this floor?" she once replied, more bewitched by him than convinced, and set her feet in their soft socks on top of his. She was a woman in a permanent state of disquiet, that was her normal mood. Uneasy because of the machines that her husband worked with, uneasy because of the horses that could kick out backward, uneasy because of the heavy backbreaking labor of pulling out the flax roots in mid-July, handwork he excelled at. In the last month he had joined the Reds and started talking about "comrades," balling his fists or holding up a finger, which bothered her even more. What would happen when the farmer, Hocke, heard about this, and what would become of Dina and her other future children if their father was put out on the street?

So now she looked at the imminent birth and felt nothing, not even the slightest disquiet. She glanced at Cathrien Padmos's face, which she had known since she was a child, saw how she was sweating, tried to hold her hand, accepted that she was pushed away by the other woman, perhaps because the latter needed to retch, and meantime was so desperately cold that she couldn't make her mind function in any normal way at all. When Lidy asked, "Shouldn't we find something we can wrap the baby in, the little child, in a minute?" she nodded.

"Good."

She and Lidy went to one of the two cupboards.

"This?" asked Lidy, holding something woolly.

"Or this?" Laurina hesitated.

A few minutes later, the women gathered around the mother-to-be and Izak Hocke, who for some reason had been summoned to join them, were able to reassure her that they could already see the crown of the little head. It was eleven in the morning. Outside the window of the delivery room was a world that nobody could now imagine being anything other than it was. Murderous, a single surge of gray and brown. That the storm had still not begun to abate after more than twenty-four hours was, meteorologically speaking, to be considered a freak occurrence.

Cathrien Padmos was the type of woman who gives birth to children on her own. She had accepted having a piece of bedding rolled up and pushed against her back, but she wanted none of the hands, the looks, the help that were intended to be of assistance to her but actually worked as its express opposite. She was at the height of her battle with the pain, that invisible enemy, also an angel who numbs and transports one to a faraway place where one can cease thinking about one's loved ones who are dead, or noticing and realizing it to be significant that the bed one is lying on is standing on a worryingly unstable, swaying attic floor. She raised her head and began to scream uninhibitedly.

The sound of a storm defies words. Or rather, the effect it has. The world makes noises. There isn't a moment of peace in which it isn't creaking or rustling or banging or talking and uttering every possible nuance of lament until sometimes it even sings. Some of these noises can wait a little, but others are absolutely urgent.

Up in the attic, everyone had gradually become oblivious to the wind. The incessant hammering on their instincts, the incessant demands on their imaginative powers to foresee what could happen if they didn't figure out a way to get out of here, had dulled their minds.

Hocke, van de Velde, Zesgever, and Cornelius Jaeger stood at the window from which, if you laid your head against the glass and turned it all the way to the right, you could see Cau's farm. Cau himself wasn't standing with them. He was down on his heels by the now abandoned camping stove, seeing if maybe there was still a splash of coffee remaining in the pot. The wind had been rattling against the roof like artillery fire for some time now. Sometimes it was there, and you knew it, even relied on it to be there, then it would suddenly stop, and there would be a pause. Even Cau must then have heard the other noise from outside, and felt it go through his very bone marrow.

His house no longer had a façade. Hocke and Zesgever, quite detached, concerned only insofar as they had to wonder if their own home was going to hold, let their eyes wander over the exposed interior of the Gabriëllina's attic as it still stood above the water. Oh, the stuff, the worn-out inner spring mattress, the cast-iron stove. The cupboard with long out-of-date and unusable cans, jars, preserving jars, horsehair sieves: it was all there in total conformity with the situation, as if the objects had just fled from downstairs to upstairs like the people. But not a trace of Simon Cau's nephew, Marien. No sign of life in the attic across the way.

But that was made up for by the human cargo on rafts that were being swept past them, and other flotsam and jetsam. Under a bad spell, bemused, the little group of men stood at the window and heard the screams of terror and cries for help, and the curses.

"Bastards! Help us or drown!"

A chunk of a roof went whirling past.

"Vipers! You're godforsaken!"

Most of its roof tiles were missing. It came, with at least eight people, perhaps an entire family, aboard, from the direction of Gabriëllina Farm and swept southward past the top floor where Hocke and his evacuees were sheltering. There wasn't even any point in wrenching open the window and trying something with a rope. The family, about to be submerged, was seized almost at that very moment by the current that was pouring past the house and away at an angle toward the grayish horizon. The screaming man's protests changed immediately, merging, as they could see from the house, with the last movements of people struggling with all their might to stay alive one more minute, one more second, and who knew, even in that last minute, the fullness of that last second—you could tell—that a child was still a child, a novice in conditions that were sometimes glaring and senseless, and that a parent was a parent. Don't be afraid, just hold tight to me . . . two of the onlookers, van de Velde and Zesgever, squeezed their eyes as the roof capsized and they heard a sort of animal howl. Izak Hocke turned around. Another similar freight was coming at them from the right.

"I can't look anymore!" he said, absolutely at his wit's end, talking to his mother's back as she wandered around in the half-darkness.

The only one left looking out into the storm now was Cornelius Jaeger. His head low, immersed in the din as if he had become its medium and was internalizing it, he stood at the window. Did he feel that at least one person had to bear witness that the high-pitched, multi-toned whistle was in the process of obliterating the communities of Dreischor, Ouwerkerk, Nieuwerkerk, and Oosterland? Midday had already passed. The tide was slowly beginning to rise again. Out on the great polder of Schouwen it crept forward insidiously across the ditches, because the sea dike that ran from the coast all the way to Zierikzee had been breached only at Schelphoek. But even on the heaving, drowning polders of Duiveland, the majority of the victims were still at this point alive. From attics, rooftops, and rafts, they did what victims who are still alive always do: they scream, and they wait for help.

Up in this particular attic, they were waiting for something that can be characterized, questionably perhaps but also not wrongly, as deliverance. The birth, almost upon them now, took precedence over the storm. The cervix was fully dilated, the head of the baby had emerged and was pointing down through the pelvic girdle. Lidy, among those surrounding the bed, was the one most involved in what was happening. Leaning far forward she watched as the little head, with its skull bones that, as she knew, were as flexible as the whale-bones in a corset and could move over one another, pushed its way forward a tiny bit, then slid back again.

"It's going fine!" she encouraged the not-so-young mother, who was looking around as if she were hoping to break out of an encirclement. She too, if she remembered correctly, had made quite a spectacle of herself during this last phase, but this woman chose from now on to let not a single sound escape her. So whether they wanted to or not, everyone could hear the screams coming from outside. Lidy looked at the red face, saw the arms that tried to cover it. With the clarity that comes with exhaustion, she registered that death cries and birth cries are similar, that they both resemble and illuminate one another.

Muffled barks from the dog.

When a child is born without professional help, those present have to use their own good sense. Unwind the umbilical cord from round its neck. Rub the soaking wet little body till it's dry. Wrap it up warmly. Clamp off the umbilical cord, cut it with something sharp. If the child is a bluish red because blood or slime is blocking its throat and windpipe, suck them out. Lidy, with a strange, salty taste in her mouth, heard the child whimper a little, then scream. Cathrien Padmos had given life to a healthy boy.

Moving heavily, weak at the knees, she went from the bed to the window, where the strange deformed boy took a step to one side to make room for her. She leaned her forehead against the window. Feeling light-headed, she sank back for a moment into what she had not forgotten, home, Nadja, Sjoerd, her sister, her brother. One could not describe it as coherent thought. It was more a knowledge, certain but as vague as fantasies of heaven and hell, that they were there, in some unimaginable place in safety. She forced her eyes open and craned her neck, for in the middle of the stream of debris that was sailing past her on the waves she saw a raft with a high rim around the edges, maybe the upturned roof of a hut or something like that, and on it was an animal, alone, motionless, it looked to her like a pig. Before she could wonder if it was still alive, she saw the animal lift itself a little on its front legs and then tread forward into the water in a way that looked intentional.

"My God!"

Now there wasn't a human being or an animal to be seen any-where. Not even a bird.

Utterly shocked, she turned away. The boy, right next to her, looked at her and she stared back into the eyes under the continuous line of the eyebrows, at the mouth, already with a hint of fuzz on the upper lip. Nadja? Sjoerd? Sarphati Park, number 36? A paradox of danger and safety: there had to have been a moment of clarity, a short leap between its onset and its end, that was a rude awakening for her. The world was under a flood, the universe was turning in the wind, and they in this attic were the only ones to have been spared.

24

My Wife Doesn't Understand Me

One beautiful day in May 1962, in an Amsterdam bedroom, a man who could only describe himself as contented and happy both in his private and professional life awakened with the immortal words in his head: *my wife doesn't understand me*. Nonplussed, he rolled onto his side. Armanda was still asleep, on her back, chin pointing up in the air, a position she'd taught herself to use, initially with playful light-heartedness, after reading a newspaper article about double chins. Where did these words come from? Heavy and awkward, they ran through his mind. He stretched out an arm; she was wearing a short nightgown she called a babydoll. He could see the beginnings of her responsive smile, because the unbleached linen curtains let a lot of light into the room.

"Yes, that's better," she'd decided when they were settling on the decoration of the new house. "Now maybe we'll wake up early by ourselves as the children do."

His hand slid over her sweet, soft belly. Since the birth of their youngest she hadn't quite managed to get back to her old weight.

At breakfast half an hour later, the words were submerged but didn't really disappear in all the busy activity of a family starting a new day with quite a lot of noise. On top of this the radio was on, to give them the news. French underground atomic test in the Sahara. He reached for the milk bottle—the first thing he did every morning was drink a glass of cold milk—and looked absentmindedly at Armanda in her blue mohair bathrobe as she cut a piece of buttered bread into little pieces for Allan, sitting beside her all big and plump in his high chair. Some men love their wives less when they're sitting opposite in their bathrobes, unwashed and uncombed, but he had always liked the blurring of this line between table and bed. "Stop it!" she was saying to an angelic little blond girl as she took the tin of rusks away from her without even looking—his favorite, four-year-old Violet, who gave her father a smile as soon as she saw him looking at her, with such sparkling eyes that no movie star could have topped it.

"Open your mouth and close your eyes!"

It was Nadja, smelling strongly of eau de cologne. He obeyed. Last downstairs, Nadja laid her cheek against his and put a piece of nougat, her passion of the moment, into his mouth. Since the move, during which she had come across the photo of her mother in the Hotel Kirke, in a cardboard box full of old odds and ends, she had, amazingly, become demonstrably more loving and good-natured.

Heaven knows why, but he got to his feet to turn up the volume on the news. Chancellor Adenauer considers the conversations between the U.S. and the Soviet Union over the status of Berlin to have lost direction. Dutch troops dispatched to New Guinea on the frigate *Zuiderkruis.* The Upper Chamber, by a vote of 78 to 58, has passed a revision to the law permitting the sale of fresh bread to begin at 9:30 in the morning instead of 10 a.m.

He raised his head to observe an area of the wall above the radio: the building of a dam to control the Grevelingen at Schouwen-Duiveland has been resumed after an interruption. The Delta Commission expects this fourth major stage in the eventual closing of the sea arms of Zeeland and Zuid-Holland to be completed within two years.

"The weather . . ."

While he listened in the bright dining room—Armanda was going to have the wall broken through to the kitchen before fall—to the forecast about the cold front from the northwest that would envelop the country during the course of the day, he was seized by an impulsive fantasy masquerading as a totally rational decision. Quite strong winds in the coastal provinces, he heard, as he wiped his mouth and got to his feet. The Grevelingen was an easy drive if you took the highway through Noord-Brabant.

Shortly afterward he was in the car on the Rokin. He parked in front of the entrance to the bank and went to the room adjacent to his office on the second floor to give his secretary instructions for the day. A quarter of an hour later, en route to The Hague, he was hearing the words again that he had woken up with this morning. And the gentle, inviting, absolutely undramatic nostalgia that they contained. Sjoerd Blaauw and Armanda Brouwer had now been married for seven years. This was a fact. But when he, Sjoerd, thought consciously about himself as a married man, he automatically included in this a previous past, as free as a dream that he yearned for, the way you yearn for something that one day slipped between your fingers and is gone.

Armanda was lovable. She was damned difficult. She was an angel in bed. She stuck her head in the pillow and complained in a muffled voice that she had a headache. In the first years her eagerness when he came home was sometimes so blatant, and she let herself fall into the sofa with her arms outstretched in such open invitation that he actually felt more like having a simple conversation with her about, say, football. "Did you know they're broadcasting a big match—*mmm*—tonight on the radio?" Baffled look from her, and he turns toward the living room table and goes on: "Starts at eight." Six months after Violet was born, she was back to teaching three mornings a week, and the moment his mother-in-law came in to look after the baby, she disappeared to the Barlaeus school, in a rush, cheerfully, dressed appropriately in a tweed jacket that seemed made for a young English teacher.

Then came the time she liked to provoke him with the question "Who am I?" and lay her hands over his eyes. Playful results, of course, and a suitable response from him that necessitated no compliments. Shortly before Allan was born, she said she wanted to move, and immediately. Bad evening. October, wind howling on the roof. They were building or hanging something up in the attic, doesn't matter which, when she laid the hammer aside. After they had looked at each other for a moment, listening to the wind, and she had said,

"It's too Lidy-like for me," he had snorted once in the way that was typical of him and then replied idly, "Oh—maybe it wouldn't be such a bad idea to look for somewhere on the ground floor."

"Not a bad idea," she continued as she turned around heavily to go back to work. "And we're not going to take a thing, not a single piece of furniture, from this house when we go."

Nadja thought it was terrific. An eleven-year-old girl—skinny as a beanpole, but with a red plait down her back as thick as your wrist, and absolutely no freckles—can happily say Yes! when told that her entire life is going to be stood on its head. When it took place, her little brother, Allan, was three years old. While her mother did a drastic clean-out of the attic, stuffing photos, letters, schoolbooks, and reports into garbage bags, Nadja was on her knees in the rectangle of light thrown by one of the attic windows, with a photo in her hands.

"Hey, Mama!"

Armanda went over and immediately recognized the family photograph that Jacomina Hocke, with whom she was no longer in contact, had sent her as a keepsake.

"Who's the child you're sitting *there* with?"

Armanda, without hesitating, her voice involuntarily outraged, said quietly, "That's not *me*."

"Not *you*?"

The astonished forefinger of a girl who has never been told a thing about an exchange of mothers. In the beginning her father and the whole family were in too much disarray; later, having accustomed themselves to the slightly edited family story, the new version with all the details that fit perfectly, had even been added to, they never got around to it. But in their hearts they surely must have known, didn't they, that at some point they would have to tell Nadja everything.

"Just a moment," Armanda had said, reaching for a packing chest so that she could sit down. Bent over next to Nadja, she was better able to look at the picture, and did so, suppressing the first, instantaneous, strong impulse to tell her adopted daughter straight out, without the slightest psychological subtlety: "That's your real mother." She knew the corner from which the photo had been taken, the year before it had been snapped, she had after all been there herself. From the Winter Garden of the Hotel Kirke, you look into the reception room with the tables laid. There are draperies to either side of the staircase, and there's a palm tree. Given the backdrop, you wonder what the two people in the foreground, in adjacent wicker chairs, have to celebrate in such a grand way: the little gap-toothed girl, laughing shyly, and the woman, Lidy, with eyes that look slightly tragic because of the lack of lighting, and a smile around the lips that you'd have to know in order to interpret as "All very nice, but tomorrow I'll be home again."

"That's your real mother," said Armanda.

"Goodness!" said Nadja.

That is how it happened.

In the fishing village of Bruinisse, on the Grevelingen, a complete working harbor had been built to block off three miles of water by means of a dam. It was late in the morning. Sjoerd Blaauw, like a tourist, politely stopped a workman in overalls and boots to ask if they were making good progress.

"Let me through, friend!"

Quite right. He took a step to one side and lost himself for a moment in contemplation of the phenomenon in gray and blue-white, the two in spectacular contrast to each other, and which he would have loved to have explained to him. Gray was the color of the quays (which were also loud and dusty), full of asphalt, steel cables, blocks and tackles, trucks, and machines that looked like military equipment, and gray was the color of the contours of the construction site a little farther off, in which a tide lock 450 feet long by 55 feet wide was already in operation, and also the portion of the dam that was slowly advancing from Flakkee. The row of caissons lying ready in the water next to the quay were also gray, a beautiful example of hydraulic engineering to instill respect, but naturally a joke, a child's toys compared with the Phoenix-A-X caissons, as tall as high-rises, which would shortly be sunk directly at the edge of the sea in an opening several hundred yards wide by fifteen yards deep with a tidal range of eighteen feet. With a warm breeze in his face, Sjoerd looked up high. Blue-white (the quiet, independent, comfortable, tolerant blue-white that their national culture demands) was the color of the all-encompassing cloudy sky of the Dutch Masters above it.

A faint feeling of dizziness. His eyes moved down again. At an angle to the quay, with its bow toward the caissons, was a ship the color of red lead, a totally normal domestic ship with a cabin, named *Klazina*. Sjoerd turned to a man wearing a greenish leather jacket and tugged on his sleeve.

"No, back here," the man answered in response to his question as to why the dangerous arm of the sea was not being blocked off directly at the shoreline.

"But why?"

The man adopted a more comfortable stance as he explained to Sjoerd about the separation of the floodplains of the Grevelingen and the Oosterschelde. And about the injection of millions of cubic yards of sand, the building of entire asphalt mixing plants on-site, a foreign cable railway in our polders and watery lands, and about piers and caissons and abutments and swing bridges and sluices in the Har-ingvliet, where enormous shields would be steered from seventy machine rooms. . . . "Oh, mister, have you ever thought that the nightmare of 'fifty-three, back then, was the beginning of a damn magnificent dream?"

"Dream?" Sjoerd's face had taken on the well-known expression of schoolboys and students who want to learn the mandatory stuff for a test, while their hearts, otherwise occupied, do what hearts want to do: swell to bursting.

When did *my wife doesn't understand me* begin to echo in his ear again, like the line of a poem? When his eyes turned away to look at the powerful little ship that was in process of taking one of the cais-sons in tow, a red ship with a deckhouse on top and a name that was the only female presence in this world of men—*Klazina*?

"So, would you like to come along?"

The man, about to say good-bye, had noticed what the other was looking at.

"Can I . . . could I really?"

"We'll fix it."

Not long afterward he was standing on the foredeck of the little tug. Sjoerd, on the water again where he'd been once before. Noticeably calmer, the water, noticeably bluer than it had been when it engraved itself in his memory. Close behind him they were busy with chains and winches, was he standing in the way? No, the crew paid no attention to the strange, tall, blond fellow staring at the expanse of water as if he were staring at a world that had long been denied him. All the same, a boy brought him milky coffee in a pale pink mug, said, "Please!" with quiet warmth, and let him alone again with the vibrations under his feet. He lit a cigarette. The water between Bruinisse and Oude Tonge glittered, reflections, shouted orders, echoes: everything, all of it, exactly mirrored—even if in a fashion one couldn't have guessed—the words he had woken to this morning.

Lidy, look at me. Do you remember how we went to Ouderkerk? You were already weeks late with your period. View of the bend in the Amstel. Freeze-frame of Rembrandt, down on his knee, drawing this view. And you with your news. Do you remember how I got the fright of my life, and you turned around to pick some flowers and to murmur: "What I'd like is . . ."

"Yes?"

"Is for you to make the same face you made back then when you caught that pike."

We sat down on a bench at the entrance to the Amstel park.

That evening Sjoerd went on a date and cheated on his wife for the first time, and it isn't clear that the one thing—his experiences of the day—had anything directly to do with the other. It simply happened that as he sat down in Amsterdam in the wonderful evening air on the café-terrace of the Hotel Americain, he made eye contact with a woman who happened to be passing. Slender, wearing a green dress. Who next moment was coming to sit next to him at the round table. Large, shiny shopping bag on the ground between their chairs.

"Good?"

Sjoerd had ordered a glass of claret for her too. The weather had ignored the forecast on RNMI all day. It was warm and wonderfully sultry.

"Mmmm."

Not the slightest awkwardness between them. What did you do

today? His question to her, slightly narrowed eyes. Worked (in some institute), bought shoes (in the bag), talked to old friends on the phone (in Vienna). Like a woman letting her fantasy run at the first meeting, she didn't look at him directly; instead her eyes seemed to go through him to someplace behind him, as if through a fog.

"And you?"

He began to talk about the construction in the delta as if he'd been waiting for this opportunity, his voice unusually emphatic and excited. And she listened, her arm next to his on the table, and twisted her wrist, because everything was already conspiring to have their hands end up on top of each other. (Later she would tell him she had fallen that evening for "the gleam" of his desire, his masculinity without even a trace of typical Dutch dullness in the way he looked at her or the way he spoke.)

"More than a billion cubic yards of seawater with every tide!" he almost shouted, telling her about the Oosterschelde. "They close it with a forty-foot-high dam smack up against the sea! Don't think that's easy, it involves an estuary with a mouth more than six miles wide! First they import enough sand to create three new islands, then in the channels the wild current forms as a result, they build thirteen gigantic towers on sills of steel and reinforced concrete cased in stone!"

They made a date for the next afternoon.

When Sjoerd came home at around eleven and went into the living room, Armanda stayed sitting close to him on the sofa and stared at the tips of her shoes with a tragic expression.

"What is it?"

He had called her that morning from Zeeland to say that that was where he was, and told her in good faith that he didn't know yet when he'd be setting off back to Amsterdam.

So now this situation. Remorsefully Sjoerd sank down halfway onto the floor in front of her and looked into her face. Armanda, a little encouraged by this, immediately let loose a torrent of words, she'd spent the entire day imagining the whole area he'd felt compelled to go visit all of a sudden, just like that, the map, the layout of Schouwen-Duiveland closed in by its two sea arms.

"*Her* map," she sobbed openly. "Forbidden territory for me!"

Sjoerd had put his arms around her hips and her bottom. Now he slid onto the sofa next to her, pressed his face into her neck, and whispered, "No, no, you're crazy" so compliantly into her ear that she sat up, looked around her, all animated, and exclaimed, "And what do you say to *this*!"

Disconcerted but still remorseful, he followed her eyes.

"What's all this except *her* new house, her seven rooms, her attic, her garden to the southeast, her shed, don't pull such a dumb face, with brand-new furniture that's all the stuff she chose?"

She turned to him. The brief, hostile look she gave him said: Give it a minute before we make peace. "Oh you haven't a clue how often I've thought, This is *her* life that I . . . okay, this is all I'm going to say: these are her chocolate caramel bars I'm eating right now, I used only to like the plain ones, her extra pounds I'm trying to lose—she got slim again so damn quickly after Nadja was born—they're her brochures for the latest vacuum cleaners I'm looking at, and when I choose one, it'll be the one that'll make the least noise in her tender little ears. Do you understand what I'm talking about? This is the sixties now, the Netherlands are becoming supermodern. Do you know what I sometimes still think? Lidy's just gone for a day, and she's relying on me to live her life for her, all organized and proper, and that's exactly what I'm damn well doing."

Sjoerd listened, surrendering to her because of what he was going to do the next day. He was about to interrupt her by way of a general answer, with a quick "Hey, why don't we go to bed?" when she stiffened again.

"Do you get it? No? Okay, then I'm also going to tell you that sometimes, no, often I see every single one of our most personal memories, think of our Sunday-afternoon walks to Ouderkerk, think of our birthdays, our Christmas dinners, I see all of it as a sort of contrast stain, a measuring stick, against her water drama in God knows how many acts . . . you're shaking your head."

Sjoerd pulled her head toward him. Pushed his nose against her ear. She said some more sad things, then indicated she was ready to go to bed with him.

.   .   .

Dark. The intimate world of a bed with soft covers and sheets. No caresses. Or?

Well, yes. Sjoerd, unscrupulous or perhaps full of scruples, saw no reason to pass up the cornucopia of aroused hormones, warmth, and tenderness of a wife who was back in a good mood again ("Oh, what does it matter, he doesn't understand and he never will"). Afterward, like any real man, he immediately fell asleep. Armanda spent a little while thinking about the menu for Sunday, when the family would be together for lunch again, this time here in their house, and pictured her table. Father and Mother Brouwer, Betsy and Leo with their two boys, Jacob, now twenty-two, with a very fat but very pretty girl with milk-white skin, Letitia, and her family too.

Asparagus? wondered Armanda. With plain boiled potatoes, thick slices of ham, an egg, and hollandaise sauce? And with it some bottles of Gewürztraminer. Or better, maybe a Riesling?

25

The Last Lunch

"Well," she would have said, "the whole time we were sitting there that Sunday at midday, eating, you have to imagine the insane noise of the storm. The way I'm talking to you now, in my normal voice, it wasn't possible. So remember that during everything I'm telling you about, everyone was screaming the whole time at the top of their lungs. It just stormed all through the middle of that day without letup, I'm not going to keep repeating it."

That is what she would have said if at that moment a boat from, say, the river patrol had appeared at the attic window, which is not completely unimaginable, and she could have given an account later on of her anxious hours. There is quite a difference between recounting an adventure to an interested audience after it's over, embellished here and there with a couple of invented details and facts that came to light only afterward, and living one's own mortal danger, which must remain unvarnished, unimproved, and, *basta!*

"You're probably thinking," she would have said, "how could you eat in such circumstances, but we could. The table was a chest with a cover over it, there was a knife and a breadboard. The farmer's wife had carried everything possible up the night before, including a bag with precious things like eggs, butter, brandy, and a spice cake, because she'd been intending to go after church in Dreischor to visit a woman who'd just had a baby. How did we sit together? Imagine eleven poor devils, gray faces, a floor that everyone knows is swaying.

Horribly cold, of course, and very dark, even at noon. Cathrien Padmos, in the bed with her baby. Soon the Padmoses' boy Adriaan crawled over to be with his mother and baby brother. It had begun to snow. We saw the window gradually become coated with snowflakes, which didn't bother any of us, because nobody wanted to keep looking out anymore. What could be done? It must still be ebb tide, but the water was barely going down at all. Though enough that over the road, at Cau's house, some iron palings were sticking up out of the water, and trapped in them was the body of Marien Cau; you could see deep holes in the side of his head.

"So Gerarda Hocke fried eggs. She fried them on both sides, after breaking the yolks, tipped them out of the pan onto slices of bread, and said, "Zesgever?" Or "Laurina!" What? No—nobody betrayed obvious signs of anxiety. Where that came from, I have no idea, but that's how it was. Probably the cold made it impossible. If your body is already trembling with cold, it can't tremble with anything else. I know that Cornelius Jaeger checked the water level from time to time. He opened the attic door, peered down the stairs, then came back again. We looked at him, agog.

" 'So?'

" 'Roughly one step lower.'

"Maybe because I learned nothing else about him, I remember very clearly the way he looked. As if he had no substance, no past, no future, other than his appearance that day at noon. Aside from the hump on his back, it was his face that was the most distinctive thing; he had very prominent cheekbones, one of them closer to the eye socket than the other, his irises were almost black, and then he had this little precocious moustache, the child was twelve, a year younger than you were, Jacob. A body full of errors, like a very remarkable charcoal drawing.

"Most of us had already had a few mouthfuls of cognac. Two glasses made the rounds. It goes straight to your head, and everything starts to spin, if you're in the kind of situation we were in back then. I think we all felt we were still part of the world, but it was like being on a mountaintop—we were also a long way out on the edge. I still see Izak Hocke rolling himself a minuscule cigarette, with a little piece torn off one end of a paper. One of his eyes was swollen shut, half his face was a violet-blue, yet he radiated some sense of salvation the entire time. Now in his gesture as he took a few drags on the roll-your-own and then passed it on to his foreman, van de Velde, I saw something that was not perhaps so unfounded in these circumstances, namely a kind of calm despair: life has its own time limit, we all know *that*, but as long as we're here, we're here.

" 'The people in The Hague could send us a plane, dammit!' Nico van de Velde exploded at some point. And we looked up and saw an angry grumbler who was forgetting that the government doesn't work on Sundays.

" 'Or a . . .' came the prompt riposte from the birthing bed, 'or a . . .' and we all turned round or to one side and saw—I can't describe it any other way, the bliss of Cathrien Padmos. Her large eyes were sparkling as she stared at us, her face was flushed with the slight fever that every woman experiences on the day she has given birth. Ignoring the fact that everything was pointing to the imminent end of the world, she was in that state of rapture induced by her optimistic, death-defying hormones.

" 'Or a helicopter . . .'

"As we looked at her, she looked down, but then there was another smile: she was reassured to discover that the baby was already suckling energetically at her breast. Now all we need is a modern miracle like a helicopter, she must have thought, and we'll all be saved. But quick!

"That is how it was. An impossible situation that changed us all forever. I see us still sitting there in a sort of circle, marking off in the following order, if you imagine the hands of a clock: Cau, talking to himself, Zesgever, me, van de Velde, Hocke, his mother, Cornelius Jaeger, and Laurina van de Velde, who stood up from time to time to shuffle over to the godforsaken space between the two clothes cupboards, but nobody paid much attention. What is grief? Is it something that shows in a person's face? Mrs. Hocke was the only other one I ever saw bending over that place, the others . . . didn't want to? At least half of them almost certainly knew how things were with their own loved ones. So what were they supposed to do about this one death, such a tiny one, right next door?

"But the old woman did. I would never have thought that gold can contain its own light, and yet it must have been so in the two spirals that hung down to the left and right of her forehead. How otherwise could I remember so clearly how she looked? Her jaw muscles clenched as she bent over the place where Dina lay. Did she ask herself, I think she did, where this poor invisible little thing that she would certainly call a soul had gone? She belonged to the ultraorthodox Zeeland sect, so don't be too quick to say: 'to heaven,' please! The catastrophe was still unfolding, houses everywhere were collapsing, when sermons started being preached again two days later.

"Imagine a barn, wet to saturation point, and a preacher on an upturned water barrel. When the congregation who have been standing shoulder to shoulder go their separate ways again, what they know is what they already knew. The flood—so says their dogma of guilt and punishment, and they deviate not one iota from it—is God's spectacular but measured answer to our own provocations. I ask you seriously (Father, Mother, darlings, you're both shaking your heads in exactly the same way), doesn't this indicate an extraordinarily arrogant view of life? Punishment and guilt: the interaction of two great forces. And did you know, moreover, that brides from families who adhere to this sect wear black when they marry?

"Yes," she would have said, "there's a wedding photo of young Gerarda with her bridegroom and both their families. From left to right in front, on chairs, sit Cornelia Hocke-Heijboer, cousin of the bridegroom and sister-in-law of the bride; Sara Heijboer-Bolijn, sister of the bride and sister-in-law twice over of the bridegroom; Anthonie Hocke, the bridegroom; Gerarda Hocke-Heijboer, the bride; then the mother of the bride, Lena Heijboer-Koopman, widow of the mussel fisherman Iman Heijboer, and next to her Anna Leendrina Bolijn, aunt of the bridegroom and cousin by marriage of the bride's mother Lena Heijboer. Behind these six seated people stand four men, of whom all I know is that they were brothers, brothers-in-law, and brother-in-law's brother of either the bride or the bridegroom. The weather is splendid. The wedding guests have positioned themselves in front of the façade of a house or a farmhouse, shadowed by a tree in full flower. All of them without exception are wearing black. The five women have their hands in their laps, but Anthonie Hocke, the bridegroom, sits between them with his legs spread, his shoes shined to a mirror finish, and his hands in their thick knitted gloves on his knees in a pose that radiates masculine energy. Gerarda too is wearing black gloves. Of all the women, she, the bride, is padded out in the most clothing, wearing a long coat with lapels, and underneath it a dress that goes all the way to the chin. It is only Sara Heijboer, whose Zuidbeveland traditional dress includes a shawl that covers the upper arms, who lends the photo an idea of soft welcoming female flesh.

"Funereal? No, but serious. The scene isn't funereal for starters because of the women's snow-white caps, which separate the standing and seated wedding guests—four men and five women with the bridegroom in their midst—like a beam of light. With the exception of the Zuidbevelandish cap, in which the woman's head and neck are framed like a shellfish in its opened shell, the caps stand away from the face, looking like bright starched veils made of floating snow-flakes. How wonderful it must be to wear a crazy headdress like that! To hear everything grave and difficult in life discussed from inside the absolute privacy of such a white, translucently fine object cradling one's head!

"Not all of them, no. Only the two young women, Sara Heijboer and the bride, wear the gold above their ears. And when I look at the only smile in the photo, on the face of the bride's mother, and at the padded bride next to her, I know that the little ceremony has just taken place, in which the mother gives her daughter the precious head decorations like a dowry. She is to wear them, take care of them, and at the appointed time she is to give them to another young woman in the family."

"As I already told you," she would have said, "we all—every one of us—found ourselves in thrall to the situation. And the situation was the storm. And as we sat there the eye of the storm was, in some sense, us. Silent, empty, for one endless moment devoid of all charac-ter and devoid of all passion. How often do your eyes exist only because they're looking, and your hands because they feel cold, and how often does the house you're in exist all on its own, just because it's still standing and will hopefully continue to do so, if God is good, until this terrible flood recedes again?

"But afterward . . . I know for sure that since that moment none of us is the same person we once were!

"And there were things to note about Simon Cau. Who was he? Was he a man of property, a dike sheriff, someone who attracts a circle of people wherever he goes? Extreme alterations in character seem to occur less frequently in reality than they do in books. But look at this! Simon Cau stands up, because he needs to use the bucket that's behind the door to the entrance to the attic, with the sea splashing not even two steps below.

"He stands up, goes to the door, and closes it behind him, which it won't do properly anymore because the frame is no longer aligned. It must be about four o'clock; the noon tide is very high again. When he comes back, he's not looking down, as he did before, he's glancing around searchingly, as if he'd forgotten where he'd been sitting. Then he strikes out. The bird, the goose, was just sitting where it had been sitting since the beginning, on a sort of hand-knotted Smyrna rug (Mother, we made one at home ourselves once, do you remember, that little runner of stiff white canvas and the strands of wool, about three inches long, that we threaded through it and tied off on the back?), but Cau kicks the creature away and makes for his chair as if he has a right to cut his own diagonal straight across the room. He sits down in exactly the same position he had before.

"Oh. What's your guess? Fear? Losing a grip on himself? My own guess is that he thought the flood was his own doing. That he was absolutely reclaiming the responsibility for it himself. Not just for the water and, God help us, its effects, but also for the utterly unfamiliar meteorological conditions this weekend, including the astronomical forces associated with them, and the oceanology, because this water had come a very, very long distance.

"Grandiose? But fear *can* also occur on a grand scale. He arrived too late, *basta*, at this ramshackle section of the Grevelingen dike which, mind you, he had recently discussed one afternoon in the tavern De Galg with three technical engineers from the hydraulics department, venting his worry and frustration over the state of the embankment, the stone reinforcements, and pushing back against their doubts and fruitlessly pious hopes that all this was surely first and foremost the responsibility of the national authorities. So he reached the dike at a point when all was already lost. Can you imagine this? The wind that was blowing there wasn't a force of nature, it was the force of his own bad decision, fool that he was, to ignore the classification of 'dangerous' that was being broadcast on the radio, put on his good suit, and head for the Hotel Kirke in Zierikzee with his neighbors.

"Cause and effect. They are the Furies, Siamese twins. . . . This would not have happened, *if*. . . But enough of Cau. I stopped watching him, decided that what I wanted was a mouthful of cognac, but there was none left.

" 'Here,' I heard. It was Albert Zesgever, passing me the tail end of a cigarette that I could still manage to puff on two or three times if I held my fingertips right up to my lips.

"I looked at him, full of sympathy. Tall man, maybe forty. Red face, dark hair that seemed to grow up out of his neck like tarpaper. He was a very coarse man, a poacher, but also someone who could apply artificial fertilizer so finely and evenly by hand that Hocke, for this reason alone, had not yet acquired a mechanical spreader. I am guessing that Zesgever for the rest of his life became someone other than the man who messed around with his wife, which everyone knew, just as they knew how things had got totally out of control the night before."

"Oh, you mean, the night before, when . . ."

"Yes," she would have said. "As the wind reached hurricane speed. You need to know, before I tell you how things went when it hit force eight in the night of January thirty-first to February first, that Zesgever was a drunk, and when he had been drinking, he beat up his wife, Janna Maria. There are always things that set a man off, Albert Zesgever was that way too, and when he was loaded, he always knew whom to blame.

"That evening Janna Maria was sitting at home with her elbow on the table. A kerosene lamp that was turned way down illuminated her face and, to either side, her hands, along with a piece of clothing she had been altering. Outside the window one of those storms was howling that occur every year. It was close to eleven at night, the two children were asleep in clean, ironed pajamas, Zesgever was out somewhere. Because she knew that her marriage was the part of her life that often ended in a thrashing, and because she also knew that this could sometimes be avoided if she appeared to be asleep in the dark, she decided to pick up the lamp and climb the ladder. But suddenly, he was there. A length of the roof guttering was rattling, so she hadn't heard the front door scraping across the floor. She half turned toward him and saw from the game bag hanging slack across his shoulder that his drunken state was that of a man whose gun hadn't brought him any luck. The salt marshes behind the dike along the Zuidlangeweg were underwater. What Zesgever, for his part, saw as he came out of his haze was a creature who was radiating fear.

"He was well aware that the whole world, which is to say this little hamlet, saw and judged his abusive conduct harshly. He himself could no longer understand his own rage once he sobered up and came back to his senses. But then he had to endure for days, sometimes even weeks, that Janna Maria's black eye and split lip made his neighbors and acquaintances lower their voices whenever he was in earshot.

"So tomorrow—Sunday—his father-in-law was supposed to come pay them a visit. Zesgever was terrified of this man, a dike worker and excavator at a nearby freight harbor, thoughtful and friendly to one and all, and he was always at his humblest when they encountered each other. But for now it was still Saturday. The wind is blowing almost relentlessly, but aside from that, everything is quiet. Zesgever takes a few steps, asks something, Janna Maria's answer is not to the point, and also inaudible over the howling and thundering of the storm. Zesgever immediately focuses on Janna Maria's white, damp face, and something inside him erupts.

"This time it lasts longer than usual, and is more ferocious, perhaps in tandem with the violent weather. Blows can be delivered with a hand or with a fist. When he stops to catch his breath, she can no longer stand. Then she begins to vomit, lying on her back.

"At first, when he crawls into bed under the eaves still fully dressed, he's cheered by the rising force of the storm. Janna Maria, dragged upstairs, is lying beside him absolutely motionless, but still warm—isn't that how it was? Yes, that's how it was, he knows it, and imagines that for the rest of his life he will know that her head is so close to his ear that in more normal weather he would have heard her breathing. He stretches out and begins to sleep off the booze. What is the happy thought that sticks in his head just before his legs start to turn heavy?

"It's not hard to guess: the old man won't be coming. In weather like this, the old man absolutely won't be able to leave his harbor!"

"And you?"

"What do you mean, 'and you?' "

"Well, how have *you* changed since then?"

And then she would have looked away from Armanda for a moment (for it would have been Armanda asking these questions) and into the sunny dining room. Next to the window, a vase of purple tulips from the garden. A sleeping tomcat, a fat red thing, lying among the toys on the floor. The smell of freshly brewed coffee wafting in from the kitchen.

"Oh." She would have reached for the cigarette just lit by her husband. "God, I've no idea."

But Armanda would have kept looking at her, interested. Until, a little light-headed from the Riesling in the middle of the day, she would have come up with an improvised, but honest, answer.

"If I think about it—in every way. In all the hundreds and thousands of shitty little things that make up life and that you feel, since that time, are actually part of something else entirely. Something terrible, that involves only you, and that you can't talk to anyone about, because you were the only one there back then."

And she and her sister, suddenly overcome with emotion, would have fallen into each other's arms.

The present had other demands. Four thirty on the dot. Dusk was falling, it was high tide again, and the weather forecast for this Sunday was the opposite of mild. In De Bilt, the national meteorological office was warning all regions of the country, once again, about a severe storm coming from the west-northwest. What this meant for the attic in Hocke's farmhouse was as follows. A blow struck the house without any forewarning. There had been no particularly powerful gust of wind, but the blow unleashed such a huge wave of pressure that they all could feel it in their eardrums. The first thing they became aware of, in almost the same moment, was four or five gray projectiles suddenly shooting at random around the room. Nobody had time to realize that these were bats, abandoning their winter hibernation spots under the roof beams: what everyone saw was a network of cracks spreading across both side walls. The glass in the window exploded. The roof was torn upward, part of it disappearing to make way for a pile of black clouds. The house twisted and came off its foundations.

26

About Nadja Blaauw

Coffee cup in hand, Armanda sat at the table between the living room and the winter garden, which was lit at that moment by a ray of the morning sun. It was eleven o'clock. She was wearing thin blue trousers, cut wide, and a red blouse with rolled-up sleeves. As she was getting ready she had taken the scissors to her hair, still loose on her shoulders, to trim the ends and her fringe, in a routine intended to preserve this look for the rest of her life. The color would also remain the same: a medium chestnut brown, according to the description on the package.

On the table were a letter and a newspaper, both still unread. After her children had left for school, she had picked both up off the mat, and her eye had been caught, for a moment, unavoidably, by the large headline. Wednesday, 11 August 1972, seven people had died in a wind funnel the previous day that had struck a camping ground in Ameland. Uh, uh, uh, she had thought vaguely as she looked at the envelope with Nadja's writing on it, and decided to leave it unopened for the moment. News that one hasn't yet read hasn't yet happened, in a way, just as truths set down on paper in heaven knows what frame of mind have flowed out of one heart but have not yet reached the other. Armanda stared into her lush, unkempt garden. She hadn't seen Nadja for weeks.

It was her day off. While she hung out the laundry on the drying frame in the stairwell, she let her thoughts wander to her odd fate and that of her daughter Nadja. Nadja was a lively girl with a luxuriant mane of red hair, who was studying history at the University of Amsterdam, more or less diligently but not with any great urgency. The remarkable thing that Armanda was thinking about was the fact that Nadja, although she was her stepchild, was closer to her heart than Violet, a delightful teenager, and Allan, who since the divorce had so clung to his mother that when he went off to school, he always knocked one last time on the window from outdoors to wave at her and be sure she noticed.

Armanda shook the folds out of a pillowcase, remembering the day when Nadja had lain on her stomach on her bed, sobbing with fury, while she sat next to her discreetly on a chair in the dim light. It must have been in November, after school, it was already getting dark. While Nadja was telling her in all its miserable details (his bed was in the same room as the Bechstein grand) that it was all over with the piano teacher, she had really had to struggle to suppress the feeling, as she stood to stroke Nadja's hair, that her hand was not part of her body but belonged to the doppelgänger who had remained sitting on the chair in the half-darkness to watch how she was getting on with this growing daughter.

Good, Nadja had soon got up again to switch on the light and wash her face and tell her lightly that given her lack of genius she'd prefer to switch from piano to history. "Wait, take a look at this." She had turned round to look for something.

A picture, a beautiful but terrible picture, torn out of a book and drawn by Rembrandt, of an eighteen-year-old girl, executed by strangulation by the City of Amsterdam for having killed her landlady by hitting her over the head with an axe. She and Nadja had looked together at the little body bound with ropes. The mood in the room was one of Crisis Over—Life Goes On. In a tone that sounded like an explanation of something, Nadja said, "One of the jurors at her trial before the sentence was carried out was named Blaauw."

The doorbell rang. Armanda set down the basket with the rest of the laundry and went downstairs to open up. Jan Brouwer was on his morning walk.

"You need to get something done," said the old man, right in the middle of the sidewalk, pointing up at the façade. The white climbing rose, which had come loose in yesterday's bad weather along with its trellis, was hanging over forward, baring a house wall that needed replastering.

"I know, Father," said Armanda, pressing a kiss onto the freshly shaved cheek. As she went back inside she made a mental note to call the builder that afternoon. Sjoerd and she had been apart for almost three and a half years now. Exterior work on the house had always been part of his responsibility.

Now for the letter! she thought, as she chatted to her father about the weather, now back to normal (warm; weak wind from the southwest, stronger along the coast). She glanced from the envelope on the table to her father, who simply by being there miraculously transformed whatever might be contained in the room into a moment of present calm: two cups of coffee, a bowl of cookies, and a great streak of sunlight across the floor that was targeting a male leg dressed in gray lightweight flannel. Months before, she and Nadja had had a conversation in which Nadja announced she was going to move in with a man in Bijlmer, a Surinamese, and there had been a big scene.

"There's a letter from Nadja. Should I read it out?"

Oh, Grandpa Brouwer's open, benevolent look! He settled himself comfortably, ready to hear how things were going with his beloved eldest grandchild.

Dear Mama,

It's three in the morning. I'm sitting at the table wearing the winter coat he left behind, over my pajamas. I can't sleep. You were right, I think, he's left me. I didn't know it, but the early morning bus trip last week through the Bijlmer was our good-bye. It looks absolutely awful there, Mama, unfinished apartment houses and otherwise nothing but sand, though at least you see corn poppies and stuff growing on it. He leaned over to me, all confidential. I'll never say it out loud, he murmured in my ear, but the Netherlands are beautiful. I find the Netherlands beautiful. We were on our way to the University Hospital.

I was going along to keep him company, and then continuing on to my lecture. You know, or actually you don't know, so I'm going to tell you, he's a senior male nurse in Paramaribo, and came here for a specific time to work at the U.H. in the intensive care unit. For further training. How was I to know that the time was up?

So I've been absolutely flattened for the last six days, and I've done nothing but think about him, it's unbearable but he's still mine and he's black as black can be. (Once we were walking down the Warmoesstraat when someone in a group of guys from the Antilles or Surinam yelled something at him, some curse word I couldn't understand. Sranan, he said, when I asked him what sort of language it was in, and he burst out laughing when he told me what it meant: horribly black!) Once when we were in bed, I made some sentimental remark about this black/white contrast thing in our relationship. While I stuck out my leg ostentatiously and held it next to his, I was carrying on about "isn't that beautiful" . . . and at the same time I was thinking secretly that blackness isn't something external, it's inside him, he lives in his blackness. And in the same moment I felt I was flying across hundreds of years of West Africa's past, that I was sailing across the ocean in the blink of an eye, to land in Fort Zeelandia in Surinam, our colony of traders in coffee, cotton, sugar, and slaves in our fine Dutch seventeenth century, where our souls would meet.

That thoughts are thoughts and words are words is something you can figure out just by looking at the idiotic difference in the speed at which they move, you know? The only thing I said about all this wonderfulness was "isn't that beautiful?" Nothing more. And Mama, the words were barely out of my mouth when I looked sideways and you know, he was absolutely furious. Suddenly I was looking at this man on the pillow and the sheets who was very angry, angry up to here, even his shoulders were rigid. Am I your first nigger? he asked.

I told you we first met on a sightseeing boat. It's the best student job anyone can have. You stand with the microphone in your hand and your back to the captain, canals, bridges, to your right that's a mug of coffee, and for the rest of it you simply tell whatever comes into your head. He was sitting right at the back. He looked from the merchants' houses to me, from the drawbridges to me, from the whole labyrinth of waterways and water lanes that winds through old Amsterdam in all its alarmingly crumbling glory when seen from this side, and eventually empties into the IJ—from all of that he looked at me to watch (or so I thought) the words coming out of my mouth. Next day he was sitting there again. By chance I was in really good form and babbled on about our great trading city, the jewel of our blessed little Repub-

lic, that once set the tone for the entire world economy: first, as I explained superenthusiastically, thanks to the Dutch sailors who so loved going to sea that they didn't care about being paid; second, thanks to the windmills, such clever technical doodads that could be harnessed to saw wood, grind corn, pump out polders, you name it, they could do it; and third, I said briefly, because what did I know about this stuff, thanks to slavery. On the third day, when he looked at me, I looked back at him. And I could feel that he didn't understand a word of my set text or even guess what any of it was about, he was just looking at my mouth.

Mama, have I ever told you that I almost never felt attracted to any of the boys at school, and I don't really feel attracted to any of the guys in my study group at university either? Too much like pals or brothers. I never once felt my heart go thump! After our third trip on the Queen Juliana, *he and I went into town, ate at a little table, and took the bus to the apartment he'd rented from friends for the duration of his stay in the Netherlands. Oh, I know, you just won't get it. I was out of my mind with love. So where did my wedding night take place? In an apartment in a new block, with a fancy roofline that makes it look as if it's standing up at an angle on the flat polder like a boat that's sinking.*

When he'd gone to sleep, I leaned over him. Is it true that the first thing you fall in love with is a face? But can that be something other than the eyes and the mouth? I think it was already quite clear to me as he lay there, sleeping sweetly, that he had an expression of his, you have to say it out loud in an earthy but friendly way, but that he really did try to reach for my face through my words. And I can visualize them, all in a row, the young guide's words, out of which all you needed was some intelligence and goodwill and you could conjure a complete merchant fleet sailing laboriously against the wind, and the harbor of Hoorn in bad weather, and Amsterdam harbor half frozen in winter in the eighteenth century, and the storehouses, packed full of produce from the colonies, the churches, the grand houses on the canals with their blazing reception rooms and their women always standing at a window and reading a letter. Luxury, calm, and lots of tea, in mid-May you could watch all of Amsterdam boarding lighters to sail to the tea pavilions and summerhouses on the Vecht and all the way to Haarlem, returning in the fall. I mean it when I say that it was all streaming through me like a dancing river, and now through him as well.

Mama, something's weighing on me. I think it's dreadful, but one time I had a really hard time suppressing a pang of pity for him. We were coming home after a late movie. Did I feel like having a late-night supper? He's already pirouetting toward the kitchen. How about oysters? Of course. And he comes back with a glass full of vinegary pickled mussels, gray blobs of crap in a glass that he holds up like a trophy. My king of the primeval forest. Poor sweet guy. Then he puts a bottle of white wine on the table that's been stand-ing next to the heater for hours, switches on the main light, and goes to work with a corkscrew. At that moment I would have given anything not to have remembered that a few nights before, in the dark, he'd said to me: You touch the blackness in me. And how blissfully happy I'd been, and had thought: how great, there's this naturalness between us, and we don't know each other's weaknesses, though they certainly exist, and we can just leave it alone, leave it alone! Oh Mama, don't be surprised by this letter, it's night, and I'm very alone, I was so captivated by this man!

At this point Armanda raised her head and met the eyes of her father. He was crushed, but still benevolent.

"Shall I pour us a quick cup of tea?" she asked gently, thinking of her father's prudery, and how he was so stiff-necked in his rejection of all modern developments.

"Oh, finish dear Nadja's letter."

His voice, unsure as it always was when his feelings became con-fused without any prior warning, led her for a moment to her own love life. It was good that a lover was no longer called "lover" these days, but, more modestly, "friend." Her father liked the disheveled mathematics teacher, one of her colleagues, whom she had brought with her to number 77 on several Sundays now.

"All right." She picked up the sheets of paper again, hunted for a moment, then resumed her reading. "Now I must tell you something that you couldn't know back then, but your rage probably picked up on already: he's married back home."

Without looking up, she saw her father stretch out his arms, and she knew how shocked he must be.

"Oh, my little one!"

She read out the rest of the letter.

.   .   .

And I want to tell you, there's something else, something strange, that I went through with him. There was a party in the garage in our apartment building. He asked if I was coming. This party was going to be a winti-pre', *an African idol celebration. Do you believe in them? I asked him straight out. He gave me a warning look. Believe? Do you mean believe? You don't, do you? He began to laugh, poked me in the stomach with his finger, and went to the light switch to demonstrate something to me. Okay, the ceiling fixture in this room uses three bulbs, two of which are burned out, but I could see, couldn't I, that the light switch itself was working. Don't ask how . . . he said maliciously, already dragging me toward the elevator. Basement.*

So where are the cars, I thought, as we entered the concrete cavern that took up the entire space under the building. Larger than ten churches. Entrance and exit ramps, pillars, neon lighting, painted numbers identifying the parking spots, everything very orderly, yes, but not a car to be seen. What there was instead, somewhere in these catacombs, was an enormous but invisible drumming; we really didn't need to ask the way. The Bijlmer, Mama, is terrific, it shows a real vision. Until the last ten years, more or less, there was just a village here on a sandy road between Weesp and Amsterdam. Then along came the architects and drew some enchanting apartment buildings like honeycombs, with garages underneath, in a paradise of meadows and poplars and new stretches of lawn. God, how beautiful, it was supposed to become a city where living, working, and enjoying the fresh air on weekends are separated by nothing more than a few crosshatched pen strokes. But you've no idea: right now almost the entire middle class of Amsterdam is sitting on the waiting list for houses with gardens in Purmerend. And I'm looking at people here, striding out to the sound of the drums with towering headdresses. . . .

So, we went to where the party was in the garage. There were around a hundred people, all of them black of course. Excitement and drumming and a lot of jumping around by a band called Boeing 737. Very appropriate, it seems to me now, because basically what they were doing was picking up somebody's ancestors from the primeval forest and transporting them at warp speed to a polder southeast of Amsterdam. We moved into the middle of the crowd. My beloved was already doing little steps forward and back.

Winti, *he said, when I asked him afterward, means: a spirit of your ancestors who moves as fast as the wind. Very simple.*

*It was next day before I got any more details about these spirits, all per-
fectly normal according to my guy, one huge family according to him, that
also included Voodoo. Oh, but aren't they really dangerous, I asked. What?
he said, the Voodoo* wintis? *And he told me how back home on his farm an
iguana with revolving yellow eyes had sat in a tree for weeks, and there
would have been no point in chasing him away. But there are also lots of
examples of well-intentioned spirits, he said, and named some water sprite.
When such a* watra *takes up residence in a person during a party, he or she
always asks right away for a bottle of rum and a box of cigars. At the end
you must banish him or her, because water sprites love social gatherings. I
know, the whole thing's madness, but it interested me, because I thought: it's
all him.*

*So, I wanted to tell you about the party. Everyone in the place was danc-
ing. And did it get hot! Then the thing everyone had been waiting for happened. Crazed yelling. A boy, not even ten years old, I think. Began stepping
backward, tried to say something: um, um, as if there was a name he
couldn't remember. Then this child asks for something in a booming voice,
really overwhelming, sounds very heavy—and he gets it. When will I ever
see a child glug down a glass of beer that size again, his hands already reaching for another which also goes down at one go? It was one of those* watras, *it
really was, Mama; he came, he said in this huge voice, from Alkmaar, no,
no, not our nice little town near Amsterdam, this Alkmaar was once a sug-
arcane plantation, a vast stretch of land on the banks of the Commewijne.
People were passing on in whispers everything he said, as translated by an
interpreter, because the boy, who was possessed, was speaking in an African
language he himself didn't understand. Never knew that what we call the
factual is such an elastic concept. The ancestral spirit first complained at the
top of his voice about the neighbors around the coffee plantation at Nijd-en-
Spijt, then cheered up a bit, looked around, said hello to his family, and asked
them how things were going.*

*I couldn't tell you how the party ended and whether the spirit really did
leave. I needed air. This* watra *also gave off a particular smell, formalin, you
know, the smell of new schoolbags. And what was I thinking as I stood there
all on my own in the grass all covered in the evening dew? Absolutely nothing! I believe the way we're supposed to use rational connections when we*

think is completely overvalued. It hardly ever happens. I, for one, don't like it and I only do it when I have to write something for one of my study groups at the university. I just stood there in the cool and looked.

My neck hurts. My fingers hurt. I'm crushed by this dreadful unhappiness. Am I empty enough to go to bed now?

I give you a hug. Don't be angry anymore.

Nadja

P.S. It's late morning, the day is bright. I was thinking about my mother, Mama. Where she actually is. Became a spirit far too early. And I didn't just think about her, to tell you the truth, I . . . called her. I whispered mother! mother!

27

The Collapse of the House

For a time they were side by side, being propelled forward at an insane speed. Like two boats that have cast off and started a race. She lay flat on her stomach, her head in her arms, hands clamped on the edge. It had happened unbelievably fast. When a house comes off its foundations and the roof is torn off, the entire fabric gives way. It described a little curve on the water, then the wind knocked away the walls. The floors were ripped away in sections by the current. There was no panic. She had heard no screams. Nor seen any in eyes or faces.

There had even been a kind of farewell. She saw Izak Hocke look at his mother and Cathrien Padmos look at her baby and Laurina and Nico van de Velde look at each other and Zesgever at little Adriaan and Gerarda Hocke, the heavy goose clutched to her breast, look at the failing roof of her house. She registered. It all happened in a fraction of this one second of terror. This old woman knows she's old, and close to death. She sees the floor of the attic of her house break in two, and the furniture suddenly fly into the air. An enormous force pushes the objects to the surface. Cupboards, tables, she knows every one of them piece by piece, knows what has been in them or on them. It doesn't require conscious thought. Just before a wave riding from the bottom lifted both parts of the floor and hurled them forward more than thirty feet in a single blow, the old woman saw the beds, water jugs, and the pathetically sodden featherbeds from all three bedrooms on the second floor come swirling up in front of her feet. The house was half afloat. The cellar and storerooms had already parted company with it. An inhuman situation: an old woman surviving her own home?

Only Simon Cau in his last moments, thinking of nothing and no one. He didn't even wait. Lidy, who needed all her strength to seize some outstretched hands and hold on tight, still saw him throw himself into the water. A gray silhouette bending forward, then streaks of foam.

Now, painfully, she eased her grip on the edge of the wood that was not swimming on the surface of the water but about four inches beneath it. She lifted herself a little. The raft was being propelled by a powerful current. Beneath her only yesterday, there had been a sandy road called the Captain's Road, which led, by way of many twists and turns, over the Melk dike to the main road to Zierikzee and finally to the Oosterschelde. Inching her way backward, seeing almost nothing, she became aware of the identity of her companion on this slab of flooring, on which until a moment ago an entire life had played out, as if on another planet, with its own time and laws, a life complete and full of significance, to which she now had been compelled to say adieu.

Cornelius Jaeger. She knew he was there. When the house broke apart, her faculty of observation was aborted. As if events were trying to prevent themselves from happening. And after that, as she was flailing in the water, she had only looked at his face, then his hands. To actually heave her up onto the raft had not been necessary, and the boy wouldn't have been able to do it anyway. She had crawled onto it by herself, just before a wave coming right up off the bottom had risen and taken the little nothing, the foolish chance repository that was her house and her sanctuary, up onto its back. Now, as she risked a quick glance around her and then back in the direction of the storm, she took stock of her situation. A few square feet of floating debris. On it, by way of company, in addition to Cornelius Jaeger, the Hockes, mother and son, an assemblage of shoulders, arms, eyes, trying to keep its seat.

It began to snow. Wet flakes flying past her face in a southerly direction. Everything jolting, wobbling, no purpose in life other than to hang on. Lidy, without a roof over her head for the first time since she was born, was bent on survival. As the house broke apart, her exhaustion had transmuted itself instantaneously into terror, her terror into action, and action into the absolute determination to live through this maelstrom. Nothing would be able to shake her of this. She saw a whole mass of unidentifiable objects appear in front of her, caught on a post here, a tree there, and then she was shooting past it. She saw dead cows, a dead horse, a dead man, oil drums, and knew that right behind her on the raft was a whole little family. How could it be possible? The old woman was still wearing her gold. The farming women of Schouwen and Duiveland have every imaginable way of keeping their headdresses and their gold jewelry firmly pinned to their heads. Gerarda Hocke's bonnet of white lace or finely starched linen had blown away, but under it she always wore a black crocheted undercap, which fitted tightly to the head and held the gold spirals so tightly that they could not be dislodged.

The snow was getting thicker. Five or six minutes had gone by since the small community in the attic had broken up. Even had Lidy wanted to, which was not the case, she would no longer have been able to see how her former companions were faring on the other raft. There were only two of them. Only Laurina and Nico van de Velde had been able to keep their grip on the other part of the floor, from which planks had started immediately to break off left and right. Now they were caught in an undertow, the raft tipped; they managed to pull themselves back up on it and stretch out on the wood before they disappeared forever into the driving snow with no one to witness them.

It was slowly getting too dark for anything to be visible, and moreover the screaming and howling of the hurricane discouraged any observation of their wider surroundings. In such conditions, what would be the point of trying to see anyway? Lidy kneeled there, hunched over, legs spread for balance, in the borrowed thick coat that was soaked through, and rough shoes, and clung to a plank that protruded a little above the others. What you see in such a position is mostly your hands. But her very blindness, or close to it, served only to sharpen her other senses. Some living force was coming at her, constantly shape-shifting, in curves, and wings, and foam, and spray:

it was the question that silenced all life's other questions. Almighty God, merciful God . . .

Did she really still believe she could manage? Or was she sensing the road now opening to her at such speed? It doesn't matter. Ignoring everything a rational person knows in principle, she held fast with all the skill she could muster, as if someone had just taught her the lesson of a lifetime. She knew her fingers had become very bony. A few minutes before, she'd seen that she'd lost her ring, her wedding ring with the little ruby. And she had actually thought, Oh, what a pity!

On February 1, European time, at 5 degrees latitude, the sun goes down at 17:27. And now she really couldn't see her hand in front of her eyes. The cloud layer was so thick that even the moon couldn't penetrate it.

28

Oh, My Papa

Exactly a week after her father died, and three days after his funeral, Armanda awakened with the uncontrollable urge to tell anyone and everyone that her father had died not once but twice. It was a particularly beautiful autumn day, sunny, with a hint of sweetness in the misty air. An hour later, when she stood in the street and saw the men and women coming out of their houses to head for work—on bicycles, on foot, or, some of them, by car—she wasn't sure whom to impose her urge on first. Everyone seemed absorbed in their own thoughts, and she wasn't accustomed to striking up conversations with just anyone. The first time her father had died was over a year ago. A malignant tumor on the pancreas, a seven-hour operation, a partial recovery, but like everyone he had understood and accepted that the only use of his recovery was, quite properly, to hold his wife, his children, and his grandchildren close and take his leave of life. Emaciated, gentle to the point of formality, he lay on his deathbed, prayed with the minister, looked deeply into the eyes of each of his loved ones, thanked Nadine with "you were my whole world," closed his eyes for three days, his pulse meantime almost imperceptible, and opened them again on day four. Blue, clear, focused.

Restless and impatient, she walked toward the Rijksmuseum, with a white cloud standing above it. The sunny city felt cold and unwelcoming. Looking around her, she wondered which of all these faces could be the one to talk to. Her father had died again the week before, swollen and struggling. He didn't want to go. And went when no one was there with him. She came to the underpass to the museum. Even before she entered it, she was assaulted by the sounds of the accordion player performing sentimental German pop songs. As she paused under the domed ceiling, the volume was overwhelming. She stood still, glanced around, and listened to the song. She was forty-nine years old, had renounced more than a few desires and suppressed others, as who hadn't in this phase of their lives—but this one?

There must be some important exhibition, she thought. On the other side of the building, in front of the entrance, was a rather disheartening queue of people. She joined it next to a tanned, quite young guy with long blond hair and muscled arms, in a T-shirt, a sort of Viking type, and said to him: "Oh, oh, this is going to take a while, isn't it!" After some desultory chitchat, she got onto the subject of the double death of her father, Jan Brouwer, seventy-six the second time around.

"Not a bad age," said the Viking. They hadn't advanced a single step.

"Maybe not," she said, "and yet deep in my heart I count it as seventy-five for the first of his lives, and a year for the other."

The Viking looked at her eagerly.

"Well," she said. "Can you imagine it? Completely changed."

"How—changed?"

In a tone that suggested she was having to explain the obvious, she said: "I mean that my father, a retired cardiologist, was a highly intelligent, rational, devoted man, focused on his work and his family. There's a certain kind of person who's born to live a happy life."

"True."

"So, after his first death, his character, his behavior, even his appearance, changed completely. I mean, he even started tying his shoelaces differently, making two bows first and only knotting them afterward."

The Viking stared at her for a moment. Then made a face, a sort of grin of recognition.

With a hand shielding her eyes like a bridge, for the sun was climbing in the east, she said: "Father began to eat. After two months he was a little, fat old gentleman, still very friendly, but friendly in a *different* way, restless, and his face got redder and he wore these funny checked shirts. And he started taking walks all on his own for hours at a time, and when he came home he wouldn't say a word about them to my mother. If he'd been younger, you could have imagined—well, you know. Once . . ."

Suddenly the queue was moving. That always makes everyone start itching to cover the full distance right away. Conversations cease.

"Once," Armanda finished her sentence, "I see him in the city, he's walking ahead of me, quite fast, given the way he is, for Father was always someone who would step aside politely rather than get into a showdown about who-has-the-right-of-way-on-this-sidewalk, but now he's making a path for himself across the Vijzelgracht by dint of staring grimly straight ahead, or so I guess, and he comes to the Rokin, then the dam, then he goes all the way down the Damrak as far as the main station, which he goes into by the front entrance, then out again on the other side, and then on the Ruijterkade, quite by chance, as far as I can tell, he meets a big, untidy-looking woman, who speaks to him, to Father's initial embarrassment, I think, but then it's as if she's given him a password, she suddenly gets this really friendly smile out of him and they have a cheery conversation for a good ten minutes. So, after they shake hands and say good-bye, part of me wants to catch up with him and say, Hello, Father! but another part of me is inclined, given how arbitrary the whole story seems, to just watch where this suddenly new and resurrected father of mine goes on these private walks of his, so I follow him and see him, a minute later, pushing open the door—"

She had reached the ticket desk. The girl looked up. Armanda said over her left shoulder, searching for the Viking, who was nowhere to be seen: "—to the tavern, the one on the corner, you know, it's all done up to look old, and they still scatter sand on the floor."

The girl, hand ready on the till, asked: "For the exhibition or just for the museum?"

"Just *The Night Watch*."

While the girl entered the price of the ticket, Armanda felt a surge of ugly obstinacy. It was as if the conversation she had had with her father shortly before his second death were now jabbing her in the side. She had gone into De Laatste Stuiver. He had seen her at once, and although she too had immediately spotted him at the window, in front of a backdrop of gray houses (it was about to start raining), she looked around the room at first, as if hesitating. Fine, they were both soon sitting in front of a drink, and her father was telling her wasn't it extraordinary, he'd just run into one of his old patients for the nth time, who was feeling great and had charmingly reminded him about the prescription he had written for her fifteen or twenty years before.

"Aha, and?" she'd asked, as someone was already bringing them another round, and she was thinking: who knows, maybe the way he walks and looks and talks and thinks these days reflects his real self? So? Isn't it time I recognize this second-class father as simply my *father*?

He had said he'd finally worked out the meaning of a day in the life of a man.

"And what is it?" she had pushed him.

Like a bird, he took a sip from his glass with a movement that was rather extravagant for someone in his condition. When he looked up, he began evasively: "You know, this patient, who's been following my orders to swallow a modest daily dose of twenty milligrams of dipyridamole for the last twelve years—"

She'd interrupted him.

"Father, you were going to say something else! Some definition of the core of daily life, something nice about how small it is, something logical about this horribly and yet pleasingly sticky coating on our everyday routine, and I really want to hear it from you!"

Then he had stared at the ceiling and started to talk about eating food out of the garbage, about using a black bolt gun to stun cows so that they collapse without making a sound, about sitting in a chair on rainy days watching the windows in the house across the road steam up. . . .

Armanda stared at the cashier as if in a trance. The girl was holding out her ticket.

She said, "Absolute nonsense! Of course I knew it was Father Number Two talking!"

"What are you talking about?" asked the girl suspiciously. "Please pay. You're holding up the entire queue."

Short pause, in which nothing happened. Oh, that's how traffic jams start, thought Armanda as she dug around in her purse for a two-and-a-half-guilder coin. Then she went up the stone staircase, followed a sign with an arrow, and soon was in front of the enormous canvas that took up the entire back wall of a rectangular room full of seventeenth-century masterpieces.

"Dear God!" she murmured, astounded by the scale of the painting.

Next to her was an old lady, small but dignified, with gray hair wound in plaits around her head and horn-rimmed glasses perched on her little mouse face. A former presser from one of the oldest cleaning establishments here in the city, as she learned, after they had struck up a conversation; she would have guessed an old baroness. Still possessed by the need to tell her story, she gave the other woman a pregnant look and then turned back to *The Night Watch*.

"Incredible figures, aren't they?" she said. "Just look at the way they stand together so proudly and joyfully! In a moment they're going to exercise and shoot. Isn't it sickening what's become of Amsterdammers since then?"

"Oh yes," said the old lady in a voice like a little silver dinner bell. "There are moments that come over you like a cloud of hot steam and then vanish again, when you think, What kind of a city is this now, so devoid of really rebellious ideas or even a hint of class warfare." She snapped her fingers and pushed her glasses higher up on her nose. "But this painting isn't about Banning Cocq and his men, it's about that little fleck of light, that bizarre child pushing *her* way up out of the darkness."

"Shall we sit down for a moment?" Armanda proposed.

A few minutes later she and the old lady were on a blue velvet bench right in front of the enormous canvas, agreeing that there was nothing this city needed more than *The Night Watch*. And in the same breath Armanda had kept talking about what was weighing on her heart: "Twice! Imagine! And the second time, mind you, he was all pink and fat!"

They stared at each other searchingly. "For my mother," Armanda continued a little less agitatedly, "it was much easier to keep seeing this resurrected husband as the same man she'd loved before. Maybe because she's a more generous person than I am, that could be, or maybe because she had been breathing together with him every night in the dark. That would have maintained some sort of relationship even if, let's say, he'd turned into a dog. But I'm pretty sure of one thing: she felt as uneasy as I did. And this unease of hers, like mine, didn't just spring directly from the change in all these externals, because when you look at it, the change wasn't really that large. It didn't come from him getting up at the crack of dawn, it didn't come from his loud 'good morning' over an extended breakfast, or his new brand of aftershave, or his switch to paper handkerchiefs, or the way he turned up the corners of his lips when he laughed; he got fat so quickly, started buying dreadful new suits without consulting her, but he remained a very lovable man, really, and a well-meaning husband, bought flowers on Saturdays, went with her to visit relatives and friends, accompanied her to the theater, where he simply forgot that she was used to him helping her into her coat in the cloakroom."

The old lady cleared her throat and stood up, smiling politely. Armanda stayed sitting.

"Oh God, no! All that wouldn't have bothered us at all. But how can I explain to you, it was his godforsaken uninvolvement in everything. Sitting in the corner full of energy and all alert, arms and legs spread, his hiking shoes still on his feet, while Mother and I were in the same room and hadn't the slightest connection to whatever was going on inside him!"

Unbothered by the fact that the lady had left, Armanda stared at *The Night Watch*. She and the great canvas, it seemed to her, were both on the same *level*. But after a quarter of an hour she'd had enough. I'll buy a couple of pretty postcards, she thought, feeling idiotic because what she really meant was: I've got lots more to tell!

In the museum shop she saw a familiar figure.

"Betsy!"

Why should she doubt the one real reason why her friend and ex–sister-in-law had come? Betsy turned round, holding the card she had just taken out of the rack. (*The Jewish Bride*, Armanda saw at once, flashing on the unconnected thought that Betsy was named Rebecca after her grandmother Vaz Dias.) They greeted each other affectionately. "Shall we do something?" "Do you have time?"

The museum cafeteria was a space as large as a church, and at this time of day no sunlight came through the painted glass windows. They ordered coffee and began to talk, what about was irrelevant, they knew almost everything about each other. Betsy and Leo's twin sons, Wim and Stijn, were students and thank God they still came home with bags of dirty laundry at age twenty-three. The mathematics teacher, Cees, was still in Armanda's life, but she didn't want this fair-weather friend to move in with her. Sjoerd had got married again in 1978, he was working in a high-level job with Labouchère in Paris and was always on the phone to his beloved half sister about this or that. Violet was doing an internship at a bank in London; Allan, who lived in an extremely comfortable squat, was getting more simple-minded by the day, and Nadja had been living for years now with a sculptor.

That left the real end of Father Brouwer.

If Jacob had been at home more often, Betsy and Armanda wondered, would he have seen that Father, who was now refusing medical supervision, was going downhill again despite how well he looked? Perhaps, but Jacob, the doctor without borders, as the family called him, had been sitting in some godforsaken corner of the world for almost a year, and barely made it to the funeral. Okay, Armanda said now, but shouldn't she have seen it as a warning that in the last weeks he kept calling her Lidy?

She lowered her head in thought, and wondered, "As if the person he really wanted to remind was himself . . ."

"Dammit," said Betsy, "he'd forgotten her, the first time he died."

"Yes, as if in his heart she'd ceased to exist for him who knows how long ago. None of us noticed at the time. It was all so peaceful. I can remember thinking: How lovely to end your innings that way, so friendly, so nice, so serious. And a last heartfelt word for each of us. But yes, *one* name was *explicitly* left out. . . ."

Armanda and Betsy looked sadly and quietly at the cups on the table in front of them. There had been nobody at the next one, at deathbed number two. So it was inevitable that everyone would start imagining all sorts of things, whether they were applicable or not.

And it hadn't been a deathbed but a half-worn-out Bukhara rug on a herringbone parquet floor. Jan Brouwer was lying next to his desk, in the undisturbed consulting room on the first floor, when his wife found him, after calling and searching, at around four o'clock on the twentieth of October, 1980. The light in his eyes was already gone, but because of the bizarre course of events in the last year, she couldn't believe it without further checking. She telephoned Doctor Goudriaan at once, couldn't reach him, and called Armanda. Armanda had knelt down and was looking at the worried expression on her father's face, with its eyes still open, making him look as if he were objecting to something, when the doctor on call came into the room. His rapid examination was no more than a ritual, an answer for wife and daughter.

"God, we were in such a state," said Armanda. "I remember the two of us kept asking in unison: So? What do you think? Shouldn't you call an ambulance? Shouldn't we lift him onto the sofa? Couldn't you do CPR right now?"

29

Out on the Oosterschelde

The mat of reeds sailed on. Hocke lay pressed tight against her back and hips. He had wrapped his left arm over her body and stretched his right arm next to hers and up over her head. She had let go of the stalks to twine her fingers into his. Lovers lie like that. The heavy black sleeve of her coat was pushed up a bit. The storm raged on unchanged, with wind gusts of seventy-five miles an hour over the water; it was simply shifting a little from northwest to northeast. The moon had reappeared with a bluish cast that negates all sense of depth and volume and gives everything a particular visibility, so that space itself acquires a perspective all its own, in defiance of all normally accepted theories. Lidy's wrist, as bony as a child's, trailed in a witch's cauldron of sheer brute force. She had forgotten what a house is, or a marriage, or a family—that kind of thing is quick to go.

Lying in a reed bed engenders a sense of earth, of land, even despite the wetness. But this part of the landscape was moving, and moving with some speed, in a southeasterly direction, which didn't mean much to Lidy anymore, as she had lost all idea of land. For the space in which she found herself alive, depleted and exhausted, but nonetheless alive, was an enormous unknown. The whole system—focal point, outlines, verticals—was heaving and surging in the uproar. Moon, clouds, and stars, which she had always believed belonged in the firmament, came up at strange angles out of what had become a wild waterscape to right or left. Yet her heart beat on, without anything she could have described as a fear of death. Her fingers held tight to Hocke's. She had not forgotten what it is to want to live.

An hour passed in this fashion. Dusk. From time to time another squall of snow. About three feet away from her, another figure was lying in the flattened reeds. Gerarda Hocke. Lidy wasn't clear, nor was she even wondering, if the old woman was still among the living.

The hunchbacked boy had been gone from them for quite a while now. When they lost him, it had been pitch dark. The section of floorboards they had been sitting on found itself above the dead-end street of Paardeweg near Nieuwekerl, a village in the process at that very moment of crumbling street by street. The floor planks went shooting over a flooded network of ditches, eddies, and little bridges, which together were causing an angular momentum, not that powerful in and of itself but wide-reaching. The shaking of the raft doubled and redoubled, because there was no letup. Visibility was almost zero. Yet as Cornelius Jaeger rolled off the raft, Lidy saw it, and saw for the first time that the child was in fear. Eyes are fine lenses, they don't just capture light, they also emit it. As the boy lost his grip on the planks, he sent up a wordless plea for help with every ounce of will left in him. Lidy saw a pair of shiny green eyes, little facets, flat not curved, that contained nothing in the world that could be described as a look or an expression, just simply a signal that read Mayday, help . . . and indeed she literally flung herself forward.

Save him? Her? Action? To weigh this in a fraction of a second, in the belief that she was responsible for the suffering of the little hunchback? Not a moment later, she herself was thrown from the saddle.

Half water, half land. A hybrid of coastal vegetation that came from a bay on the north side of the polder of Sirjansland, part of which bordered the Grevelingen. The mat of reeds had already come an unimaginably long way. Lifted up and then helpfully supported by the flood, this mere line in the air had traveled ten miles to give three drowning people, Hocke, his mother, and Lidy, the feeling that they were crawling onto land. There is no need to remind anyone half drowned what that is. Land means territory, something in principle you can stretch out on. Even when it is saturated with sea and river water and the ever-thinning layer of silt. Formed by the North Sea, really no longer being held together by the roots underneath, you can drag yourself onto it, using your knees to work your way up, and feel you have reached dry ground. The old woman was more or less thrown onto it by a wave. Hocke and Lidy had to search for each other amid the floating wreckage of the storm, clutching then losing each other again among the cartons, branches, chests, sacks of potatoes, clothes, corpses, and bottles and finally just hoping for the best. The false island of reeds was still roughly seven feet by ten as it continued its journey. Lidy, very sleepy now, closed her eyes. The wind roared in her eardrums, the snow tasted of salt. Barely conscious, she knew that she and Hocke, wrapped in thick wet layers of fabric, made a single body. God, they were saved!

That had been an hour ago. But what is an hour when one is humbly embarked on the road to infinity? From now on, time, an element that is supposed to "pass," would be absolutely worthless to both of them. A pair of lovers. Enclosed by sky and sea. Two beautiful people, in fact. Each potentially widowed from the first moment they met. As a boy, Izak Hocke had always assumed that when the time came he would marry his great love. Thereafter he remained a bachelor for years. Was there such a girl anywhere? Lidy, on the other hand, had been madly in love two or three times, when her impatience—and, naturally, her ovulation—made a decision one day at the end of February 1950. What are they doing here, body against body? Lidy, a tall white child of the city underneath her dark clothes, and Hocke, a farmer?

They don't sleep, they're at least half-awake. He lies there, his nose in the hair of the last woman of his life. The wind is like a sword slicing over their heads, there is no question of any caresses between them. But does that imply the most cold and cynical way a man and a woman can be with each other, with a total lack of "I love you"? Their bed of reeds is beginning to calve dangerously, particularly on Hocke's side. Another moment or two, and they will interrupt their sentimental journey without much ceremony and go their separate ways. Lidy felt him from time to time pressed close against her back, and then for a time she wouldn't feel him at all. Holding fast to his will to live, nourishing herself on it, continuing to do so whether the end of days had arrived or not. Lidy kept her fingers interlaced with his; cramped with cold, there was nothing else she could do.

They should have stayed like that. As if someone had set a glass bell over the two of them and arranged things so that ordinary time ceased to exist underneath. The two bodies bedded in the reeds no longer looked like those of ordinary mortals. Rather, they resembled sleepers in a fairy tale, in suspended animation, sleeping on in their muddy, ooze-filled clothes, dreaming on, existing in a tempo all their own. Later, weary of this pathos that seemed already carved on a tombstone, they would stumble into time again. Or would they?

Meanwhile, time itself was not going to be stopped. Where there's time, there are tides; it was almost ten o'clock and this one was already moving fast. That the mat of reeds came apart, and the section that Izak Hocke was lying on was too fragile to stay afloat in the power of the undertow, was attributable, first and foremost, to the moon, which dictates a timetable of six hours of rising water and six hours of sinking. Hocke loosed his fingers from hers. He needed them in order to cling onto something else. It's ebb tide. Low water, a good thing, one would think, but in this case not. The water begins to try to find its way back to the sea through the opening in the dike. The flood turns and twists but is caught by the storm, which isn't running out of time, and keeps on blowing with a relentlessness unknown to anyone who has lived here even since childhood; the water goes on being replenished from the north and continues to pile up.

The small portion of the mat of reeds broke off and sank. Hocke drowned. He swam a few strokes, but very rapidly his muscles became too cold.

She didn't notice. As the reed island began to rock like crazy, she had thrown herself about and rolled away, because her inner command to herself was: Survive. She was caught and held by a soft figure crouched down like a hare, but still recognizable in the faint moonlight: the old woman. Who was looking over Lidy's shoulder with terrible concentration in her eyes. Oh God, had she now risen again as one star in another constellation of two? Each incomplete without the other. Daughter, look, over there in front of that backdrop of hell, your mother. Sunday evening, a quarter past eleven: Gerarda Hocke and Lidy Blaauw found themselves in a swirling current moving toward something that would later be called "the hole of Ouwerkerk," one of the largest breaches in what was originally the eighteen-foot-high dike of Oosterschelde.

They both felt it. Their mat was breaking up and more water was coming through on every side. As they were lifted on the crest of a wave and banged against a V-shaped double pylon reinforced by a crossbeam, the two women were immediately of one mind as to tactics. Up on their knees, they threw their arms around the rock-solid structure. In that moment, as the wave retreated again, they were able to pull themselves onto the crossbeam, where they could sit, suddenly a good three feet above the grip of the water. Thin cords whipped their faces. In the last moonlight that would shine through tonight, they saw that these were made of wire, torn telephone or electric cables. Lidy grabbed for them, wound them round the old woman's waist and shoulders, and tied her fast. The next hours reduced her to a creature that could only fight against sleep, struggling to keep her eyes open regardless of the utter darkness all around them.

Did she go to sleep? Or simply remove herself for a moment from the uncertainties of the present as a way of making the best of her situation? Without being able to remember them, she was completely in the spell of the hours that passed, filled with snatches of the howling songs of the wind. Until, suddenly coming back to life, she felt the water slopping over her knees. The tide and the weather were running their course and the next one was coming in.

Lidy managed to untie the old woman in the dark. Standing on the crossbeam, they both felt the water, with a temperature of 36 to 37 degrees Fahrenheit, come creeping up over their knees and hips. Lidy wasn't sure whether the high-pitched, mad singing that came from her right from time to time was real. The melodies, some familiar, some not, seemed intended to fix certain facts in her mind: the torso in her arms was going slack. Gerarda Hocke had lost the power to fight. But before she slid downward, she did manage to push two small objects into the other woman's hand. Lidy's fingers recognized the gold headdress clips. She shoved them into a coat pocket and realized that the old woman was no longer there. It would have been around three thirty in the morning when among all the flotsam and jetsam a door came sweeping past, within reach. Lidy was standing up to her shoulders in water, and she had to jump. In the attic of a farmhouse about to collapse, about a hundred yards away, a large family was still singing with all their might.

Lidy had not been particularly religiously brought up, but she loved songs, the more melancholy the better. So she carried the melodies of the psalms quite well in her head, and the words too, even if in fragments, and these words, as is often the case with songs too, when combined with the notes, come across as totally real, indeed believable. The family in the farmhouse had been singing psalms for hours, loudly, and intent on getting the words absolutely right. They were doomed, they probably knew as much, but were clinging to something beautiful, which might or might not be meaningless, but which they had built into their lives as a Given, to prevent themselves from being reduced to common clay. Lidy had managed to keep holding the dying old woman tight for a long time. During this interval, appropriately, given what was happening to the two of them, what had been echoing over in their direction, perversely but comfortingly, was "For he saves thee from the bird catcher's net. . . . The days of man are but grass . . . take up Thy shield and Thy weapons. . . ." The psalms of David, in the rhyming translations sanctioned in the eighteenth century by the ministers of Friesland, Gelderland, Zuid-Holland, Nord-Holland, Zeeland, Utrecht, Overijssel, and Drenthe.

So now she was on the door. A heavy, precious front door carried her along stretched out on her stomach. Monday had arrived some time ago. Monday morning, the second of February, 1953, between half past three and half past five. She kept her eyes open. She felt clear headed, focused, and full of memories. What does "forever" mean? Lidy remembered and would for the rest of her life remember the place where she was suddenly left totally to her own devices: an invisible place, although one with a faint blue glow circled by snatches of music that rose above the wind and came to her with the texts that had been sung so often in the course of time that they had become independent entities conveying no more than the quintessence of eternal longing.

It isn't far from the area around Ouwerkerk to the Oosterschelde. Nonetheless it took Lidy about an hour. The raft kept bumping into things, spun around, was carried westward, then east, or came up against some passing object, a chunk of a barn, a sluicekeeper's hut, a telephone pole, that came out of the black nothingness and disappeared back into it again. None of it bothered her. She seemed quite patient as she went into the last part of the night.

Thus it was that everything she still experienced was accompanied by the texts and nourished by them, as they echoed and reechoed in her head. "Take up Thy shield and Thy weapons . . ." Defiantly, shrilly sung verses that in no way decreased the howling of the wind, God knows, but acted as a commentary on it. A projectile slammed into her leg, she flinched in shock, but it didn't really hurt. Once she got a brief but absolutely clear look at the overpowered landscape around her, the dikes heaved this way and that, the remains of farmhouses from which loud cries for help still came here and there. Then she had to reach wildly for whatever was at hand.

She was there. A kind of waterfall was pulling the door downward, but miracle of miracles, she didn't fall underneath. The breach in the dike at Ouwerkerk was so huge that it could no longer be called a breach, there was simply no dike left. Half past six. The flood tide was still high, and the storm was still relentlessly driving the water from the north. Lidy lay half on her left side, her face on one arm, her legs spread, her feet turned to the side. Her little boat, with neither engine nor oars, obeying the current and the wind, was on direct course for the Oosterschelde, which leads straight into the North Sea. She was trembling uncontrollably, long past the point now where she could ask herself who she was, but still saying softly in her heart: "Here. I'm here!"

30

Ousted

It was one of those suddenly very cold December mornings that transport a country into a state of excitement, disbelief, good feelings. The weather reports for the beginning of the week had used words like "dry," "overcast," "mild," and had spoken of a moderate wind out of the southeast. The idea that the day begins with frozen water pipes and ice blooming on the windows of your car, which refuses to start, is therefore pretty far-fetched. Nadja and Armanda were in the train going from Amsterdam to Goes by way of Rotterdam and Bergen op Zoom. The rush hour was over, and the carriage wasn't that full. They sat in facing window seats, looking out at the patches of white and the quiet sky, an optical phenomenon that struck them both as having a remarkable affinity with the purpose of their journey. A funeral, but not of anything that could be understood as a dead person or even a dead body. After more than thirty years in silt, what remains of a human body is little more than some bones, two jaws, a skull. Armanda and Nadja stared out at the thin, fresh layer of snow, the result of a trough of pressure that had moved southward over the North Sea during the night, and let their conversation lapse for a while. Since Monday of the previous week they had known that Lidy—maybe—had been found.

Their shocking return to her trail, long abandoned, totally lost, had begun a month before. On the aforementioned Monday afternoon, Armanda had received a call from a representative of the local police, who asked her if he was speaking to Mrs. Brouwer. Within the hour a man in street clothes, with soft gray eyes and a sailor's beard, was sitting at her table. He informed her, wanted at least to give her the information, that they had first gone looking for Mr. Blaauw, then for the Brouwer family, who had once lived on Sarphati Park, but then quickly switched to the question that was burning in her eyes. Lidy Blaauw-Brouwer. Indeed. You would like me to tell you where?

A short silence. Another glance. In the mud near the Schelphoek, the construction site behind the secondary dike on the northwest bank of the Oosterschelde, right near where one of the three great river channels, the Hammen, drains into the estuary and where they've been building the gigantic flood barriers for years now—

She interrupted him. "How . . ."

He waited while she bent down to scratch a bone in her foot, then stared up at him, motionless.

"How is that possible?"

"You're right," he'd replied. "On the face of it, it's impossible." He seemed to be searching for the facts. "Totally impossible, so I've heard."

She leaned over the edge of the table, as if taking a first step toward this barely credible possibility, and waited. A backhoe was the first detail that she could get hold of, and then she had a mental image of the practical little Bobcat which a skilled operator can maneuver with real speed and agility. It had been in the middle of the previous month, one afternoon around five. But isn't it dark by then? It had been getting dark. And the skull that had been dug up had been stained very dark by the earth it had been in, all that silt and heavy clay and peat, too.

Her sister, if indeed it was her sister, must . . .

She made a gesture. A moment please.

"At five o'clock there's nobody still working on a building site, surely?"

The plainclothes policeman had looked at her thoughtfully, brought up short by her question, then he'd gone back to talking about the backhoe operator. Who had summoned a coworker still running around on the mudflats, the eerie area at the mouth of the Ooster-schelde, dug up and dug over for years now as they tried first one method, then another, to effectively block the arm of the sea. They used scoops to collect a few skeletal fragments, which they laid out together in the open air. Their workday was over, but they managed to find a construction foreman still in a trailer with a telephone. Shortly before total darkness fell, the national police came and put all the parts in a plastic sack and took them away, including a small, eroded piece of metal, some kind of hinge or spiral, possibly a clue, which had evidently, as was visible in the flashlit photo, been lying there too.

Yes. Exactly. Pause. Mutual appraisal. Then Armanda watched as the policeman removed a piece of paper from the little portfolio he had set down on the table as soon as he arrived. He unfolded it and pushed it between them in such a way that both of them could have read it if they so chose. The attorney general, Armanda understood, twisting her head sideways to stare at the sheet, which appeared to be a form letter, a typed report or some such, had given his authorization for the transportation of the body parts. Authorization, aha. Her eyes fixed on the paragraphs of type, she withdrew herself somewhat from a situation that on the one hand spoke of an end to a great and apparently insoluble riddle—whatever confusion might accompany it— and, on the other, phrases like "the judicial laboratory in Rijswijk, that usually requested Leiden's help in the business of attempting to make reliable identifications." She didn't look up again till her visitor said something that seemed to connect with the known world.

"Your sister, if it is indeed your sister, must have been buried in a layer of mud very quickly after she was washed ashore."

"Yes?"

Then came explanations to clarify that not one single person missing from 1953 had been found in the last ten, no, twenty years. "It's a real miracle, lady," hard to imagine just how fast a body disintegrates in water, particularly seawater, till there's absolute nothing left. "Five, six months at the most," depending on the factors involved. Armanda, who was maintaining an air of great interest but couldn't keep up with the dizzying speed with which thirty years were reduced to zero in a single blow, heard phrases like "low or high water temperatures," "polluted water," "crabs and crayfish," and "ships' propellers." There was no doubt that it was thanks to the mud and its capacity for preservation that so much of "your sister, possibly" had survived.

But not enough.

"Can you give me a photo of her to take with me?"

The policeman asked this after he had made a dome of his fingers before setting his hand down over the paper on the desk. Based entirely on the long bones and the pelvis, the hand went on, Leiden had decided that what was involved here was a female, twenty to twenty-five years old, height approximately five foot ten, probable date of death, 1953, since the cartilage had stopped thickening. Armanda was on her feet. Yes, just a moment, please . . . yes, a photo! A photo they could lay on those dark, cold long bones and that pelvis that are such good indicators of probable age! And wasn't it high time she should offer her guest a cup of tea?

She was already at the door when the policeman gave her one more instruction. It had to be a photo of Lidy laughing.

"Laughing," she said. "Yes, of course!"

Then she thought, Why?

The train was approaching Rotterdam. Nadja and Armanda got up, like most of the other passengers, put on their coats and gloves, and waited with their bags on their laps until the rattling over the points had ceased. On the platform, they were surprised all over again by the cold. They went to the departures board and saw that the express train to Vlissingen must already be standing at platform 10.

"So they couldn't say for sure," Nadja began, after they'd found an empty compartment at the back of the train and shut the door.

Words. Which gave them a certain sense of looking-things-straight-in-the-eye. The dubious identity of this dead person of theirs. Which not even the teeth in the photo of the young woman with the radiant laugh could change.

"So what did he actually say yesterday?" asked Nadja.

"The day before yesterday," said Armanda. Nadja nodded. "The day before yesterday, I went to"—she hesitated—"to collect the photo, for today."

This could be true. She saw Nadja nod again and nodded herself. She had gone to the police laboratory in Rijswijk to collect the photo that she was going to put secretly, even illegally in the eyes of officialdom, into the coffin with Lidy's bones or the bones of some twenty- to twenty-five-year-old farmer's wife from Zeeland. What a terrific idea, she thought, if she got the opportunity! In reality, she had done nothing two days ago other than speak to the pathologist. Why? Because. His expert report, even after seeing the photo, had remained on balance that "we cannot come to any definite conclusion."

"Oh, it was all so complicated. He said the process of ossification of the bone . . ."

They looked up—what did it mean? The door opened. New passengers were looking for seats, even though the train had been moving for some minutes. One was a little gray lady who sat down in the corner by the aisle, after slipping out from under the arm of the other person, a tall man who was loud in more ways than one.

"So, people," he said, rubbing his hands, after hanging up his coat, "the only problem we have left is when are they going to come round with the coffee?"

The gregariousness of a train trip in winter. The soft seats, and everything outside white, gray, cold. The little woman in the corner stared straight ahead like a resigned animal, but her companion was a man of alarming charisma. Within a quarter of an hour, before Dordrecht, even, Nadja and Armanda knew that he was an expert in hydrodynamics, that he worked with the authorities in "delta services," that he was getting out at Rilland-Bath, and all this interested them in a certain sense. Up to Zeeland, in the beat of the rattling click-clack of the train. Nothing there, none of it, is the way it was before the flood, said the hydrodynamics expert, take a good look as soon as we pass Bergen op Zoom. Were you there this summer? No. Oh, the whole country has made incredible profits from it in the last years. Acre after acre of landholdings, all looking exactly the same, all the way to the horizon, yes, dammit, and in the middle of each a brand-new farm, freestanding barns, drainage ditches in the distance straight as a die, roads surfaced with asphalt even out on the polders, a system of canals that reaches into every corner, and none of it has cost the province more than a cent. Pigs in the built-up area? Not one to be seen anymore!

He stopped talking and glanced at the little old woman in the corner, as if by accident, but she sat up and reacted.

"There once were beautiful old mulberry trees on Schouwen."

Spoken quietly, but with a remarkable solemnity that irritated the hydrodynamics man.

"Oh, be quiet! Nature, is it? Do you think people have no eyes to see, these days?" And he started talking about how wonderful the delta works were, and their beauty, the guts it had taken to build them, and all the money it had cost.

Armanda, seeing that Nadja was maintaining eye contact with the man, turned back to the window. A pale sun was standing twenty degrees above the southeastern horizon, with the train cutting through the winter landscape on a parallel track. Barns standing out against the snow. Branches trimmed. Shrouded in the typical frosty air that seemed to come streaming right into the compartment. Her mind was so clear that the conversation between Nadja and the hydrodynamics expert transmitted itself directly into her thoughts without troubling her. After about twenty minutes the rails curved westward at an almost ninety-degree angle. The train passed the Schelde-Rhein canal bridge and entered the land where Lidy had disappeared. A cold storage locker, a mortuary.

"Caissons with steel bars in all three sluice openings, cost per caisson eight hundred forty million guilders, construction time four years!"

"Wow."

"Then the commission had another thought about putting barriers in the Roompot eddy, and quays that the water can wash right over and feed into the Schaar and the Hammen. Cost: a billion!"

Yes, Armanda thought, at the end of the day, everything in this country is now linked forever to Lidy's epic.

The poor heroine. And dear God, is it actually her, finally, in the rosewood coffin Nadja and I ordered, in which—we felt it was the right thing—we also had them put that little metal thing that was brought up into the light of day along with the bones. When they examined it, it turned out to have been plated originally with twenty-four-carat gold. Does it belong? or . . . It could just have been lying in the earth there by total chance, with no connection, she'd asked them this in Rijswijk. Right, who could know such a thing? And the pin, which was part of the traditional costume of Noord-Beveland or Schouwen, remained, in a formal sense, an element in the Lidy Problem: to be identified or not to be identified? If only the teeth had been—

". . . twenty-six gigantic buttresses filled with an average of eight thousand cubic yards of cement. You should be thinking the Egyptian pyramids!"

—more complete!

Now she was staring out of the window the same way she'd once, when she was young, stared into the mirror. The goal of her journey was no longer visible. The landscape, Lidy's property, spread out and came closer and closer until it no longer consisted of anything but a gray background. Perfect for the illusion or vision that had haunted her regularly for half her life now: Lidy conscientiously unscrewing the cap on a little bottle of whitener and using the brush attached to the underside of the cap to whiten her tennis shoes, that are standing on a newspaper on the table in front of the high window. Location of the action is some grand house with flowering plasterwork on the ceiling, not number 77 and not number 36 but very similar. There's a dog sitting on the floor. It's snowing on the other side of the window. She herself, Armanda, is also present, though only in the form of a sense of unease, an extreme anxiety that now, at this moment of her journey, was so intense that as everything outside the window reverted to normal and became visible again, the horizon with its red misty glow, the telephone poles, the fences and chimneys, all looked to her like parts of some formula that she need only simplify in order to arrive at zero. Some things had never taken place. An entire family history really could correct itself if she only made the effort. She's the one, not Lidy, who begs her father for the car and sets off on a journey to Zierikzee . . . logical, fate's original intention. Why tease this beast so dangerously with a little plan, a little prank? The engine was slowing. A bell rang somewhere.

The hydrodynamics expert was already buttoning his coat. He stretched out his sturdy arms, took his traveling bag from the rack, and said good-bye. The door to the compartment banged shut, then was immediately pushed open again.

"The sluice here in the canal near Bath. On your way back, get off the train for a few minutes. The water falls freely, there's no pump involved, fantastic sight. No time? Why? Why? Well, as you wish!"

Armanda said good-bye to him again. Nadja rested her head on her folded arms on the little table by the window, eyes closed. Five minutes later the train stopped in Kruiningen, and even the little woman left her corner of the compartment.

The train continued slowly on its way.

Then, in a velvet stillness caused by a frozen overhead cable, it came to a halt in the middle of what were either meadows or fields. Armanda and Nadja, who'd lit up cigarettes, stared at each other. Pray God we get there in time. How much longer is it going to take? Then they talked about the state of Lidy's teeth. Twelve fillings. Amalgam. Single surface, two surfaces, and one with three surfaces in first molar, upper left, and another in first molar, upper right. An average set of teeth, very well taken care of, no X-rays ever required.

"Terrible shame," said Armanda. "He said X-rays would have been the one thing that would have made it still possible to . . ." She looked rather helplessly at Nadja.

"A classification," said Nadja, remembering the word from a phone conversation she'd had with Armanda a few days previously. The forensic anthropologist had tried to effect a classification, which is to say, a scientifically provable relation between the bodily remains found in the mud, which were identified for now only with a number, and a real person with a first and last name. The latter was already supplied with a whole series of distinguishing characteristics: sex, approximate age, anatomical build, all investigated meantime and had light shed on them. The approximate date of death together with the location of the remains had naturally led automatically to the Red Cross list of thirty years ago, which still showed the names of 839 missing persons.

"Mama," said Nadja.

"Yes?"

"Do you really think it's her?"

Armanda, suddenly deeply upset, looked at her wrist, then at her watch.

"I've dreamed about it for two nights now," Nadja went on, "very intense, very insistent dreams, that it's the other one, that missing farmer's wife from . . . from?"

"Burgh," said Armanda, in a murmur, because Burgh no longer

seemed relevant to her. Having received the same details from the Red Cross, the family there had refused to accept the corpse, rejecting it on the grounds of inadequate facts and in particular because of the jewelry, which had never been part of their traditional costume.

"But it could have turned up in the ground there totally by chance, with no other connection!" Armanda had held this up as a possibility once again on her visit to Rijswijk, eliciting a rather pleading look from the pathologist who was talking to her and answering her questions.

A man of about fifty. Sitting at a desk, tree outside the window. He acknowledged her with a smile, and then stayed with the results of the expert report. The unknown woman and the missing woman could be one and the same; but with certainty—no. Absolutely not.

Armanda had looked down to see the photo of Lidy laughing antemortem on the desk. She had reached out her hand and asked what they'd hoped to achieve with the picture. A definitive conclusion, she was told, to the accompaniment of a look that was shattering in its warmheartedness and was maintained for the duration of the discussion that followed. The unknown victim's teeth were, as he believed she knew, very incomplete, but the alveoli had shown how the teeth had originally been positioned.

She had propped an elbow on the desk and stared at the doctor with her fist against her nose.

"If for example the photo had shown that there was a space between her front teeth, we would have been able to say for sure it isn't her."

At this point she'd had a coughing fit, and the doctor had fetched her a glass of water. From this moment on, his appearance merged in her memory with that of the policeman who had come to her house, honest gray eyes, sailor's beard trimmed short. When she stopped coughing, she had asked, possibly with the help of the tears in her eyes, how drowning actually happens, and how bad it is. She learned in the course of a very long conversation that there are different ways of drowning, in some of which inhaling water is involved, but certainly not always, that if water is inhaled, it doesn't mean there's difficulty breathing, because, for example, the victim may already be unconscious, and most important, when there is severe loss of body heat, which is to be assumed in this case, actual death is preceded by suspended animation, a form of slumber that can last for some time and in the course of which the process of metabolism in the brain slows down almost to zero.

So, Armanda asked, is it a peaceful death?

"Yes. Absolutely peaceful."

The bus that went to Zierikzee by way of the mile-long Zeeland Bridge carried only a handful of passengers. Up front was a group of lounging youths who had left school early, and at the back were the two women who had got in at the train station at Goes, on their way to a burial in Ouwerkerk that had required them to get a special dispensation from the attorney general. Human remains, if discovered in Westerschouwen, must also be buried in Westerschouwen in the absence of verifiable relatives. It's a requirement of the law regarding burials, because such cases make the local mayor responsible for the costs. The two women sat close together and silent, looking out of the window. They were each wearing a dark coat with a colorful shawl. Despite the first signs of plumpness, the elder of the two, with her loose dark brown hair and a fringe, still looked quite young. The age difference between her and the other one, red-haired, fine-boned, and very pale, didn't seem that great. Yet the two of them were surrounded with the aura of indefinable calm of a mother and daughter who knew that their lives, in whatever fashion, are intertwined.

Armanda and Nadja, crossing the Oosterschelde.

It was half past one in the afternoon, and the winter sun was casting an almost colorless light on the water, which was still open, still a direct conduit to the North Sea. In two years' time the work on the flood defenses in the estuary of this arm of the sea would finally be finished. Linked metal barriers of extraordinary dimensions could then be let down in those rare instances when the height of the water beyond exceeded the level on the depth gauge that triggered the alarm; this would protect the land, which needed the flow of the tides, and block it off briefly from the sea. Armanda and Nadja looked at the expanse of water shining glassily in a framework of nothingness. They were fascinated.

"Remember we should buy flowers in Zierikzee," said Nadja. "We certainly won't find any in Ouwerkerk."

The bus stopped in the center of Zierikzee, where the shops were still closed for midday. Armanda and Nadja ate a snack in a café while keeping an eye on the plants in the shop window on the other side of the street.

"We'll make it," said Armanda.

They had agreed with the undertaker that they would be there at the cemetery when the hearse arrived at three o'clock with the coffin.

"Look, they're opening," said Nadja, and stopped eating.

There weren't many fresh flowers in weather like this. Armanda and Nadja bought chrysanthemums and had some twigs of eucalyptus and sprays of evergreens tucked in with them, rather reminiscent of Christmas.

"Might we perhaps make a quick call for a taxi?" Armanda asked the shop owner.

They drove out of town in the back of the taxi, the flowers on their knees. Here too the fields stretched away, all at perfect right angles to the horizon. The trees lining the road were still small. They looked at them, dreaming of the truth and pondering what it meant. Armanda was conscious that Nadja, who was leaning against her, viewed the entire enterprise as a kind of serious farce, since she didn't know who her mother was, but found this posthumous adoption of a dead farmer's wife totally okay. She herself was holding tight to Lidy. So much so, in fact, that at a certain point the empty black and white countryside seemed to deliver its own proof: Far too much of you has accumulated in me, Lidy. Because of you, I could never become the person I was. The taxi turned left into the village, which was made up in its entirety of new, modern houses.

The entrance gates to the cemetery were a wrought-iron monstrosity between two pillars, each of which bore a sculpture of angels' wings. Armanda recognized them from the ceremony of mourning years before, when the region had reburied all its flood victims in a single service. The graveyard in the plain, which was still open to the sea dike, looked very well tended now. Armanda and Nadja walked to the middle section of the burial ground with all the simple, identical graves that would never be moved because they had been declared a monument. They saw that the fifteen-by twenty-inch gray gravestone was already standing next to the mound of earth, covered with a thin layer of snow. It had already been explained to Armanda that nothing on it could be altered: her claiming of the bones was acceptable to the state, her putting of Lidy's name to them was also acceptable in principle, but the stone, like the three others here, must remain blank. It wasn't long before the hearse arrived. Armanda and Nadja walked back to the road.

"Can you open the lid again for a moment?" Armanda asked the undertaker, as soon as he and his assistant had pushed the full-sized coffin out of the car and set it on a bier on wheels.

And with a nod of her head, she showed him the photo of Lidy.

The undertaker took it out of her hand, looked from the laughing Lidy to Armanda, and then from under the brim of his black silk hat at the row of apartment buildings on the other side of the street.

"It's totally against regulations," he said in a tone that meant "Well, okay."

The sun went in behind the low-hanging clouds as the little procession moved to the middle section of the graveyard. Once there, the undertaker used a flat chisel on the coffin to raise the lid a fraction, which happened quite easily. As Armanda pushed the photo inside, she managed a quick searching look, but all she saw was the soft, dark cloth that had been used to wrap the skull and the bones, so that they wouldn't roll around. The coffin, light as a feather, was lowered skillfully into the grave with the help of straps. Armanda and Nadja each threw a shovelful of sand down onto it. Immediately afterward the grave of the anonymous woman was filled in.

The hearse left.

Armanda and Nadja stood for a few minutes in the silence. They looked out over the stone and the chrysanthemums to the land, bordered in the distance by the sea dike, and then they too left. Armanda had wondered briefly if it was possible when the wind was in the right direction to hear the sea from here. The temperature was already dropping again. A moderate frost was forecast for tonight, but an area of low pressure over Scotland, starting tomorrow, would bring milder air, with rain and wind.

V

Responsorium

As the storm drives the clouds
Where the sea has no coasts that remain
And the heavens have consumed all their stars
The wind of my thoughts
Blows through the empty cavern of my soul.
They encounter no further resistance,
They crowd and they pile—then they are gone.

—J. J. Slauerhoff

"How's it going?"

"Oh, I had a terrible scene with one of the nurses here, the woman wanted to stick me under the shower, but I hung onto the bathroom door with everything I'd got. It happens. Now everything's quiet again. Out there, down below, the streetcar clanks by, you know, the number three, it goes to the Concertgebouw in one direction and Amsterdam East in the other. Just recently they moved me up to the top floor. The door to the corridor and the elevator is always locked, most of the people sitting here are too out of it to be able to give you their own names or write them down if you ask them. I think it's still morning. We have 'recreation' this afternoon. The staff is absolutely obsessed with the expression."

"You look a little shaky."

"Not surprising if you're spending twenty-four hours a day collecting your thoughts. I'm guessing what you're doing right now is looking at the room I'm in, with its fresh paint, and two windows that look north, two cupboards, two chairs, a table, a bed, and a blue velour sofa, which they keep telling me, no idea why, is the sofa from home. *From home*, they said at the beginning every time they came in, and gave me pregnant looks. Go on, sit down on it. Okay, then, I will, but personally I don't believe a word of it. When I took a sniff at the seat, I could smell old food and cigar butts, the smell of decline. Maybe it's because of that smell, or maybe it's also all the changes in the weather we've been having recently, or all the hours I spend sound asleep, but I sit on the couch without budging and regularly ask myself what life actually is."

"Yeah. No one has the answer to that one."

"All this sorrow, all these little worries, all these desires. When we go to the dining room at noon and we all sit down at those long tables, almost everyone keeps their heads down, we're serious and quiet, the people next to me hardly say a thing, but when the food carts are brought in, we all look up like prisoners in a penal colony who've just been pardoned. I give an absentminded smile as I lift the lid off the food tray, divided up into compartments, when it's set down in front of me. My mouth's all dry, but it responds automatically, I don't mind, my whole body says yes, but what's the point? Where does it come from, this morbid appetite, maybe it's just a desire to keep my footing on the very last step before I trip and fall into the grave?"

"You're in a really grouchy mood, aren't you?"

"Grouchy, grouchy, I sit, I look out the window, I eat. I grant you, I still love the smell of bread. I know it's a treacherous feeling, but I do still find reality attractive. Down on the first floor, in the entrance hall, there's a wooden bench along the wall next to the swing doors. When I sit there sometimes in the afternoon for a little bit, shoulder to shoulder with my fellow inmates and fellow sufferers, I feel as weary and as dull as the toothless old guys in a shady little square somewhere in Spain."

"Sounds familiar. And that blue sofa stood for years in the room at the end of the little staircase to the mezzanine."

"Really? Well, I guess that must be right."

"Yes. And at the top of the back, there by the wall there was a lamp with two shades made of wavy orange-red frosted glass, that didn't really go with it, but were perfect when you wanted to submerge yourself for hours in Russian and French novels, which we often did. Next to it were those low doors to the second, smaller, balcony at the back of our house, which we used to go out onto at night and listen to the nearby gunfire in the last winter of the war. You were twelve, I was fourteen, we were both incredibly skinny, and one night we slipped through the railing on the balcony like cats and dropped down into the garden, a pothole or two, a couple of hedges, and we were in a side alley. I'm certain that from the moment we climbed back up about an hour later, we were obsessed for days with the same question, though we never said it out loud to each other. You never ask anyone else the real questions. We'd found a man in a narrow street lined with high, straight houses, he'd been shot, he was lying on his back, and we decided to keep going. A city where the shops and buildings are half in ruins looks much softer at night than it does during the day. In the Eerste Sweelinckstraat there was a doorway and a couple necking in it. We could see that the man wanted more than the woman was willing to give. My God, the despair in the way he was clutching the girl to him with such force, you'd have thought he only had a matter of hours left in his life to do it. Is that, is that what our salvation depends on? We stood stock still and gaped at them like frogs, then headed back to bed in what pitiful starlight there was. You wanted to stick your half-frozen feet into the backs of my knees."

"And was I allowed to?"

"Of course. You were also allowed to put your arms round me. Oh, what bags of bones we were back then. It was a miracle we ever got enough calories to keep our little body heats up to ninety-eight point six."

"Okay, so that means life equals warmth, and the all-consuming struggle to keep one's temperature up. The chief cook here seems to feel that's best done with boiled and roasted potatoes and proper cutlets seasoned with thyme, and he gets money for it from the inmates. We also manage to get tulip bulb syrup from him. Excuse me for only asking now, but I promise you, it's a question I've been asking myself forever: Are you cold?"

"You could say that, yes. Terribly, actually, but at a certain point it just stops mattering."

"Really?"

"Really. I move around under the surface of the water now, which is much more comfortable than being above the surface on some wretched raft. It's crazy: as long as you're hanging onto a piece of wood, you also keep hanging onto your questions about life, no matter how cold and insignificant they've become. Just let go, for God's sake, and then you'll also be free of the last issues too, and of the raging as well, of course, and roaring thunder all around you that really got on your nerves after two solid days, and in a sense is still roaring to this day. The storm has become part of me, its gusts are my memories. My entire self is rooted in the difference in pressure between a low over the North Sea and another west of Ireland. Experience has taught me: in the end you're really not yourself anymore, you only consist of what's around you. It's ebb tide. The scale of the water level in the Oosterschelde is causing an incredible undertow in the direction of the North Sea. It's quite unusual for me to find myself here in the vortex north of the Roggenplaat, while four or five of the other cases who ended up like me in the open sea beyond Ouwerkerk were washed ashore near Colijnsplaat on Noord-Beveland."

"Can you see anything?"

"I'm tired and I'm old. No, stop shaking your head. I have wrinkles all over my body, my lips are cracked, my bones are plagued by the wet and the cold, I assume you can imagine this, have a sense of it. And moreover, if you've had an unusually intense life, you no longer need your eyes to perceive things. A ship's horn sounds. They've seen one of my beloved companions floating facedown and they're using a boat hook to neatly fish him out. Oh my love, just rest in peace, maybe you know I came only to visit, but then, as you can see, I stayed. The things we went through! In the blue twilight I can see the faces of my nearest and dearest, their teeth are chattering furiously, but apart from that they're looking at me quite cheerfully. If we'd been granted the privilege to sit next to one another on a bench back then, we would certainly have done so."

"Oh, Jesus!"

"What is it?"

"A stabbing pain in my side. I've been having all sorts of bodily complaints recently—that's what they call the pains and the exhaustion here. And after meals I sometimes get nosebleeds without any warning at all."

"They won't kill you."

"Yes they will! Just wait! I'm dying!"

"I can hear you trying not to laugh."

"I wish. I'm rubbing my lower back with both hands, the life force is about to escape, it's old and dark and wild as a boar. Well, I've really had enough of breathing. My lungs have done more than enough pumping. How I've envied my big sister these last years for her water-logged lungs! And admired her fate! While I myself in the meantime have just been continuing the whole ceremony, created by God to live, rather than live through things, that heroic version of spending the time assigned to you. All the idiotic moves I made along the way, a sort of spastic dance now that I look back on it, all that walking, sitting, kneeling, bending, stretching, putting things down, picking them back up again, putting them down again, picking them up again. I think I was always more of an activities-oriented person than, for example, a good person, let alone a noble one. Now what I'd really like to be is light, as light and free as eternity. I'd even like not to comb my hair except when I really felt like it. I would also like to have the permission of the authorities to wear my support stockings, my skirt, and my wool jacket the whole time and never take them off. Come on, let's have a glass of port. There are still days sometimes when I'm absolutely compulsive about needing to go somewhere, but as soon as the nurse on duty talks me out of it, I'm as quiet as a lamb."

"How did *you* find him in bed?"

"Please!"

"Well?"

"Listen, I slept like a dog last night because someone was dying in the room next door. Running and thumping about on the other side of the wall, as if a fistfight was going on, I don't understand why the party has to end like that. And now, when they've obviously removed the troublemaker and everything's back to normal, you drop a bomb-shell like this. It's a dark day, the weatherman pointed out little white clouds with snow and hail showers and told us they're coming from Iceland. What do you think? My memory is obstinate these days, it doesn't like releasing its load. It all comes out backward and at an angle. I wish you'd just leave me in peace. I still turn red when anyone mentions him. You know, I take it, that he left me?"

"Yes, who the hell would have thought it!"

"Not you, nobody would argue with that, but deep down I never trusted the whole thing for a second. He and Mrs. Blaauw the Third

supposedly are back living here in the city again. An old married couple, and I imagine them living in retirement in some comfortable
apartment on the other side of the Amstel. While we were still
together, your husband and I, you could see his pleasure sometimes
when he watched the sunset and the red glow of its rays as they spread
across the houses. A man out of some myth, so tall, with those muscular arms and the tiny blond hairs on them. God, I was so happy
with him! It began to happen frequently that he would come home
later than I had expected. There would be this half hour or even an
hour of anticipation, crowned with the sight of his car slowly cruising
past the window looking for a parking spot, there he is! What? Oh
yes, two, a son and a daughter. They're doing well, but they don't
have much time to take care of me, they both live abroad. Children
are the best thing, the most important thing in life, we're part of the
post-Enlightenment West but no different in this regard from someone still living in Stone Age Papua, who absolutely knows that his
family will go on stamping and yelling in primeval fashion to let him
keep sharing in their wonderful sheer *existence* even after his death.
Yes, they call me regularly. When I hear my children's voices, I think
it's wonderful, and when the conversation's over, I think that's just
fine too. I keep listening to the dial tone in my ear for a moment, or I
go to the window and look down to the street. I conclude that worry
can make you heavyhearted, and so can its opposite."

"How's Nadja?"

"Wait a moment, I think . . ."

"What is it?"

"Oh, I thought there was a knock at the door. I thought someone
was coming to vacuum or empty the wastepaper basket. There's so
much to do here. Every week a young man comes to clean the windows. He takes the flowerpots off the windowsill, they're blue Alpine
violets, and puts them on the table, where they immediately start to
give off their scent. Odd, the way they refuse to do so normally. He's
a very nice young man. He cleans the windows and scrubs for me.
Because he knows I see no reason for a conversation, he suggested
recently that he just turn on the radio. He hadn't even touched the
thing before a loud male voice was filling my room with talk about
how both his father and his grandfather had led strikes and the entire

harbor was going to be idle next Tuesday. Yes, I thought, yes of course, life means action, and I watch the boy reach for the bucket with such an absurdly, movingly intelligent expression, in order to go to the bathroom and fill it with water. I kept my own face neutral. My eyes are turned inward. The stage is empty and the lighting terrible, but now and then a shocked figure appears. I look at it blankly. Nadja . . ."

"Yes?"

"Oh, you know, basically it's always remained inexplicable. But inexplicable doesn't mean, according to people who know that sort of thing, that it doesn't happen quite often. The goal of life, which everyone makes such a big deal out of, seems to be totally irrelevant when it comes to the actual impetus that keeps the whole thing going—it must be some terrifying sort of egoism, pure willpower, that can occasionally dump the whole mess at your feet. Nadja asked for a glass of water, and someone, a lonely lady sitting on a bench with a book, so they told me, went into a pub and got it for her. She had no heart trouble, at least nothing pathological, the autopsy established that. Strange, yes. The local doctor, lacking her medical history, couldn't issue a death certificate. Nadja had driven her car to the center of the village. No, not for a long time, although she quite often came to Amsterdam while Mother was still alive. Next to her on the front seat was a folded newspaper, half read. As the traffic barriers came down and she had to stop, she may have glanced at it, but I find it unthinkable that a list of performances and events for music, art, and film could be the cause of a sudden fatal heart attack, *mors subita*, no matter how sensitive the victim was. So, to cut a long story short, the barriers went up again and the traffic moved on at a moderate pace. Suddenly I find myself wondering what novel the lady may have been reading as Nadja got out shakily and everyone behind her began to honk their horns, because they were still stopped on the train tracks. This line runs right through the village, it's a much-traveled stretch, at any moment the warning signal could sound again. And the lady was reading, undistracted, under her tree, completely transported, wonderful. You don't have to act, yet you still experience everything, you don't have to speak, yet you converse with amazingly intelligent partners on your own level, and if you don't know how to love and to flirt, well, you know now. Oh dear old Lidy, the sea-green screen between us has become completely transparent meantime. With one of us pedaling the bike and the other on the carrier, we race along the canal in the watery dusk. There's no wind, all the flags are hanging slack on their poles. Does it still matter who read which book? Who lent the other which pullover, who inherited a child and a husband from whom? In cases of sudden death, the assumption is that some emotional distress unconnected with the immediate sur-roundings simply stopped the muscles of the heart."

"Dear God, Manja, does such a thing really happen?"

"Apparently yes. Inner factors sometimes succeed in completely hollowing out the psyche undetected, and then . . . you're suddenly gone. Do you know how much the heart of an adult woman weighs?"

"Well?"

"They check it during the autopsy, they weigh the heart."

"Heavens! The scales, the pans of the scale, *the weighing of souls*!"

"It weighed twelve ounces, which is normal. You know, don't you, that Nadja, who was widowed, was in love again, and didn't want to talk about it to anyone—nor was she allowed to. So I don't need to tell you what was involved, of course: a secret, adultery, hopeless. There came a time when she started to look pale, but was not audibly or visibly suffering. God preserve us, she may have thought, from the person who spends so much time pitying themselves that the whole world has to know about it. What was noticeable, however, during this period was that she went almost every day to the long-term-care section of Tabitha House, yes, here, where I am now, to visit her grandma, our crumpled, demented little mother, now almost ninety-three. If you've been bound to silence, you can still use an incomprehensible oracle to have dialogues with. Once when I asked her—looking all sympathetic the way an insider does—how Grandma was, she reported: 'Oh, fine, we listened to a Schubert sonata to-gether.' It must have been about two months after the death of our little mother, previously known as our mother, that Nadja also crossed over and pulled the drawbridge up after her."

"She was so sweet."

"Oh God, wasn't she!"

"So unself-aware. Once I went with her to a place that sold children's clothes, where she was to try on a winter coat with teddy bears embroidered on it. She could already stand by then. The saleswoman sat her up on a chest of drawers, all jammed up in the thick, stiff coat that made her arms stand out like a penguin's, and she gave me a blank look of such force that it silenced every piece of nonsense in my head. That winter she caught pseudo-croup, and Sjoerd and I were sure she was going to die, because she couldn't inhale anymore."

"I think you're wrong. It wasn't that winter, it was two or three winters later. But it's true, we were scared to death. In those days in Amsterdam if you called a doctor in the middle of the night in a panic, he actually came, those were men—"

"They certainly were."

"—who didn't just keep the phone within reach of the bed but their shoes and socks too. 'Of course she won't die.' He picked up the little girl, the favorite of my children forever, took her into the bathroom, and ordered us to turn on the hot tap. And I'm telling you, the steam made the swelling in her throat go down immediately, her air passages were open again, and in a flash she was back to breathing normally. Sjoerd and I lay next to each other in the darkness afterward, deeply impressed by how narrow the dividing line is between helplessness and a wonderful, warm bed. I stretched out my hand. My sister's husband, I could feel it, isn't going to be able to go to sleep yet, maybe he's thinking about God and marveling at the compositional gift that He exercises when He sets life and death not one behind the other but side by side. In the morning, when I woke up, he was way over on the other side of the bed."

"We always slept in each other's arms."

"Oh, mostly we did too."

"Oh, oh, oh, we were so in love with each other! Love at first sight, colon, with this one, quote unquote. No power in the world could have aroused me like that for any other reason. Oh, that mad, grand, heathen 'yes!' That bow to nature, pure and simple!"

"Yes, and its trump card at a most particular moment is the indivisible First Person Plural. He was a horny man, wasn't he? Always ready, even when the circumstances, physically speaking, weren't exactly ideal. Advanced pregnancy, raging hangover, once the two of us had a real flu . . ."

"Well, speaking for myself, I had good experiences with the flu. There's no better aphrodisiac than one or two degrees of fever, damp sheets, and a red-hot pillow. 'I've brought thyme syrup and a bottle of champagne,' he said once, when I'd spent quite a while in bed waiting for a solicitous husband, and he crawled in with me under the covers, shivering slightly, with aching joints, swollen membranes, and a raw throat."

"The sun shone through the bedroom window, the top half of which was made of lead glass and colored everything around us cinnabar red. Free-hanging tendrils of black ivy swayed in the breeze outside the windowpanes."

"But the craziest thing I remember is when he had his traffic accident. Right-of-way ignored when turning left from the Amstel to the Berlage Bridge. 'Come here, lie down close for a moment, I'm so cold from the sheer fright.' He pushed back the covers and I couldn't understand how he had managed all three flights of stairs on his own or how the ambulance crew from Onze Lieve Vrouwe Gasthuis could have let him go. I took off my clothes and lay down, being careful of the blue-purple bruises on his hips; there was a big, white, unbelievably imposing bandage round his knee. It makes you feel quite instinctively guilty. And why wasn't I at home when he was delivered by a taxi, so wounded and pathetic, and rang his own front doorbell? Soon my hand wasn't the only thing that disappeared under the covers—my head did too. I wanted to do something, anything at all. That's just the way it is, isn't it? Something, blindly, no matter what, it's our way of rebelling against the outrage of our human powerlessness. I kissed all his grazed and swollen places and reached out my hand—"

"The way every woman does automatically."

"—for that particular living swelling in the middle, to check the state of my husband's faith in the world. So, I was holding my husband's rudder and we were already heading for the sluice, when at a certain point I became uneasy. Shouldn't I look to see what the patient's moans were signifying? I slid back out, and his eyes lit up. 'I know what you like best is you underneath and me on top,' his eyes said. My eyes answered: 'That's right.' He: 'But you can see that's not going to work right now.' What, Armanda? Oh. What then? That his half-closed eyes actually flashed, from the bottom of his heart: 'You're the only desirable woman in the world, and I'm not going to change my opinion for the rest of my life, even if they put me on the rack?' Also good. So, in brief, I made the well-known bridge over him. In the spell of some secret, guilty delight, I began to pleasure him in the most exquisite way, using the muscles inside me. Oh God, that was love! If I shut my eyes, all I saw was flashes of light, and if I opened them again I saw him lying there keeping hold of himself, and I realized there was no distinction between his pain, his enjoyment, and my bliss. I was shocked by my feelings for him. Sjoerd was a man it was usually very easy to satisfy."

"You don't need to tell me! For example, if you put a wonderful dish on the table, cod, slices of potato, rice, dill, and mustard, he would look at you with a surprised look that said 'How did you guess what I've been wanting all day?' "

"But this time, I don't know, he wanted some absolutely special effort from me, and believe me, I gave him that pleasure. Movements can take seconds, then minutes to build toward something that you know is coming with absolute certainty. The question, in which you want to the best of your capacity to retain the upper hand, is quite simple: when? When my husband and yours reached that point on this particular day, I was glad that our bedroom was up on the top floor of the house, in the soundproof attic; the roof didn't touch the neighbors', because they were hipped roofs and each sloped up into a cone."

"How old are you now?"

"Me? Not that old, I think. Don't ask me to tell you exactly. You know, in some people, the decline sets in quite early. Years ago, I was walking down the street and I looked at my feet. I saw them quite clearly, one little boot in front of the other, making their way along a pavement of rectangular flagstones, yet I had absolutely no awareness that I was going anywhere. That's it, I thought, I have no sense of speed anymore, the needle's on zero, the world is going backward exactly as fast as I'm trying to go forward. That evening I called my children and asked them to tell me straight when they began to notice

I was in the process of going senile. They promised, because what I was saying, implicitly, was that when that happened, I would take my own measures."

"But they didn't."

"Of course not. Telling you straight is only okay when there's no reason yet to have to do it. Otherwise it would be so heartless, wouldn't it, and so hateful? Looking a little confused now and then, forgetting a name here and there, it happens to everybody. But start laughing to yourself when you're alone and refusing to explain why, pretend you're hard of hearing, lock yourself in, fail to turn off the gas, go wandering through town in your pajamas and dressing gown and be unable to find your way home again, and your children will most certainly stop saying, 'Mama, we think it's reached that point.' "

"Oh, what does it matter!"

"That's what I think too. Nicely locked up in a warm building, and unable to go forward anymore, I look back. I am Armanda, the sister of a woman who was very young when she drove away one morning from a happy home and sadly never came back. Since that time she lives inside me. Do you believe that I soon gave up my favorite licorice and started eating cream fondants? Good, so, when I was twenty-eight and then thirty, I enlarged my sister's family, which had consisted until then of a husband, a wife, and a little daughter, with an additional daughter and a son. When the marriage collapsed, the world, to my astonishment, continued to follow its set habits. Action, place of action, dialogue, and protagonists remained in the absolute control of my sister. To give you an example, Lidy, take the lovers who surfaced from time to time after my divorce. As regards my sainted sister, and considering that she would have known how much more easygoing life in the Netherlands had become, would they have been accepted by her? The true nature of the sister of my sister remained: her. I maintain that the only person who ever really knew me was Sjoerd, and you, Lidy, have the absolute right to feel offended that he drew a line at our ménage-à-trois. I'm sorry, but I obviously didn't manage your husband very well."

"Oh, sweetheart, we're both only human. I don't blame you for anything. But why do you keep yawning?"

"Because I prefer to spend the day like a sleepless night. The waking hours of someone who's constitutionally sleepy are dreamless and dull, like the back side of the moon. Nevertheless my mythic sister still manages to come floating through in the guise of three dead cows or something. Hello, Lidy. How did you get into this sodden chaos again? I know there are mean tricks that can never be put right again."

"I was just wild about the idea of driving a car again, you don't forget how so easily."

"Liar."

"No-o."

"Ye-es. Oh, you don't have to tell me about memory. Just when you've lost it is when you recognize how astonishing it is. The memory of someone who at some point allowed themselves to play a joke that went completely wrong works completely differently from the memory of some lucky devil who managed always to be good and behave well. I know how to treasure your magnanimous thoughts. It's a performance I've been giving for a long time now. Oh, how you wanted to go on that weekend expedition, which was supposed to be an invitation to me—except you didn't. The most important tool of memory is the ability to forget. Remember a phone conversation, even remember part of the actual dialogue, but to keep things simple, forget who proposed what and who in a whisper begged, 'Oh, please!' The thing about forgetting that's piquant is that nine times out of ten it's not forgetting at all, simply a cut that allows you to insert something. Who in God's name wants to get lost time back, uncut? I'm old. My eyes are bad, my ears too, I stand absolutely helpless in the flow of time. But at the very last moment a motive I'd forgotten all about reenters the story. It was a kiss, Lidy, no more than that, but on pain of death, no less than that either. A hot, open kiss, a feeling of fire that I'd never encountered before in all my nineteen years, has reappeared in front of my eyes, through the thicket of years, out of the oblivion in which it had been buried. The scene was the wall under the fire escape of the Nausicaä, a dismal, dilapidated student dormitory in the Zwarte Handsteeg, where a party was going on. The time was night. The protagonists were Sjoerd, in an exceptionally resolute role—he must have worked out the whole kiss and had it ready—and your sister, Armanda, who lost the plot just at the moment when her opposite number wanted to get under her skirt, because an angry-looking guy appeared in this garbage-strewn, film-noirish inner courtyard, walking his dog. I wanted to get the kiss back, Lidy, I wanted to have it forever, in my heart. . . ."

"Well, it's not important."

"Weak. Your voice sounds weak, because you know, you absolutely know, that I spent that Monday evening pacing around my room, torturing myself with the desire to come clean about the damn kiss. One step, another step, then another, on and on. Till I'd reached the magic goal of my journey, my woman's will, and, I have to add, the center of the person I am deep in my heart, in my own opinion. I went to the telephone in the upper hall. That was me. Don't take it badly that I'm going into this with such detail, but really, I was the one who made the call and I've been horribly conscious of that my whole life long. It comes in moments that are like being jolted with a brief electric shock, and then before you can deal with them, they're gone again. Maybe you couldn't see my persuasive smile, but you could certainly hear it. You could understand my chatter and my whispers, on that Monday there wasn't yet the slightest breath of a northwest wind to drown out anything. Wonderfully precocious little wife and mother, *just listen*, is what you heard? God, you really fought back. 'Huh? What are you talking about? I don't think I feel like it, thanks.' I had to make a big effort to persuade young Mrs. Blaauw to flee the everyday grind for once. That's what happened, and alas there's no act of penance that can undo the basic maliciousness of the facts. The despicable plan crossed my path, I seized it on tiptoe, you have every right to be angry. Meantime I stand on the top floor of Tabitha House and look out like a ghost. There's an old, bare elm in front of the house on the other side of the street, and in its branches is a whole swarm of parrots, there must be ten of them, they never stop talking. Strange. I think I'll lie down now and have a doze."

"No-o . . ."

.   .   .

"Are you still there?"

"Ye-es!"

"Your voice sounds so light, Lidy, and so interested, as if you really want to know how I'm faring here."

"Yes, well, must be because I was dreaming that the two of us were taking a walk on Sunday to the water tower. There were botanic gardens for plant trials on the other side of the bridge back then, hidden behind a wall. The early sun was tinting the sky above them to a pinkish mother-of-pearl color like the inside of a seashell."

"That isn't a dream, that really happened. We were still little children. But *can* you dream while you're drowning?"

"And how. In fact, it's all you do. In the dream you're calling life, we went through the grass past the houseboats, looked at the wall on the opposite bank, and felt a pleasant, eventful sort of homesick feeling. Homesickness mostly starts when you're in the open, and then a wall is always really helpful. We got to talking about eternity, endlessness, and from there we automatically got into the God problem, you simply didn't understand why the most rational people made such a song and dance about it. You stood still, to pull up one of your white kneesocks, which was all wet through—the grass was wet, it had been raining—you were thinking, and you murmured to yourself, why couldn't there be some Being that spanned everything and guided it? Your little red patent-leather purse slipped down off your shoulder. 'I don't see why that should be so inconvenient,' you said, and hung the purse, which had nothing in it, back round your shoulder. 'Me neither,' I said. You were quiet. I could see your nose and mouth tensing. 'Why can't I read *Netteke Takes a Cure*?' you asked finally, looking at me. 'You know you're not allowed,' I replied, and named the name of a friend I hung around, not a real friend, a girl who granted me her dubious and always a little tormenting favors only during school hours. She had lent me the book under the most draconian conditions.

" 'Look,' I said, to distract you, and pointed at the afterdeck of the *General Praag* right next to us, where a black bantam cock was getting ready to fly off the deck rail between some speckled hens that were waiting on the bank, frozen in a kind of primordial terror. The morning sun picked out the small male creature with its fiery-red cockscomb, its rough plumage puffed out like an actor's cloak. 'He's waiting for a drumroll from the orchestra,' I said placatingly.

"You looked at me steadfastly. You said we had made a promise always to share everything. By way of an answer, I started talking about the two white mice, which was the stupidest thing I could have done. They belonged to you, you exclusively, which was the only thing that made my reminder relevant. You had hidden them in an empty aquarium, scattered a layer of wood shavings, and put our world atlas on top to make a lid. And yes, although you would actually have preferred that I not even look at your cuddly toys through the glass, I once lifted the atlas while you were gone to have a look from on top. Terrific, not a second later, they both suddenly got their necks broken as they were cunningly scaling the sides and got hit by the heavy book when their little mama's sister dropped it in fright.

" 'What is it?' I asked, for I couldn't read your expression properly. Somehow it seemed you were listening to the scuffling next to the *General Praag*, the bantam cock had landed. Somehow I should have known: you had picked up on my mistake, of course you had.

" 'Dumb creatures,' you said.

"I nodded and indicated with my eyes the poultry sex going on in the grass, but you shook your head. A bit irritated, or so it seemed to me, at my simplemindedness, you began to express your loathing of white mice, those little snouts, those little teeth, those little eyes, all of it dumber than dumb, and the peak of dumbness was naturally to keep the pair in an aquarium.

" *'Quelle idée!'* you said, in Mother's tone of voice, and crossed your feet in a way that meant you either needed to go really badly, or that you had come clean about something and now you were ready to fantasize a little. Oh, you were such a golden, magnanimous child! You were wearing a checked, pleated skirt that morning, a blindingly white blouse, and a striped knit jacket that had previously belonged to me. Children like you often love to theorize, completely uninhibitedly. 'People have so little fantasy,' you burst out plaintively. 'It's okay that there's a primary color we don't know, but it's just pathetic and sad that we can't imagine it.' Beyond that, I can no longer remember exactly who took which part in our dreamy, faltering dialogues.

" 'Eternity,' you said, or maybe I said, 'is that we have to live the lives of everyone who ever lived or will ever live, from beginning to end.'

"Mmmm, yes, and so interesting, isn't it? Even down to the details?"

"Even down to the details, without the slightest deviation from the facts.

"We slid around ice rinks on shoes with leather soles. We licked the metal railings on the Mageren Bridge. The Amstel froze over."

"No, it was summer. We lay in our bathing suits on the beach at Langevelder Slag."

"We put on our skates with double runners and went slicing through the flocks of gulls that happened to be so numerous that year and had flown from the IJ, which was all iced over, into the city."

"I can remember to this day our sense of pleasure—space, not a movement in the sky, our warm bodies, and the even greater warmth of the sand—as we looked over at the hazy outlines of a gray ship that stood out against the furthest rim of the sea."

"Cyclists were also crossing the river."

"We thought about the bottomless chasm there must be right behind the horizon where the ship was. An aunt of our maid had killed herself the week before, and they'd only just told us, so we were in a very solemn mood."

"We'd heard that there was such a terrible cold front approaching from Siberia that within a day or so the North Sea was going to freeze over. The question that interested us was whether we'd get absorbed into the Arctic Circle just like Canada and Nova Semlya, which would mean we'd get to see the Northern Lights—yes, it was definitely winter."

"If you say so."

"Why are you lying in bed?"

"I'm lying in bed because I'm dying."

"Armanda, you can really be pathetic."

"No, no. It's really true. The children have been here twice already to say their good-byes. They plumped up my pillow, gave me a glass of water, held my hand. Oh, darlings, I said, I'm making such a lot of trouble and worries for you, do me a favor, go into town and get something to eat. I'll be awake for a bit yet."

"Ha, that reminds me that you had to go to bed half an hour earlier than I did at home, and I never allowed you to go to sleep till I'd crawled into bed too. To control this, I used to run upstairs sometimes during the half hour and bend over you in the dark, and if I smelled from your breath that you were asleep, I'd hiss in your ear reproachfully: 'You're asleep!' You were incredibly well trained, trained against me, and you were able to say 'Am not!' so convincingly out of a deep sleep that although I knew perfectly well you were lying, I had to put up with it."

"God, yes, I remember that."

"So the young ones are in town now. Take advantage, I'd say, seize the opportunity to exit in peace, on your own. You're alone."

"Yes, insofar as anyone who has another person who's taken up residence inside them can be said to be alone."

"What? I didn't quite understand you. Another person?"

"Someone who's spent my whole life looking and listening with me. In some way, a great advantage. So my sister who lives hidden inside me is older than I am, but still a lot less forgetful. Beautiful moments that I've lived, even if they've faded, shine on a little longer through her. Did you come, I ask her now, to say good-bye or to fetch me? That well-known look of till-death-us-do-part meets mine, even if it's a little frostier than it used to be. The face is blue, which occurs when the oxygen content of the blood drops below the critical point and death is very close. As it happens, I'm an expert on this. All the same, oddly, as long as *I* live, I automatically keep her, my moribund other, alive."

"Classic thought, sympathetic too! Tell me, are you lying comfortably?"

"Very comfortably. Now that I'm nothing but skin and bone, they've laid a sheepskin on my mattress. It's delightfully warm in the room. I'm very tired already, and I just peek out through the slits in my eyelids. I have almost no eyelashes left, which means that though I'm half hallucinating, I'm spared spiders and beetles. I think about whatever comes into my head: a conversation from years back about your last moments. How they may have looked. The Dutch Institute of Forensic Medicine was still in Rijswijk then. No idea why, but I feel more comforted now by my gravity and my grief back then than I did at the time. A pathologist like that knows a great deal. A great sense of peace emanated from him while he explained to me quite calmly the actual process of your drowning. He had gray eyes with such heavy lids and a lethargic twinkle, but you imagined that already. On the table between us, the photo with your face and your absurd laugh. Surprisingly, he couldn't answer my first questions, namely whether you had gone on shivering underwater, since your body temperature had already dropped so hellishly, and whether your teeth went on chattering, the way a body always does instinctively to generate a last bit of warmth. I know it was crazy and pointless to ask, but he didn't know."

"Oh, well, I still shiver like crazy, even though I'm unconscious."

"The doctor, who saw I was fighting back tears, reassured me that you can have suffered only for a minute or two. The specific weight of a human body is higher than the specific weight of water, but not much, a little movement and the person keeps swimming. A small reserve of air in the lungs is not bad, of course, screaming and calling out aren't sensible, and I assume you didn't do it anyway out of sheer exhaustion. A great disadvantage was apparently that there was no more air between you and your sodden clothes, so I assume that you sank immediately."

"True."

"How hopeless water is! It siphons off your body heat twenty-six times faster than air at the same temperature. Twenty-six times! So is it realistic to demand that your heart keep beating normally when you're in water that's thirty-six to thirty-seven degrees Fahrenheit? That your brain keep thinking normally when it's cooling down at that speed? After ninety seconds, even your most rational reflexes are completely disrupted. What are you supposed to do with your nose and mouth underwater, breathe or not breathe? That was your only moment of despair. In the grip of a great lack of oxygen, your instinct finally said yes. A large gulp of water met the opening of your respiratory tract."

"That's right, and the respiratory tract rejected it. I can tell you, Armanda, that if your friend the pathologist were to open up my poor drownéd body, he wouldn't find a single drop of seawater in my lungs. Sometimes the larynx is so shocked by the passage of water over the vocal cords that it angrily contracts all the muscles to block it. That's what happened with me. For a moment I was panicked. Shame, shame, shame, I thought, I really wanted to try that recipe for pancakes with the little bits of ginger stirred in under the batter. I felt a hellish pain, as if my head were being squeezed together by a muscular hand, and wanted to cry out, which of course I couldn't do. Yes, yes, so where are they, the sun-flooded fields of tulips at the end of the tunnel you always hear about in connection with drowning, I thought furiously, and I hadn't even finished the thought when I noticed that the pain was gone. I opened my eyes. You cannot imagine, child, how beautiful the colder, more temperate sea under the surface of the water is! It's a well-worn cliché that what you think of as you're dying is flying away, upward, but in my opinion, heading downward is a lot easier. You weigh so little, at the end, don't you? At this moment my poor body, head downward, is spiraling toward the bottom of the Oosterschelde. My heart has already stopped beating, there's no more pulse, but deep in my brain there's still life. If your doctor were to thrust a thermometer through the top of my skull, he'd establish the temperature in there was still at least eighty-two degrees Fahrenheit.

"Suspended animation. You dream, your thinking has become totally insane. And yet, if someone were to fish you out right away and really get you warm again, you could still make it. Cold, which works so that your organs need a minimum of oxygen, like a hibernating polar bear's, is a real advantage when considered from the standpoint of a rescue."

"God forbid! If you could see what I see. . . . I had already read in the Seegeranie Foundation's quarterly that the underwater area around Schelphoek in front of the coast of Schouwen could stand comparison with any tropical aquarium. I have to say the editors were right. Whole forests of pale blue sea anemones, lilac, and yellow trumpets and red and yellow tubiflora waved to and fro like curtains in the undertow between the streams and the sandbanks. Most of us, Armanda, think that fish just swim. In the position I find myself occupying, I see dozens of speckled examples with teeth and horns, staring fixedly, and doing exactly that. But right in front of me are two enormous lumpsuckers with upstretched yellow chins, kissing. Incredible creatures! Meanwhile I'm moving slowly across the seabed. A powerful undertow will pull me into the silt there, which in turn will deliver me the following week to the marshy bottom behind the remains of the destroyed dike, where my body will find a resting place for at least thirty years. I think about my family. Odd, that I can only see their faces in such a blurred way.

"A few men, a few women, a few children, farewell! Whether I chose you or whether you were assigned to me, I somehow felt I was in the right place. At this moment I discover, quite soberly, that it's actually true what writers and prophets have been saying for thousands of years: in that other world, so close that all you need to do is stretch out a finger, you will find those again whom you want to find again, and moreover they will be—because otherwise what would be the point, you know?—remarkably well disposed toward you. Now that my soul is leaving my mouth in the form of a butterfly, just the way we saw it in the Allard Pierson Museum on one of those red-figured Greek vases, I recognize your face. Oval, with a round chin. Your smile confirms my hope that we're going to start telling each other stories right away."

"Oh, yes!"

"It turns out better than expected, huh?"

"Yes, no big job."

"No. Quite easy, actually."

"Or?"

"Mmmm."

"Oh, you're asleep!"

"Am not!"

"Really?"

"Ab-so-lutely not!"

Born in the Netherlands in 1941, Margriet de Moor led a career as a classical singer before becoming a novelist. Her first novel, *First Gray, Then White, Then Blue*, was a sensational success across Europe, winning her the AKO Literature Prize, for which her second novel, *The Virtuoso*, was also nominated. She has since published several other novels, including *Duke of Egypt* and *The Kreutzer Sonata*. Her books have been translated into twenty languages.

A NOTE ON THE TYPE

This book was set in Janson, a typeface long thought to have been made by the Dutchman Anton Janson, who was a practicing type-founder in Leipzig during the years 1668–1687. However, it has been conclusively demonstrated that these types are actually the work of Nicholas Kis (1650–1702), a Hungarian, who most probably learned his trade from the master Dutch typefounder Dirk Voskens. The type is an excellent example of the influential and sturdy Dutch types that prevailed in England up to the time William Caslon (1692–1766) developed his own incomparable designs from them.

Composed by Creative Graphics, Allentown, Pennsylvania
Printed and bound by Berryville Graphics, Berryville, Virginia
Designed by Wesley Gott